STORM OF SOULS

Don't quote me on any of this. The theory worked though, in my mind. Even if I couldn't understand the math. The evil spirits, flocking to Sabnock's version of the afterlife. The humans being led there and killed.

There was a reason Mexico felt empty, *now*.

"This might be about more than killing Sabnock," I finally said.

Jen got it. And smiled. I loved that about her. She got me and backed me up like we were two halves of the same person.

Whatever we did, Sabnock wasn't on the top of our list anymore. We weren't down here just to kill him and exorcise the dead zone. We needed to purge the dead zone, at any cost. Keep the plague of locusts from being made, being shipped out over the world.

And hopefully do it in time to save the Earth.

"We can still kill him though," Jen said, her smile a little less smiley. More serious. "Right?"

I loved that about her, too.

BOOKS BY CHRIS J. CRANFORD

THE FERGUS GRIMM SAGA

Ghost Town

Recon Team Four

City of the Dead

An Ethereal End

Crown of Bones

Storm of Souls

City of Second Chances

The Crosse Series

The Deadening Wake

The Reality Thief

The Black Horizon

Finn Gallagher

The Chronicles of the Wolf

STORM OF SOULS

A Grimm Story

CHRIS J. CRANFORD

Forged Iron Press

First Paperback Edition Mar 2025

Cover Design by J Caleb Design

Published by ForgedIronPress
www.forgedironpress.com

www.chrisjcranford.com

Acknowledgements:

The Word is the Deed.

That phrase means a lot to me. I tend to believe in actions over words, in watching how a person does a thing rather than how they might talk about it. An action describes a person far better than their own words do. How we act, what we do, this matters far more than anything we can say to others about the person we wish to be.

For me this is about writing. About being a writer. That means I can't just tell people that I write, that's not enough. I have to live my life in a way that shows it.

That realization led me to my first tattoo. A tattoo from a scene in The Deadening Wake. About a man trying to save someone, and maybe trying to save himself.

For me the stories I write aren't enough. It's not enough to just write the words down, to put a piece of me on paper. The stories only really become real to me when I complete the circle and have a resonant part of my story put back on me.

So, *The Word is the Deed*. Grimm finally comes to this realization. I guess it just took some time for me as well.

I wanted to take a moment out to thank Christian Buckingham for making the deed a reality, for his vision of the scene that meant a lot to me, and Timewarp Tattoo for the life-changing experience.

PROLOGUE

The first Christmas I really had, the first one I remembered, that I really *wanted* to remember, had been at the Coopers. With Jen.

Parker hadn't believed in the holiday. Not that I actually knew whether he believed in it or not. It was just we never celebrated Christmas at his home. I would have said, knowing the man, that he just believed in hard work. In getting the results of the work you put into something, the value of what you earned. Looking back now, Parker didn't believe in things like the giving of gifts. To him, that cheapened whatever it was you got.

Of course, Parker was dead now. So I couldn't ask him. And I had misunderstood a lot about the man, though, so I could have been wrong. Maybe he had loved the holiday. Maybe he had loved Christmas with his son, waking up to all the excitement and opening of gifts, and just couldn't tolerate the holiday after his son's death. Maybe he just hadn't wanted to celebrate it with us, with those of us he boarded: me, Danny, Nick.

So I knew about Christmas. I had heard the stories, so I understood what the holiday was about, but I really didn't *know*. It was one of those things I think you have to experience to really understand.

There is, always, a wide gulf between the knowing and the understanding of a thing.

The first year Jen had arrived in Grafton, her family had invited me over. I was a kid, so I knew about gifts for the holiday, but I was also an orphan, being raised by Parker, so I really didn't have any money to speak of. Giving gifts wasn't really done, not only because of the money, but also because of something I hadn't understood at the time: the loss of Parker's son years before.

So for that Christmas, it wasn't a lack of me being aware of the holiday, it wasn't that I didn't know I should have brought a gift, it was more just not having the money to bring one. That, coupled with a general ignorance, having never celebrated it, made me unaware of what the holiday was about.

That Christmas with the Coopers had been my first real one. It had been magical, for many reasons, starting with Jen. It was the Christmas that would always stick with me, wherever I was at, throughout my life. It was there I first discovered the magic of the *gift*.

At the Cooper's I had helped set up a real Christmas tree for the first time. I had strung red and blue and green and yellow lights around the tree, winding them around thin, prickly pine needles. Breathing in the deep, woody pine smell as I lay under the tree, trying to tighten the stand. Coming back out with the sticky pine sap on my hands and trying to figure out what actually removed that sap. Turns out, not much did. I still smile remembering Jen's laugh when tinsel kept sticking to my hands, when I flicked my fingers a hundred times trying to get the shiny silver plastic ribbons off.

I had marveled at a little miniature train set they had built around the base of the tree. A round track, with a little village, all covered in a fake snow. A train station, where the train would occasionally stop its travel if you flicked a little switch on the remote. People standing by a lit lamp, wearing plaster scarves and top hats, mouths open as if they sang.

Then there had been the star. An old, five-pointed thing, its center glowing a deep, solid white. Jen and I had to use a tall stepladder to get the star on top of the tree, and no matter how hard I tried, the dang thing always leaned a bit to the side.

It had been magical to me. The preparation for the day in the weeks leading up to Christmas. The time spent finding the tree and then creating the world in which the tree lived. The brightly colored blinking bulbs, the wood stocked by the fireplace, the wrapping of gifts. The hanging of stockings. The stocking of the stockings.

Even the food took time. There were cookies to bake, gingerbread men that I iced frowny faces on. Because I never smiled. Someone started calling them grimmerbread men, and the name stuck.

There was fudge to make, sweet square chunks of peanut butter and chocolate. There were peppermint candy canes to hang in the tree, hooked spirals of red and white, and if less canes were hung on the tree than came in the package, well no one could blame me. There were mugs and mugs of hot chocolate, and bags and bags of marshmallows. There were sausage and pepperoni rolls, warm bread filled with spicy pepperoni, and a spicy-sweet sausage.

With all that going on, you might ask how I could have not gotten a gift. How, after seeing all the packages under the tree, I hadn't gone out and got something for Jen. All I can say is that I was caught up in the moment. Bewitched by the magic of Christmas. I became lost in a world I had never known, a world that had sucked me in, and never let me go.

On Christmas Day we had sat around with mugs of hot chocolate and watched it snow. There was this feeling of peace that I'll never forget. The flakes were big and the snow came down thick; the ground was covered in a white blanket that only kept swelling higher and higher outside. There was a crackling in the fireplace from a log burning there, and Frank Sinatra was softly singing the words *Have Yourself a Merry Little Christmas* over and over, the words coming through a needle scratching softly off a record spinning on a table in the corner of the room.

Jen and me sitting on her couch, a place that felt more and more like home to me, looking out the big front window. The morning sky dark with the snowfall, dark with the fallen snow. The flakes were huge; they drifted down in front of the panes of glass, and every now and then one glittered, caught by a brief ray of morning sun. Each of us taking tiny sips of the mugs of hot chocolate, the mugs warm in our hands, occasionally licking the sweet, melted marshmallow stuck to our lips.

The singing of Sinatra, the crackling of fire, the sweetness of marshmallow, the chocolate cocoa, the feeling of peace. The big flakes, drifting down, piling on top of one another. The blanket of snow outside, wrapped around the house, keeping us safe from the world.

Like I said, something I'll never forget.

The feeling of Jen's hip against mine even then was electric. We were both young teenagers, still really unaware of our feelings for each other, just the happiness of being by each other, the tiny, stomach-jerking sensations of seeing them for the first time. The deep breath inducing, *intense* moments of when we stood too close, when our eyes connected and neither of us could look away, when, for a moment, I had forgotten to breathe.

That was Christmas to me.

I didn't bring a gift on my first Christmas. I could never really say why, although I hope I've explained it. And each Christmas thereafter, I didn't either. Even as Jen and I grew closer each year and went from middle-school best friends to high-school sweet-hearts. Not because I was stubborn, I didn't think. But maybe because it was my tradition. Just bringing me.

Above all, Christmas should be about being with those you love.

And sure, it was only a few days away. It had been hinted this year might be a good one for me to break my particular tradition. And the way Jen felt, with her struggling to figure out a what felt wrong inside her, what was missing, a part of me *knew* I might be able to help with just the right gift.

I just wished I could figure out what that gift should be.

CHAPTER ONE

I t was hot in Mexico.

It shouldn't be, not this time of year. Not in late December. Not with Mexico City being a mile above sea level. The day should be pleasantly cool, a nice seventy degrees, the sun should be a reassuring warmth on the skin. The breeze, blowing inward from the ocean, should stir the hair on your forearms, and carry a hint of salt.

There should be streets packed with traffic, sidewalks packed with crowds, there should be motors running and horns blaring and the low-lying hum of thousands of conversations among millions of people. There should be shoppers walking around in chinos and white, blousy shirts, drinking and celebrating and ducking into stores for the occasional thing that caught their eye.

After all, Christmas was just a week away.

It should have been all of that and more.

Instead, Mexico was a nightmare. It wasn't cool. People didn't populate the streets shopping for gifts. Cars and trucks didn't crowd the highways. Mexico City was empty now. Empty except for the dead zone, and the few survivors left in the country.

And empty now, because of the plague. Hot. Dry, with the brief flashes of mugginess that moisture around an ocean brings. The sun was always angry, always red, always glaring at everyone below. Clouds that formed quickly dissipated, almost in their moment of creation, the heat burning away any moisture daring to gather in the atmosphere, leaving the sky a grayish haze, as if the heavens themselves tried to hide what lay underneath.

Not that there was much left to hide.

Whatever had existed yesterday in Mexico was gone. Whatever, whoever, all of it and everything, gone. An infinite number of locusts had surged out from the dead zone in Mexico City, creatures Sabnock had created, the insects washing over everything in a gigantic tidal wave of crunching mandibles and corrosive blood, eating every building, every plant, every animal and human left standing.

Nothing had escaped the locusts.

They had eaten high-rises, leaving huddled remains of buildings where there had been tall structures pointing high in the sky. They had eaten monuments, leaving ichor-stained concrete where pieces of history had once stood. They had eaten vehicles, leaving empty, brittle, twisted frames of steel and iron. They had eaten cattle and dogs and people, leaving mounds of black shells from which an occasional white bone flashed.

There was a flutter in the air, a stirring that might once have been a breeze before it had travelled the long distance over a barren land, before the breeze had died, before it had become the gasp of something cool from an ocean too far away from here to matter.

The breeze carried no hint of salt, no taste of origin, no scent of where it had been or what it carried. It was an empty wind, a wind that occasionally stirred the empty shells of locusts along the streets like small carapace-like tumbleweeds. It was a wind that only existed to reveal what was left. What had been there. And what had gone.

The stirring of the air left just the cloudless darkening haze of late evening; the gray-blue sky streaked with purple, the purple so dark it appeared as black, and so empty the moon seemed a tiny orb perched over the horizon, a pale weak whiteness hanging in the east, unsure of where to go.

The moon hovered there. Then moved west. Slowly. Timidly. As if afraid. Stepping lightly in its journey through the night, until it found itself hovering over the once City of Spring, Cuernavaca, and a ruined building covered in locust shells, a building broken under the assault of insects, broken and buried under mounds of black carapaces.

A building with a vault.

A vault with people.

Survivors.

And me.

CHAPTER TWO

There was a hum in the vault. A nearby rumbling of a motor. The vibration could be felt in the floor underneath me, running along the underneath of my legs. In the wall behind me, slightly trembling against my back. The oscillation of something running at sixty hertz.

A generator.

It must be pretty big.

There was a hint of the motor powering it in the air. Each breath brought a scent of something sweet and diesely. Fumes. My head ached from them, and that told me the vault might not have enough ventilation for the generator. That, or it had been running too long.

An occasional slapping sound broke through the humming, distant light thwacks sporadically echoing over the thrum of the generator. A weird sound to wake up to in Alejandro's compound. Not something I had expected, when I had collapsed against the wall, after flying Gabrielle back through the plague.

We had barely made it. Me for sure, but Gabrielle, almost not.

I opened my eyes. The light was dim in the large room of the vault, what I thought of as the party room. A place for everyone in the vault to congregate, a large area with couches and tables and a long bar across from the elevator.

Michael sat there, much like he had before, when he had told me to go to sleep. When he knew, and I knew, there was no way I could make it back to Jen and save them. That whatever had passed up there had passed, and there was no way I could change it.

This time he had company. Tabitha next to him, cross-legged on the floor in much the same way, her face concerned behind her glasses. Gertrude, behind both of them, on her knees, the hilt of her sword and axe poking out from her shoulders.

They all froze when I opened my eyes. It looked as if they had been talking. Otherwise, it was quiet. The room was silent around us, other than the hum of the generator. Maybe a smaller hum of people speaking across the room.

The lights... trembled. Wavered. Grew brighter and dimmer. And then steadied. The three of them looked up, but only briefly. As if the lights were something they all were used to, and maybe they wondered when they might dim for a last time.

I nodded, wincing a bit at the knotted muscles at the back of my neck. All my muscles were tight. Like my whole body had had one big cramp. My voice sounded rough. "Water?"

There was a six-pack of bottles between Tabitha and Michael. Three of the plastic loops were empty, hanging in the air, but the other loops all held tall, cold bottles. Long, bold words down their sides, white words on a background of a light blue raindrop: Smartwater.

Smartwater with antioxidants.

Michael broke a bottle off one of the loops and held it out to me. I chuckled. The chuckling hurt. My body was tight. Sore. But I took the Smartwater—with all of its antioxidants—with a smile. Hell, I could use them.

The bottle was icy cold in my hand. I opened it with a grimace. My body ached, and even the plastic top was hard to twist off. Then I took a sip. The sip became a deep swallow. The swallow became a continuous stream of swallows, big gulps.

Smartwater with antioxidants was pretty tasty.

You know, for water.

I looked around. The whole corner of the large room had emptied. There was me, where I was leaning back against the wall, Michael, Tabitha, and Gertrude. The couches and seats closest to us were empty. The vampires and humans that had been there had apparently moved.

The rest of them watched. From a safer distance.

The three of them, the angel and the witches, looked worried. Concerned. About me or the situation, I wasn't sure. Tabitha had a pile of stuff next to her. Another folded towel. A shirt and pants. And shoes. I realized then that somewhere during my flight I had lost one. I had just one sneaker on.

I placed one hand over the key. It still radiated the slightest warmth into my palm. Something I knew, I felt, would always be there between Jen and I. It was faint, but there.

It was the deepest of reliefs for me. The feeling was better than the first taste of the Smartwater, although I took another sip. My voice, though still rough, was stronger. Sounding more like a mild case of strep, less like I had smoked a couple of cartons of cigarettes. "They're still alive."

Michael nodded, as if he had expected no more and no less. Tabitha's face showed a mix of relief and puzzlement and worry. I understood Tabitha's concern. A mother for her daughter.

I wanted to reassure her, but the only assurance that even I had was the thought that if my friends were alive, they would have kept Zoe alive, too. That was all I had, and that wasn't enough to stay alive. It was just enough for the belief to run, unsaid, an undercurrent to our conversation. Let it lie there, and let it be believed.

The earth witch's face looked torn. As if she didn't know whether to be happy or not. As if afraid to grab the tiny lifeline handed her.

I understood.

It was best, in these times, to do what you could do. I asked about Gabrielle.

"Alive," Gertrude said. "I'm told. Sleeping."

Gabrielle had bled a lot. I could still feel her body jerk in tiny motions under the biting of the locusts. My hand closed, briefly, on its own. I hoped vampires had a store down in their vault. Some kind of blood bank. I hoped. If she was sleeping anything like I had been, it had been the sleep of the dead.

Speaking of, I got the fresh towel from Tabitha and poured some of the water on it. I tried using it to clean off my chest. The towel came away with spit and some of the glop of the locusts' insides. I kept up the cycle, pouring the water on my chest, bracing myself for the chill of it, then kept finding a clean corner of the towel and wiping off what I could.

Mostly I made a mess of things. But I felt a little cleaner. A little.

I was still tired. Not falling-down tired, like I had been back in the elevator. Just incredibly-tough-to-get-up tired.

The lights flickered again above us. I looked up, but the three of them didn't. Like they were used to the dimming and brightening.

How long had we been running on generator power? How much fuel did we have? Why did the lounge smell like diesel? Most generators had an exhaust piped up to the outside.

I drank more water. Cleaned myself some more. Michael gave me a second bottle when I finished the first. Tabitha helped get a button-up shirt around me. It was a dressy shirt, white with long sleeves, and I ended up buttoning just a couple buttons before giving up.

My next task was the pants. It took some work and a lot of wincing, but I was able to slide off my jeans. Or was it jean now? Was it always plural, or should I remove the S when just one leg was there? Or were jeans always plural, with either one leg or two?

I mean, I was pulling on the pants. They were plural, and had two legs. Just like jeans. If I happened to rip off a leg of these, and the way things were going I might, would I call them pant instead of pants?

Someone once told me that what the brain thinks during your most exhausted moments, when you're the most empty of energy, is the real you. It's the thinking that comes uncluttered by other thoughts and worries that isn't tinted with past or present or future. It's a direct stream of consciousness from the part of your mind that's usually hidden, that only comes out when everything else is too tired to overshadow it.

I hoped not. Because the plurality of jeans and pants didn't seem to be a critical world-destroying issue, I might be the only person to ever think that thought in the history of mankind.

I thought I'd leave it that way.

The lights kept up their dimming and undimming, occasionally brightening too much in a big glow, rarely going completely dark, and for the most part they kept the room illuminated. Tabitha was nice enough to do the socks and shoes. The shoes were a little tight and pinched my toes together. But they'd do.

I watched her tie my laces, like a mother would for her kid. Laughed a bit on the inside at the image. Felt bad because I knew she must have been thinking about Zoe. And kept a blank face when the earth witch glanced at me.

I finished the second bottle of Smartwater. I couldn't really feel the antioxidants working. They weren't ganging up on the oxidants.

Maybe that was stuff that happened later. Maybe I shouldn't feel them working at all. Maybe antioxidants took all the oxidants out ninja-style.

Come on brain. Get with the program. This jean/jeans/antioxidant shit is getting old.

I groaned. Or maybe shouted, in a groaning way. And shook my head. Moved to get up, fighting the sleepy brain and the achy body.

I found it still was harder than I would have thought. My whole body felt like it was coming out of a hundred-year slumber. Everything was slow and thick and sore; every muscle responded only after a moment's thought, and then weakly.

Note to self: becoming a flying battle tank takes a lot out of you.

I had not felt the same way before, when all the plates and the wings had come out of me. When I had become the armored angel back in the factory at Grafton. And people had been shooting at me at the time. Bullets had bounced off me.

It had been a gunfight. And there had been a lot of people shooting at me. A lot of bullets striking my armor and bouncing off. I would have thought that would have been harder to protect myself from an infini-million locusts.

I would have been wrong.

I must have used a lot of ethereal energy. My hand moved around for the Five-Fold blade. Gertrude saw me looking for it and understood the motion in the way warriors do. She handed it over, the blade in a new sheath, which I found a nice gesture.

The sheath had a couple of straps so that I could strap it to my leg. Which I did. Maybe I wouldn't lose it this time.

I slid the blade out, just a bit, until I saw the Five-Fold symbol. It glowed there, but it was weaker. Much weaker than when I had created it. I flickered my ethereal sight there, and the five circles almost seemed to swirl like a funnel. Like a little tap of energy of its own.

I couldn't see that before. The symbols had been fiery with power. The swirl now spun slowly, like the slow spin of a whirlpool. Glowed less brightly. Before, in my ethereal vision, it had been almost blindingly brilliant. Like an ethereal sun.

How much had I used?

Was it access to that energy that had helped me to become the armored angel? The battle tank? That large tap?

That didn't strike me as right. I had pulled a lot that night back in the factory. In Grafton. I had killed a lot of people then, bad people, evil people. I had killed them for their ghosts, and I had used their spirits for energy, in order to save Jen.

It had been a lot of energy.

Maybe not the same amount as I had pulled from the Five-Fold blade. I just didn't know. There was no power meter, no gas tank needle, measuring what I used. It was just a feel. I did what I could in the moment and hoped we survived.

I hoped Gabrielle really was okay. She had been alive, well as alive as vampires could be. Surely that was enough to get her healed.

Would Johnny care if she died? I hoped so. Something about them, about he and Gabrielle, was sad to me. Maybe because I had found Jen, after ten years apart. Maybe I wanted the same for my friends. Johnny and Gabrielle. Nick and Sarah.

Even in our darkest moments, we all want the best for those we love.

The lights flickered again. Briefly. Swelling and then dimming. The generator's hum choked a bit, like it had coughed. A slap or two, back from the elevator bank.

"The locusts," Michael said, as if *that* could explain it.

Maybe it did. The flickering of the lights, all the people down here, maybe we were at the edge of the load the generator could carry.

Still, why were we on a generator at all?

What the hell could these locusts do?

"How long?" I asked.

"A couple more hours," Michael said. "It is evening, now."

I hadn't been asking how long I had been sleeping. Though it had been a long day. We had driven down before sunrise. I had thought it might have gotten to mid-morning when I went into the dead zone. So I must have come back with Gabrielle around noon. By the best guess of my one-legged-jean mind.

"I mean, how long until we can leave?"

"Until it is finished," the angel said, like it was the most apparent thing in the world. "Likely the morning. The center of the plague is above us now. What you flew through earlier, that was the outskirts of the swarm."

I knew how that had felt. And if that had just been the outer edges of the plague, I shuddered to wonder what they could be doing above us. Even if they were just insects. "What can these things *do*?"

His eyebrows lifted. A very slight motion. "You will be surprised, if we make it to morning."

I didn't miss the *if*.

It wasn't a when-we-leave. It was an if-we-make-it. A very big difference.

An image appeared in my head, of the plague of locusts eating metal and brick and people alive; of insects the size of my fingers, swarming my friends and taking hundreds of tiny, blood-filled bites. Just as the locusts had tried to eat me. Just as they had taken those same tiny bites from Gabrielle.

The generator's coughing, the flickering of the lights, the smell of diesel, that all meant this wasn't over. The exhaust made more sense, now. I wondered if the tube was getting swarmed by insects.

If they were pouring down the exhaust in order to keep it from breathing. To choke it to death.

Or to come eat us.

I looked past Michael. Back the way I had come, from where Michael and Gertrude had pulled me from the elevator. A few people stood there, vampires and humans, holding books and rolled-up magazines and even, in one case, a two-by-four. They swung occasionally, at something in the air, and the slapping sounds came from when a book or magazine hit the wall.

So the vault wasn't really a vault. It wasn't a safe place, though it had gotten us this far. It had a couple of weak points. The elevator bank, coming down. The exhaust tube or tubes of the generator's motor. The insects were coming down in those places.

What else might we be missing? It wasn't like things today were built to be insect proof. Ants, cockroaches, gnats, these things could make it anywhere. Why not hungry locusts as well?

The fight wasn't over. We still had to last the night. Or however long it took for the plague to spend itself out.

Dammit.

Here I thought I could take a break.

I pushed myself up. Not letting myself feel the exhaustion. A large groan burst from me. I'll say groan, and not moan. Or cry. It definitely wasn't a cry.

The three of them looked up at me. Then got up. It was a lot easier for them than me. None of them mentioned it though. I still thought they were bragging.

"What are you doing?" Michael asked.

"Finding a way to stop the locusts from coming in." I said. Or asked. I wasn't sure which.

"How?" he asked. He was calm, but Gertrude wasn't. She was hiding it, and maybe the lights had hidden it, but she was pale. Worried pale.

"I'm assuming you think they can eat their way down to us?"

"It's not out of the realm of possibilities."

"Well, we're buried in the earth," I said, and pointed at Tabitha. "And we have an earth witch."

Tabitha was shaking her head before I finished. "I've tried. It's too much earth. Too much to harden. I just don't have the strength."

I understood her worry and concern now. It wasn't just concern for Zoe, a mother's concern for her daughter, but it was also the worry that Tabitha wouldn't live to see whether or not her daughter was alive. Whether she could make it in time to help.

I grinned a bit. I could fight. I could always figure out a way to fight.

"Maybe you didn't then," I said, holding up the Five-Fold blade. "But you do now."

CHAPTER THREE

Yeah, I wasn't sure it would work either.

Ethereal energy was a domain I worked in. It was a power I used and controlled. As far as I knew, with my mother and father gone, I was the sole operator in the landscape of ethereal energy.

Maybe, though, all I needed was a shift in perspective. After all, I had used the power to heal Jen. And Johnny. In the aftermath, both of them had mentioned hearing, seeing, feeling spirits I had used. Johnny could still see them, at times.

Jen had actually used ethereal energy when she had been trapped in the key. Used it to fuel her power. Used to help me fight the geas, used it to fuel her lightning storm at Red Rock.

She had used her own pool of the energy, at first. And then had used some of the ghosts I had tapped once she had understood. Once she had figured out how I accessed the ethereal plane, she had piggybacked off of that.

I had evidence other people could use ethereal energy. Even though Jen and I were... unique. Our bond, there was nothing like us. Like her and I, and the key. I would argue there was nothing like Jen.

I could use ethereal energy. I could access that power through ghosts, through living their histories, their memories, their lives. Other people could use that energy, though, once I accessed it. To me, the Five-Fold blade was that. It was a pool of energy, clean, stripped of the memories of people, of all the evil they had done.

I hoped that once those lives were lived, once that debt was paid, anyone could use the energy left. Kind of like jumping a dead car battery. All a person needed to access the energy was a set of cables and another battery, another car.

I thought it was possible. The other car was the blade. The set of cables was me.

Simple is as simple does.

It seemed possible. Plausible. At least, I felt like it was worth a try.

At first Tabitha protested. The normal reaction of people when first asked to do something way outside their comfort zone. Outside the norm. The first thing they say are things like: *I'm not* sure, *that's not how it works*, or even a *hell, no*. Maybe, if they were being polite, they'd say something like *maybe another time*.

I couldn't blame her; we were talking of power, of a different type of power, of combining that power with hers, and merging powers in new ways might have a disastrous consequence. There were all kinds of unknowns in the equation.

In Red Rock, those consequences had been beneficial. Pushing the ethereal energy to Jen along our bond had allowed me to handle more of it, but it had also allowed her greater power, and together that had helped me fight the geas. It also had allowed her to rain down lightning. And had, unfortunately, shown her how to access her own ethereal energy.

Here, it could allow Tabitha enough power to keep us safe. Keep the vault sealed. Keep the locusts out.

As if echoing my thoughts, the motor powering the generator coughed a couple of times. I heard and felt the sputters. Saw the results as the lights flickered, not dim and brighter, but on and off.

We gained nothing by not trying. Even if Tabitha wasn't, I was kind of a leap-before-I-look kind of guy. And, in the end I had an effective counterargument, "Do you want to live, so we can find Zoe?"

That got Tabitha on board.

Not fully. Not all the way in. But enough to try.

I looked over at the earth witch. She was not looking at me. She was looking ahead, focused on the vault around us. Focused on the earth and all the metals surrounding us.

We sat together, her and I. Gertrude and Michael standing behind us, closer to the center of the room. Alejandro as well. All waiting, watching, maybe hoping.

We all were back by the elevator bank. The center of the vault. Both of us cross-legged, next to one another, sitting amidst the choking of the generator, the dimming of the lights, the chittering skittering sound of locusts, as they snuck out the elevator doors, followed by the pounding slap of a book.

Not the ideal place to concentrate on melding different powers, I'll grant you that.

The Five-Fold blade rested in my hand, the hand away from the earth witch. The symbol on the blade glowed a light blue that swelled inside the darkness left by the flickering lights. I watched the ethereal tap there, the slow tidal spin of energies inside the symbols, in a moment of wonder.

Tabitha held her focus in the hand furthest from me. Her talisman, the large rock. The stone cracked and lined like it had come from deep within the earth. Polished in some places, sharply edged in others. Old.

We held hands between us. Her hand was smaller than mine, cool, damp. Her fingers were more lined. Wrinkled.

Still, her hand gripped mine, tight.

I gripped hers the same. "Ready?"

Tabitha nodded. Her eyes closed. Tightly pressed together.

I began to pull energy from the blade. As I did, I pushed it through me. Through me and into Tabitha. Like I had when I had healed Johnny back at the airport in Denver. Like I had with Jen.

There was a moment of resistance. Like pressing up against the outside of a bubble. There was a slight wall between us, something thin; it gave as I pressed. I pulled more ethereal energy. Increased what I pushed into Tabitha. The bubble bowed inward.

I increased the energy flow a little more. Kept increasing it in slow, tiny increments.

Tabitha's hand spasmed.

The bubble burst.

The energy poured into the earth witch. Or rather, she took it, pulled it from me, from my hand. The energy zipped along my nerves, my skin, my bones. Lightning struck the Five-Fold blade. I was the conducting rod, and the bolt coursed through me, tingling my spine, and zipped over into the earth witch.

Who vacuumed all that energy up.

Large cracking sounds came from the elevator. Screams of metal bending beyond where it was supposed to be bent. Cracks and pings and tings and squeals echoed down the shaft.

Tabitha's eyes remained scrunched together. Her face paled. She weaved a bit while she sat. Gertrude stepped up from behind her, afraid to touch her.

A moment later the lights went out.

The generator gave a last cough.

Voices came from the lounge behind us. Small exclamations of surprise.

Tabitha's hand gripped me harder. Power flowed through me, the hairs on my arm lifted with it. They floated in the air, trickling with power, for a moment or two more.

The metal squeals slowed down. In the background, behind us, I heard similar crunches and pings. Tiny sounds in the air, like a hard rain hitting a piece of sheet metal, the pings scattered at first, and then thrumming into the metal as the rain came down harder and harder.

A sound beat in the air, like a metallic, rolling thunder.

Then a final large pinging sound in the room. My ears popped as the pressure changed in the vault, and a ringing echoed through them. I worked my jaw a bit, trying to get my hearing back.

Tabitha let go.

"It's done," she said. Her voice exhausted. "I closed everything. Plumbing. Vent shafts. Elevator. Then burrowed some new ventilation, a large enough hole from here to about a mile away."

I couldn't see her. But her voice felt like it was aimed in my direction. Answering my question. "We've got to breathe. If the locusts can find that shaft and then get back here through it by morning, we're probably dead anyway."

"I can't believe that worked," Gertrude said. Her voice wondering, somewhere above us.

My mother would have said we had become more.

Michael might have said something about forging.

I looked down at the Five-Fold blade. The blue energy still swirled there in my sight. Slower still. Like it was almost empty. I sheathed it with a grimace, snapping a little piece of leather over the hilt to lock it in.

Beams of light flashed through the room. Someone found a portable lantern and lit it. The glow weakly illuminated the center of the lounge. Shadows hid the faces of many of the vampires and the humans in the room. Briefly a beam flickered over us, highlighting those around me: Gertrude's expression of wonder. Tabitha's exhaustion. Michael's thoughtful look.

Me, I was with Tabitha.

I pulled myself up and staggered down the wall a bit. Away from the elevator bank. A sound still came from it, a high-pitched whistling, as if millions of insects were screeching above us, as if that sound echoed its way down to us below, through whatever seals and metal barriers Tabitha had placed there.

I wanted a bit more peace than that. I had started to dread the screeching of the insects, the reminder of the train whistle, a memory of that ghostly train I had heard in my fight with Hector.

Unseen, but heard. Unknown, but felt. A constant pressure from a place I couldn't find. I just knew it was there.

Where was my corner of the room? I searched; my eyes were adjusting to the dark, to the tiny glow of light provided by the portable lantern, the edges of the room staying dark in the shadows. Part of me kept hoping to have Nick pop out of one. Tell me everything was okay. That they all were safe.

That didn't happen. I didn't know if it was because he couldn't find a place he had never been to, or if it was because they were busy themselves in a fight for their own lives. I worried, and only a hand occasionally pressed to the key kept me from worrying too much.

I kept on. One hand on the wall. Looking, but not looking, for Nick.

I was surprised when I found someone else, instead.

A form materialized out of the shadows, much like Nick would. At first I thought it was him. Nick wasn't built like a linebacker; he was lean, like this body in front of me. But this form was even leaner. A little more slight. Shorter.

Gabrielle.

Her face was pale, even in the shadows. Her eyes dark, so dark in the blackness of the room. Her skin crisscrossed in scars, tiny white things that hadn't yet healed. The scars on her skin reminded me so much of my mother, I paused there. A wash of anger came over me, anger with nowhere to go, and in the end, I directed it at Johnny. Where the hell had he thought playing thrall to a vampire would go?

You stupid fuck.

Then I took a breath. Another. He needed time. Who the hell was I to say anything to that?

Another form was behind Gabrielle. Millie. Her scar much more prominent, though, for once, the young vampire did not look so angry at me.

Gabrielle's voice was hoarse. Much like mine had been. "I wanted to thank you."

I did my normal thing. Which was to shrug off the thanks. Wave it off. I did what anyone would do. And so that's what I did.

"No," Gabrielle said, in a rough voice. As if forcing out the words. "I understand what people think of us. What humans think. And, sometimes, we give them reason."

Her eyes shimmered a bit in her pale face, black shiny pools in the shadows of the room. Her hand reached out and grabbed my arm. Her fingers were weak, but they dug into my flesh just the same.

"I didn't know what it meant to be a Wolverine," she said. "I didn't think I was really a part of you. Part of *this*."

Ah.

I was a little ashamed. A little. I had never tried to welcome Gabrielle. It wasn't something I had ever thought of. That was maybe more a Jen thing. I had just made her a part of our circle; it was always her and Johnny together in my mind. Maybe the vampire was worried, with Johnny being in the middle of what he was thinking, that she wasn't as much a part of the group as *his* part of our group.

I placed my hand over hers. The one holding onto my arm like it was the only thing holding her up. The fingers felt thin. The hand felt cool.

Still, I gave it a slight squeeze. "Well, you know now."

The shimmering swelled in her eyes. I looked away before it became catching, blinking myself a couple of times. Patting her hand in that odd way people did when they wanted to comfort someone.

Gabrielle's knees gave out. Millie caught her more than I, as if she had been ready.

"She needs more rest," the young vampire explained. "And more blood. She only took enough to keep her alive."

Millie said the last in anger. As if she was angry at Gabrielle. I realized then Millie was more mad at Johnny. Because Gabrielle was still hanging onto whatever it was they had between them.

I wondered if Johnny was stuck on a similar precipice. I understood his fear. The world would view him differently, after he bit someone, after he took their blood. He would change into what the world viewed as a monster. Not only viewed as a monster, but actually a monster, if he ever let go of his thirst. If he ever got so hungry he tore a human apart in his need.

Gabrielle had shown me something different. She had told me, in very certain terms, back in Grafton, her family's relationship with humans was different. And since then, I hadn't ever seen her feed. Not in a battle, and not afterward.

Not even now.

Maybe Johnny was worried about the wrong thing. Maybe he shouldn't worry so much about how the world viewed him. Maybe he should worry about how Gabrielle viewed him.

Maybe he should worry about how he viewed himself.

He had told me the sex had been good. Johnny had loved providing his blood to Gabrielle. It had been a high for him, and something he thought had been special for them both.

That wasn't enough for a real relationship. But I didn't think that was all Johnny wanted from Gabrielle, or her from him. There was more there between them, more of something *real*, even if the sex and the power that came with being a thrall had been the initial lure.

There was fear there for Johnny. Fear of change. Fear of becoming a monster. Fear of what Gabrielle might see in him when he was no longer the human providing her blood. All little fears, things people used as excuses, when the real question was, did he love her or not?

One thing was for sure. Gabrielle loved him. And that love would continue, whether he was a human or a vampire. I had that kind of love myself, and I recognized it in others. Especially my friends.

Johnny, I thought, my eyes pooling with a wetness. I worked my way over to my section of the wall, planning on sleeping as much as I could. Planning on being ready to leave the moment the plague passed. Planning on heading back to our hideout, of being back with Jen, of feeling her arms around me, a place of peace, and wanting the same for Johnny.

You dumb fuck.

Jen's fingers twined in her sister's, Sarah's form next to her, her head lying on Jen's shoulder. They held each other, the grip no longer tight, but the loose clasp of people who were tired. Exhausted. Weak.

An icy chill remained in the freezer, even if the power was out. The group huddled together on the floor, side to side, back-to-back, in the darkness. Pressing themselves together against the cold.

The scent in the air was a weird mix of warming frost and frozen meat. The icy, chilled smell reminded Jen of freezer burn. The scent was something they got used to, but occasionally she would take a deep breath and it would hit her again, fresh.

It had been a long time. Hours. It was sometime between midnight and morning. All they could do was wait. The door was locked from the inside, the handle on the outside seemed to be missing, or eaten by the locusts, and even though the screeching outside seemed to be dying away, they were trapped.

And the sound was dying away. The screeching was definitely less now. At least it wasn't the same pulse-pounding screaming as earlier in the night. It wasn't the screeching of insects, the fluttering of a million wings, the zipping of bullet-sized creatures racing by Jen as the group had run to the bar.

Jen shivered. And squeezed sister's hand. "He'll be here soon."

They both knew who Jen meant.

She had spoken the words softly. The air in the freezer seemed to be getting thin. The mix had certainly become more carbon dioxide than oxygen. There might have been some air coming in somewhere, but if so, Jen couldn't find where.

The freezer had kept them safe. For the most part. There had been one time, a few hours after they locked themselves in, when the locusts had found a way through. They had burrowed into the ventilation duct. Had eaten their way into the softer metal of the duct between the freezer and the refrigeration unit and made their way into the freezer.

It had been hard to hide the panic then. All they could hear was the skittering of the locusts, wings and carapaces bouncing off of walls in little ticks and tacks. There was no light; the group was all huddled together, each of them jerking and yelping when they got bit. One yelp became another. One scream led to a second, then a third. The whole group shifted around, and at the same time tried to press themselves tighter together.

Lucky enough, it was still cold in the freezer. If not freezing, the freezer had been built well enough, so it still retained a chill inside, even with the power out. That chill seemed to slow the locusts down as they trickled in.

Nick had tried to solve it first. He shadow-walked with his Five-Fold blade, time after time, looking for a way to close the hole. Or even find it. All he actually did was bring more locusts back with him, hanging on his clothes, skin, and hair. Those locusts buzzed around the darkness, until they landed on someone and bit them, then there would be a surprised cry and a slapping sound and, sometimes, more buzzing.

Nick was getting ready to go out again when Jen stopped him. Hating the locusts. Hating the bites. But hating most of all the fear they brought in her, the memory of the insects zipping by like the black bullet that had killed her.

"Nick," Jen finally said.

"I know," his voice was dark. Cold. Angry maybe, that he couldn't fix it. "It's just the one spot. I can't figure out how to close it."

Outside would be the refrigeration unit. A big box mounted up to the side of the freezer. Some hoses maybe, and a duct leading from the unit. It was likely the duct was tucked behind the machine and the wall of the freezer, and hard to get to from that side.

But not this one.

Jen let go of Sarah's fingers and got up. Slowly. One of the chickens hanging there bounced off her head, leaving her hair covered in a slimy frost. She tried not to think about it and began weaving her way around the wall.

"What are you doing?" her sister asked.

Nick had paused his assault on the locusts that had come in with him. He stood there, and Jen bumped into him before working her way along. Shushing Nick before he spoke. Quieting the group.

Jen shushed them. Listening for the hole. The screeching of locusts, heavily muted by the walls of the freezer. She closed her eyes, even in the darkness, and listened. Past the quick breaths of Nick. Past the deeper whistling breath of the bartender, with his broken nose.

She listened until she could hear where the screeching was loudest. Until she could hear the little feet of the locusts, as they crawled inside, as their wings fluttered and tapped against the metal of the freezer. Until she was feeling the wall with one hand, the metal freezing her palm, and she found the hole the locusts were sneaking through.

"Everyone, close your eyes."

She could feel the question coming from them. Waited a moment. "Close them tight. I'm going to count to three."

A locust bit her hand then. A sharp bite. Jen slapped her palm against the wall and felt the insect pop there. Leaving a messy goo on her skin.

"One…"

She slid her hand along until her palm covered the hole again. It was square and maybe a little smaller than her hand. There used to be a fine mesh there, but the mesh was gone, leaving tiny strands of torn metal that sharply poked into her skin. Along with other things. Moving things.

"Two…"

Something bumped up against her palm. Bulbous and prodding. Something—*a mandible?*—scratched lightly against her skin. It was hard not to jerk her hand back. It was dark. Cold. Freezing, and with the screeching outside and the tapping of locusts against the inside walls of the freezer.

The thing bit her. Jen smiled and tightened her eyes. "Three."

She called her power, and a ball of lightning appeared in the center of her hand. For just a quick moment. There was a zap, a loud popping sound, a flash of light burned brightly through her eyelids, and the smell of ozone flooded the freezer.

Then Jen pulled her hand back. Waited. The metal sizzled and burned in the darkness; she could hear it kind of bubbling. The ozone smell became something acrid. Jen couldn't see what she had done, but she hoped whatever hole had led to the outside, she hoped she had sealed that hole.

"Everyone take little breaths," Johnny said, and then laughed. It was a dark laugh, from a man who used to always have a quick quip ready.

Someone moved. Or jostled. Maybe elbowed. There was a grunt.

"Sorry." Johnny's voice again.

They waited after that, Jen finding her place between Sarah and Johnny. As far as she could tell, they were in the center of the floor, everyone almost back-to-back. There really wasn't a good way to share warmth, other than putting their arms around each other and huddling up.

Jen reached around her sister and Johnny. They huddled tight together. Sarah shivered a bit. Johnny held himself tight, as if afraid to move. Or holding himself so tightly he couldn't move. She could feel his arms, knotted up as if he clenched his hands against the cold. He was so thin under Jen's arm. Brittle.

Jen hadn't paid enough attention to him. Like Nick, Johnny had always been solid. Always been someone who could handle things. But he was in a fight now, a fight for his life, and with everything going on, with the brave face he had put on, they all had ignored him.

She could feel it now, in the tightness of his corded muscles. The brittle feel of his bones. The strain, in every breath Johnny took. Jen could feel it, but didn't know what to say. Especially here, now, trapped in this freezer, with dwindling air and a sea of insects waiting to eat them outside.

Insects that—to Jen—sounded like a million bullets, all aiming for her.

She hated it. Hated her anger. Hated her frustration with herself. And hated the fear. All of it stole time from her; Jen worried more about herself, and how she felt, than her friends.

Not that she ignored them. But she wasn't what she had been for them. And the anger, the fear, the frustration, all of it overwhelmed her sometimes. Jen didn't know how to face it. She could throw lightning, blow everything up, but the tiniest zipping sound, maybe someone zipping a bag up quickly, all of that would bring her fear back to her. The fear of a bullet tearing its way through her body before she could see it.

She had been so sure of things before her death. Sure of herself, sure of Gus, sure of her friends and what they could do, standing against Raphael in Grafton. Standing against Azazel in New Orleans.

And now, standing against Sabnock here. The glinty man, she was sure, in the storm of locusts outside. The demon trying to kill her.

And she thought she knew why.

Just like Azazel, Sabnock wanted to rob Gus of her.

That made her angry.

But also afraid.

Because the demons had won, once.

The fear waxed and waned in her, while they all waited. A tidal effect from an orbiting body she could never see, only feel. It ebbed and flowed, disappeared for days, then crashed into her at the oddest times. Those times the feeling was so strong it pushed away her thoughts of her sister, of Johnny, of the things her friends might need.

"Jen?" Sarah said, softly. "You okay?"

Jen realized her hands were balled tight. The tension radiated from them down each arm. Including the arm wrapped around her sister.

She pulled her arms back. Huddled them around herself, held herself tight. Trying for all the world to unball her hands, to relax. To feel her sister, worried next to her. To feel Johnny's shuddering, his fight against his hunger. Jen tried, after long moments, to focus on them, and push her fear away.

Hopefully, none of them weren't so far gone in their fears, their worries, their problems, that none of them couldn't be saved.

CHAPTER FOUR

Michael had been right, when he said I would be surprised at what the plague of locusts could do. Maybe I hadn't entirely believed him then. I hadn't even believed him after surviving the flight back with Gabrielle. But I should have.

The world had changed overnight.

I guess I should be used to that kind of thing. The world had changed in big ways for me lately, with Grafton, New Orleans, Colorado. And now here.

But I wasn't yet. I hoped I would never be. But there was a part of me that knew I should prepare for this. That something was happening the world over, that there was some force racing us all to a destination, that more and more changes would happen in the coming war between demons and the humans left on Earth willing to fight them.

We had left the vault as soon as the screeching had stopped. The cry of locusts had died off into a whistling whisper, leaving a sound like the faint ringing in the ears, and then maybe the ringing was gone. I couldn't tell if the sound was real or not; the screeching had been that loud, for that long. It was like getting a hearing test, wondering if you were hearing the ping in your ear, then wondering if you were just hearing the memory of the ping.

We had to break the elevator shaft open. Michael and I. Tabitha had sealed it good and in turn, she had to weaken the metals enough so that Michael and I could rip the doors apart. As carefully as we could. After all, we might need to hide back here again.

Then the two of us had to do the same thing to open the top of the elevator cab. As soon as we cracked the roof, dead locusts fell through. The shells piled over us, black husks streaming down like cereal pouring out of a box.

A lot of cereal. Into a very, very large bowl. Parts of mandibles and shells all mixed with a little green insecty-inside glop rained down on us both. Sometime in the middle of the pour I desperately found myself wanting a shower.

Still, we worked through all that. Then climbed up the emergency ladder, the ones they built into the side of elevator shafts. The sides of the shaft were sticky with popped locusts, my hands and feet were covered in the ichor by the time we got to the top. The rungs of the ladder seemed weak, pockmarked with the goo, but whatever corrosive effect the bodies of the locusts left behind seemed to fade after their death.

Then a short walk down a hallway covered in the same thick shells. My feet kicking a few, crunching others in my too-tight shoes. The front doorway gaped open in front of me, the door gone, missing, the sunlight shining through the hole dimly, as if the sun itself did not want to shine too bright a light on what had happened underneath it.

I walked through the open doorway. My hand tight on the Five-Fold blade. And broke out into the world, under a sun that had just finished rising in the east. A cool breeze—at least, cool in this weird-ass Mexican winter—blowing across my face. Bringing with it a musty scent, dusty, like old death. And a little sweet, like a wound that had gone gangrene.

Like a city, dying.

Dead.

Cuernavaca would never recover. It was gone. Forever.

All the buildings around us, brick, metal, wood, had been eaten. Every face of every wall was pockmarked, as if with age. And stained, stained with a greenish-rusty goo. The same ichor that coated my fingers, my pants, my shoes.

Millions of black wings everywhere, with tiny dark claw-like legs, and shells, all covered in that green goo ichor. The carapaces lay everywhere, as if the creatures had eaten their fill, then eaten more, eaten until they had burst. As if something had driven them, as if the insects had lost what minds they had. Ruptured bodies of locusts, almost popcorn-like, piled over the walls, across the streets; the shells crunched on the ground as I walked out the front door, they massed over a mound that looked suspiciously like a cat, though I didn't look too closely.

The tall towers in the middle of Mexico City made sense now. The bulbous, green-ichor stains I had seen at the top. The high-rises, they were nests. Nests for these locusts. The plague. How many of these locusts could each of those buildings hold?

Looking around Cuernavaca, I could only think, enough. Enough to do this. Enough to destroy everything, every person, every animal in Cuernavaca.

All the glass in every window was gone. Any thin material, like cotton or fabric, missing. Here and there might be a flap of the edge of a shirt. What was left of a belt buckle. And the buildings themselves. Made of iron, stone, and brick, even those had been worn down under the sea of locusts that had crashed over them.

After the glass, the curtains, the doors and windows had been eaten, after the two-by-fours and the drywall and tile had been nibbled on, well then the acid of the locusts had gone to work. Seeming to eat through iron and brick, stone and rock, only thick, humped remains of apartment buildings, leaving huddled homes without roofs, vehicles without tires.

I was suddenly glad my Camaro, the old '68, was hidden up in the United States. Because the newer one would never roll down a road again. All that was left of the car was the heavy metal of the frame and engine block. All the rubber hoses, the leather interior, the tires, all of that were gone. Even the seatbelts had been eaten.

Jesus, what could these locusts do?

I had asked that question a few times already.

Seeing was believing.

The angel had told me. And even now stepped up beside me. One eyebrow raised.

"Yeah," I said. "I understand now."

The plague was a real thing. The destruction might have hit hardest here, because we were hiding in the vault. But it spread out, further than I could see, and I imagined the entire city of Cuernavaca like this.

Just gone.

Destroyed. Eaten. Buildings, cars, pets. People. Everything looked pockmarked. Eaten. As if the city had aged thousands of years in the roughest weather, overnight. Covered in ichor and black shells. And sticking out of mounds of black shells, in places, whitish objects that I didn't look too closely at. Even so, I could see the empty orb sockets of a skull sitting on one pile of shells. A femur lying out of another. Even tiny white bones, like fingers, spread out of a scattering of black carapaces, like the last reach of a person buried under the plague, trying to claw their way out.

The key was warm on my chest. Calling. Beckoning.

The rest of Alejandro's people were coming out. One at a time. He had stayed at the top of the elevator to help those climbing up, and most of the vampires and people coming out, they were shocked. Stunned. I could see it in their faces, looking at the catlike mound, and glancing at each other.

It would be a rough way to go.

The swarm had been violent. Deadly. Its winds had hit Cuernavaca like a cannibalistic hurricane. Everything the plague had swept over was destroyed. Dead. Gone.

Gertrude and Tabitha came out of the door. The two stood in front of the truck they had been about to weld plates to before the plague struck. Standing in front of the truck where I had parked what had used to be a Camaro beside.

The welding machine was still there, a square box, the metal casing eaten, the two rubber wheels gone. Part of the metal frame looked twisted in the back, and the bottle that had been holding the gas was missing.

Tabitha looked at me. I knew what she was wondering. I needed to know the same.

It was like Michael had read my mind. "All of Mexico will be like this."

"All of it?"

The angel nodded. "Everything the plague touches. Everywhere the storm blows. Until the locusts eat themselves up."

I couldn't envision it. Not all of Mexico destroyed like this. In one day.

I mean, Mexico was big. BIG. How could it all be blown away, eaten, gone? This was a horrifying example of what was in store for the world. If Sabnock could do this here, then what were the other demons planning? How soon before Paris fell? Or Italy?

Had they already?

How long did I have to save the entire world?

Michael's face told me his thoughts ran along mine.

My eyes caught Gabrielle heading out of the front door of what used to be a building. She was just one refugee now in a stream of vampires and humans. The vampire had a quilt wrapped tightly around her, one fist visible above her breast, fingers tight around the blanket. Could vampires get cold? I didn't know, but the quilt was thick, something checkered in orange and yellows, which seemed very un-vampirish.

Her face was exhausted. Thin. Wan. The vampire was maybe too tired to be shocked or surprised at all the destruction around her.

After all, she had lived it.

"You are leaving soon?" she asked.

"Now, if I can help it," I said.

"Before you do." Gabrielle motioned to the Camaro. The truck. Or the humped metal-eaten shapes they were now. "The convoy."

Dammit. The Mad Max plan. I had made it flexible, so that we could adjust it on the fly. I had been a little proud of that part, truth be told. Especially since I wasn't a mastermind of those things. But if every truck and car in Cuernavaca was like this, if every car in Mexico was like this, well, I was pretty sure the plan wasn't *that* flexible.

I blew out a breath. Wondering where we were going to get any cars. Wondering how we were going to get to the dead zone and attack the Crown of Bones. Wondering how the plan would happen, with me having to fly up north.

"It'll have to wait."

At least until I got back. Maybe by then I'd come up with something.

Gabrielle's lips curled a bit. She looked south a bit, then back to me. As if she already had something in mind. "We will work on it."

"You have an idea?"

"Maybe." The vampire shrugged. "Go. Get your friends. Then come back and see."

Your friends. I hadn't missed that.

"It's our friends."

Her eyes flashed a bit. She went to say something. Her face was tired, exhausted, and her irises shimmered with the slightest bit of wetness. As if the vampire was forcing herself to not think about him. A thousand things went through her face, and she said none of them.

My heart raced to go north, but I stayed a last moment. "Wolverines, right?"

The thousand things flashing over her face stopped, like a slot machine, coming to rest on an expression I would have said seemed wistful. She nodded, though. Perhaps a thankful nod. "Wolverines."

Michael came up to stand beside us. His gaze north. Like me, I think he burned to go. The trip wouldn't be long, not the way we planned on travelling, but still I paused one last time. Whatever Gabrielle had planned, I wouldn't be here to help with. Or protect. The vampires here, and their humans, it would be them on their own.

An irrational need filled me, to be by Jen, *now*. To never leave her again. To never leave my friends on their own, to never leave them where Sabnock or Azazel or a thousand other things could kill them. Maybe not so irrational need as a rational one. A very Grimm one.

Michael's face twisted, as if he knew what I was thinking. The angel's actions made more sense to me now. Why he had retreated from the world. There could only be so many times you couldn't be around, so many times someone died because you were helping another before you began to step away from that pain.

"Just be careful," I told the vampire.

"Careful." Gabrielle's mouth twisted. Looking around. Waving a hand, half-heartedly, at the ruins we stood among.

"I know." I smiled her smile, something harsh and distant. Careful was relative.

"Be more than careful," Michael said, breaking into our conversation. His voice deep, his words slow. As if he was dredging up an old memory. "Sabnock does not do things by the half."

That figured. The demon wouldn't just think his plague would finish us all off. He would send someone, or something, to check and see who was left. To check and see if *we* were left.

Which left me with the burning need to get to Jen.

It was time.

"Listen to the angel," I said. "Whatever you're doing, stay low. We might be a few days, but we'll be back." My eyes met hers so that she would understand. "All of us."

Gabrielle nodded, not saying anything. I echoed her motion, not trusting my voice. Seeing the thousand things back on her face. In her eyes. Wet, but determined. Intent, but angry. Purposeful, but unsure.

She had made a decision, and whether it included the locusts, Johnny, Sabnock, the Mad Max plan, I couldn't tell. I hadn't a clue what she planned, or who she planned it with. What she moved forward with.

Whatever it was, I knew one thing. I knew resolve when I saw it.

Time passed slow in the freezer. It had warmed; Jen no longer shivered. There was a sweet, coppery scent in the air. Locusts stumbled around, fluttering a bit. She heard them, in little flickers of wings. An occasional hissing.

Much fewer now than earlier in the night. There had been more fluttering things, like giant flies buzzing. There were more yelps, more slaps, as the locusts bit someone. A swear or two.

Over the hours though, all that happened less and less. The fluttering wings. The yelps. The slaps. Most of them were silent now, Fernando and Zoe, Nick, Sarah, but they were also awake, awake and waiting in the warming freezer.

Would that be a waezer? A frarmzer? There was no way to combine the two words right. It worried Jen that she still was giggling inside at the thought. Maybe even giggling outside. Because she wasn't a giggler.

Everyone knew that.

Somewhere outside the sun rose, and they only really were aware of that from Nick. At some point there was enough light outside to keep him from shadow walking to the front of the fridge. He could feel the change as night faded away to dawn. At that point, he didn't have a place he felt safe walking to. Not in the bright light of day.

"It's different out there," was all he had said. "Sunrise."

Over the night the screeching had died off. Like the locusts had left, or perhaps were dying. Jen felt it first as a lessening of pressure, a lowering of volume in the screaming of the insects, a reduction of the bass-like pulsing underneath whatever drove the locusts.

It all faded, like all sound did, when you were in the drifting of that time and place right before sleep. It faded, but something else took its place. A pressure, a warm pressure, like a heavy blanket had been placed on them all, weighing each and every one of them down.

Jen was relaxing. And couldn't tell if it was because she was sleepy or cold. Exhausted or frozen. The blanket of pressure seemed to increase, and it didn't seem as cold in the unit anymore. The smell inside had gotten… meatier. As if the chicken and the beef were thawing.

"So hungry…" Johnny's whisper felt tight. Small, as if he hadn't wanted anyone else to hear them. As if it was something he had said in his mind and hadn't wanted the words spoken aloud.

Jen patted his leg. Lightly. His hand found hers and squeezed hard. She thought she could feel Johnny shudder, his body shook just a bit, and she thought he was crying. Silently.

She squeezed his hands back.

Her whisper could be heard by everyone, but she kept it low, just the same. Meaning the words just for him. "Are you okay?"

Johnny's reply was low, torn. The kind of sound that came from the chest, from a cry inside that never stopped. "No."

"What can we do?"

His head shook, she could feel it. "Nothing… Nothing. Nothing anyone can do, now."

"Johnny."

"Quiet," he said. A beg. A command. "Quiet. Just let me fight it… Just let me fight it."

Fighting the hunger. The thirst. Jen knew what he fought, but maybe it was time for him to give in. Before it got so bad that Johnny couldn't control it.

Her hand tightened. It wasn't fair. It wasn't fair. Not to Johnny, not to any of them. The group, the friends, they had come so *far*. And for it to end now, for him, in this freezer. For him to turn and become something he didn't want to be, maybe turn and hurt one of his friends, it wasn't right.

It wasn't fair.

Life wasn't fair. Jen knew that better than most. Knew that just because Gus had saved her once, had brought her back from being a ghost once, there was no guarantee he could do it again. Knew she could die, she could be bit, she could be eaten by those insects in the next few hours, just as easy as anyone else.

Quiet then, quiet with an occasional sob from Johnny. Otherwise, quiet. Quiet enough to hear little ticks and tacks of the few locusts left outside, flying and striking the freezer door. Quiet enough to hear the ice inside the freezer melt, to become water, and for the water to drip and plop on the freezer floor. Quiet enough to hear each of their breaths, slow draws in, quiet exhales out. Quiet enough to hear Johnny cry.

She didn't know how to help. And she desperately wanted to. Johnny had almost died, coming after Grimm, coming to try to save her. Jen wanted to help him, *needed* to help him, but like a lot of things lately, what she did seemed a little off. A little not right. A little not her. "I'm sorry Johnny," she said, forcing her hand open. "So sorry."

Johnny huddled in tighter. His moan seemed to come from inside him, like he had pressed his mouth over his jacket. Jen reached out, pulling her hand back as an ethereal blue glow lit the inside of the freezer.

Her keystone, lightly glowing that blue-white glow. Dim, but so bright in the dark freezer. The glow outlined the shuddering Johnny. The glow also revealed Nick, a few feet away from Johnny, his back to the wall and his hand lightly holding the hilt of his Five-Fold blade. Nick's face was a mask, his eyes hidden behind the light reflecting from his glasses.

Johnny moaned on, low, quiet sobs. Jen's face warmed, and she tucked the keystone inside her shirt where the glow lessened, and returned the group to darkness. She held her hand there, pressed against her shirt, pressed against the key.

Gus reached along the bond. Faint, still far away. But headed this way, and from all the ethereal energy he was burning through, all the ghosts he was living, he was headed this way fast.

Okay?

Okay? Jen thought. *But hurry.*

There was relief from the bond, a feeling of gladness swelling between them. Then, as if Gus had just got it, a question.

Hurry?

Okay, Jen repeated. *Just hurry.*

"He's on his way," she said.

There was a deep breath, and an exhale. Jen realized it came from Johnny. And at that, the whole group seemed to relax. Jen felt the bond and reached back along it, just letting Gus know they were okay. Though there might be a need to hurry. Nothing urgent; they were safe. But hurry.

Jen didn't want to warn Gus that they were low on air. And that Johnny was hurting. And that hurting could lead to something worse.

But she had said the hurry word too much. She knew Gus would hear that from the bond and know. He would fly faster now.

Though he may not enjoy her back-seat flying.

She giggled—she *never* did that—and realized she wasn't hiding anything along the bond. That Gus could feel what she was going through and was already worried. And she didn't want to worry him; he would get here when he got here.

There was no need to burden him more.

The air must really be getting thin.

She fought another giggle. Felt the pressure in the freezer return, slowly, a tiny drawing of the heavy invisible blanket over her. Felt Johnny, still huddled on the floor of the freezer. Felt Nick look at her with his mask of a face. Even felt her sister looking at her in the dark.

Jen tried to be more serious. It's what she should be.

"He'll be here soon," she said, she thought for the third time. Or the second? Jen couldn't remember. She kept her eyes closed and just rode the bond, feeling Gus getting closer and closer in the air, shooting across the horizon like a missile. Homing in to where she was and flaring ethereal exhaust behind him.

It was just a waiting game now. They would be okay soon. So no more back-seat flying from Jen for now. No more frantic worries to Gus. She sat there and tried her hardest to radiate a *we're here* along the bond, followed by a *we're okay*.

Letting Gus follow that thread to them.

CHAPTER FIVE

I flew.

The pull of the keystone drew me like a fisherman drawing in his line, a steady, inexhaustible force. I was pulled northeast, always northeast, and I followed the pull, hoping not to find a net at the end, but my friends. Happy. Healthy. Safe.

As fast as I flew, the line seemed to pull me faster. Always faster.

I was worried. Jen hovered in the background of our bond; she had both told me not to worry, and also to hurry. Neither message made me feel like things were happy, healthy, or that my friends were truly safe. Now she just rested, radiating an *okayness* that was likely to be more fiction than fact.

I couldn't help but feel the confusion in her message, a light-headedness to her thoughts, even a slight anger, an unfairness. So I pressed on faster. And faster. And faster.

And as fast as I went, the invisible pull of the bond, the line between Jen and I, drawing me closer, never slacked.

Ghost after ghost zipped by underneath me. I tapped each,

quickly. The air whipped past me, clouds burst as I passed through them, and somewhere behind me there might have been a slow roll of thunder, a sonic boom.

At those speeds it might have been easy to miss the devastation below.

It wasn't.

I just got to see more of it. I just got to see how far the destruction went. How deep Sabnock's strike had cut. How much the locusts had eaten, how many people the swarm had killed, how much now was just... gone.

The locations of the dead zones had made sense to me. Places of high populations. Places that had been around for a long time. Places that had maybe more dead buried around them than people alive. A resource for the demons. Live bodies. Dead bodies. Ghosts and spirits of the undead. Things that could make easy, standing armies.

There were definitely fewer people alive now than dead. We had seen a lack of people here in Mexico. Part of me had wondered about it but had shoved that wonder behind other more pressing problems.

There were no people around. There was no army invading the dead zone. The cartels weren't battling it out with the demon. Or even helping Sabnock. There was a lack of people here, a lack of presence that I hadn't given enough thought to.

Where were they all? The hundreds of millions of people that should live here? They couldn't have all fled; there was no place for them to go. The border to the United States would have been swamped. The ports. Everything.

Instead there was no one, anywhere. Just the people in the lines in Nick's pictures. A lot of people, in the stadium, in the Crown of Bones, but surely not everyone in Mexico. That would have been standing room only. Not only in the stadium, but in the entire city.

If you turned on the news right now, there would probably be something about the dead zones on every channel. There would be announcements from the president of the United States, trying to make a treaty with Azazel and New Orleans Zone. There would be updates from the government and their new task force, still trying to determine everything that happened in Denver and Red Rock. You might even still see a ticker scrolling by as that same task force searched for us. Me and the Wolverines.

Flipping through the channels you would also see news flashes about the French army in Paris, still in a deadlock with its dead zone. Shots of the Louvre on fire. The *thing* flying in the sky, what they were calling a dragon, nesting in the Eiffel Tower. Similar updates would come from Hong Kong, though minus the dragon.

There would be a deep dive into Rome. About what they were calling the Lost Templar Army. The Lost Crusade. The templars had gone in, trying to make it to the Vatican, and never come out.

But you wouldn't see anything about Mexico City. Not anymore. No details, at least. No video, no reporter calling into some news show up in New York. There wasn't going to be a news flash on the screen, no scrolling across the bottom of the television. No camera shots of the Crown of Bones or the people lining up to go inside it.

Mexico had gone dark. There wouldn't be any video shots, no people uploading clips from the phones because there weren't any phones. No phones, and no people. No people, so no reporters. And nothing for the reporters to get around in, even if they were here. No news vans or helicopters or cameras.

There was nothing to be reported, because there was nothing and no one available to do the reporting. And, if there had been someone, there was no way for them to broadcast the report.

It was just me, now. Just us. The Wolverines, some vampires in Cuernavaca, and an angel. Maybe the last angel.

Michael and I had circled wide of the dead zone. Keeping as far from Sabnock as we could. I thought, I hoped, the demon thought we were dead. Blazing a trail across the sky over Mexico City would be a good way to screw that up.

But I couldn't slow down. Now that the night of the plague was over, I wasn't waiting another moment more than I had to. I poured on the speed and damned the consequences.

We both flew. Me and Michael. He with real wings, me with my ethereal ones. Him a brightly shining sun, me more of a blazing light, trailing ethereal sparks. From the air we might have appeared like a meteor. A ball of light streaking north across the sky. A shooting star framed across the rising sun.

Beneath us was destruction on an unknown scale. The plague of locusts hadn't just come after us in Cuernavaca. It hadn't just come after Jen and my friends in our hideout town. The swarm had spread outward from Mexico City like a cancer, eating everything surrounding the dead zone, washed outward like a ripple from a pond until the wave of insects died out, hundreds and hundreds of miles from the city.

It was a hell of a thing to witness.

Every town, large and small. Every home. All eaten away like it had been ravaged by time. Walls left barely standing, roofs eaten and open to the sky, everything pockmarked with bites, covered in the green ichor the locusts left behind. Hard things, like bricks and metals, pieces of those things were left. But soft things, like cotton or cloth; thin things like glass, and fragile things, like people.

All that was gone.

And the sight of it all only made me fly faster.

I reached northeast on my radar. Found a ghost. Tapped it and used the ethereal energy there to build up speed. There was a quick flash of a memory, a scream of pain, a thought of *something bit me,* then a slap of their hand. The ghost ran, shoving aside someone, trying to get inside as the blue sky overhead became overwhelmed by a screeching cloud.

The ghost pushed another person down. Stepped on them, trying to get inside a home. Slapping themselves and screaming. Panicked thoughts *oh god something is biting me*, repeated over and over, followed by a painful, huddled death as locusts swarmed them.

I wished that had been the only memory like that I had lived on this trip. But that memory wasn't the exception, it was the rule. I wasn't using the knife. The Five-Fold blade. There wasn't much ethereal energy left in it. I had leaned on it too much in the past day, and now I worried it didn't carry enough energy to help me in the dead zone.

I was back to tapping ghosts. Cringing as I lived their memory. Waiting for one of the really evil spirits to come after me. I hated it, and I hated having to live the memories. The stain on my soul felt much like the towns below me, pockmarked and eaten, mottled, smeared by an ichor that would never wipe away.

All power should come with a price.

I guess I had known that. And whether I paid it in one go, as I had with Hector and the ghosts around him, or I paid it in little installments, I always had to pay.

I could pay that price. I would pay any price. I wouldn't like it. I never liked it, and I would always wonder what it did to me, the clawing of Evil, dragging me down into its depths. Maybe the stain would stick one day. Maybe the stain would grow, maybe the abyss would keep staring until I finally became the thing I fought.

I would always wonder what it did to me. But I would pay it in spades to make sure my friends were safe. That Jen was safe.

We homed in on the town with our hideout apartment building. I could never remember its name. Michael following me. An angel, and a guy pretending to be one.

Jen was quiet now. Sleeping, napping, or unconscious? I flew faster. She stirred weakly. Sent me a mixed signal, the same signal I had been getting from here, something like *we're okay* mixed with *hurry*.

Then she fell back asleep.

At least, I wanted to hope it was sleep. I tapped another ghost and flew faster. Michael dropped a little further behind me and hurried to catch up. We blazed across the sky until we got to the safe house town.

Which was a disaster.

I recognized it only because of the main street. Not the street itself, but the pattern the main streets had. Like the patterns of any main street, in any town. The feeling of this street ran a couple of blocks *here*. The building, nothing but a slumped shell now, used to be *this*. There was a pattern of buildings, a row of brick construction three or four brick stories high, where they funneled Main Street past the bar right *there*.

There was a row of buildings, missing roofs, humped blocks of brick and empty frames that might once have held stucco or stone. There was the grocery store on the block, right past the bar, the tiny square store all by itself on the corner. Or at least, what the building used to be, and now was nothing but missing glass windows, an open roof, and walls eaten until they were nubs.

At the far end of Main Street, the northern end, was the gas station. The sign there with the gas prices actually remained standing, untouched. It was the only thing left, the pavement around where the pumps had been was now blacktop covered in blacker burn marks. There was a hole in the ground where the gas tanks had been. And around the hole a big blot of blackness, burned into the blacktop, like the gasoline there had erupted in a gigantic explosion.

I slowed down above Main Street, locating things I knew used to be there. I found our apartment building, what was left of it, and dropped down through the sky, aiming to land by the alley door.

Halfway down I realized the bond wasn't leading me there. Jen wasn't in the safe house.

Though she was nearby; I corrected course and dropped in front of the bar. As I lowered down I saw the scorch marks everywhere. Black streaks on the pavement, on the walls in front of me. Black burns around the shattered bones of a broken roof. There were hundreds of black streaks, maybe thousands, and landing I got a big breath of a heavy ozone scent.

Jen.

The glass in the front window of the bar was gone. The neon sign above the door with the yellow letters, the red A, gone. The door, gone. And parts of the roof. The sun overhead broke through the ceiling and illuminated everything. There were walls there, in a faint resemblance of the shape of the bar. A low hump in front of the side wall where the tequila bottles had perched above the bar, those bottles gone now, though the sunlight caught a few bits of brightly colored glass, mixed in with the bodies of the locusts.

In the corner there, far across from me, was the table Jen and Zoe and I had sat at, just a few nights past. The table was no longer there. The *tables* were no longer there. All the stools were missing too. The jukebox by the front had been eaten to its feet.

Black carapaces were everywhere. Dark hulls crunched under my feet as I worked my way into the bar. Following the bond. *Crunch, crunch, crunch.* Letting the pull of it lead me to Jen. Trying not to worry.

The pull of *her* was strong. It led me past the bar. I crunched the whole way.

There had been a door behind the bar once; the door was gone now, leaving an empty hole and open sightline into what used to be a small kitchen. There were things there that could have once been pots and pans, what was definitely a large cast-iron skillet, and a long metal table, like those in commercial kitchens.

All of the metal there was pockmarked. Eaten. And covered in the green goo. The cast-iron skillet was the only thing I really recognized, and only its shape gave me the idea that the other things were pots and pans. They couldn't be skulls.

A twinge of fear ran through me. Even though I felt Jen, nearby. The metal table had a long black mark down its middle, something that zigged and zagged all the way along its surface, with the same scent of ozone near it I had found outside the bar.

There was crunching behind me. Michael. His feet made the same crackling, hull-crushing sound mine did. Something between a crunch and a shushing shuffle as the two of us worked our way deeper into the kitchen, past the long half-eaten table with the light-ning mark on it.

In the back was a door. A real door. One of those thick stainless-steel doors built into a walk-in freezer. The latch on the door was missing. Eaten. Gone. The metal of the door covered with pock-marks, stained in the ichor, the locusts had battered themselves against it, trying to erode the steel in waves. Eating it with their tiny supernatural mandibles. Bodies bursting and leaving goo everywhere.

The pull of Jen ended at the door.

I sent an *I'm here* through the bond.

A feeling like relief echoed back. And maybe a giggle?

Jen didn't giggle.

I took a peek at the corners of the door. Where the stainless-steel freezer had been mounted into the wall. I was able to work my fingers into a corner, and I reached out to grab a ghost as Michael grabbed the other corner.

I counted to three, then we both gave a good yank.

The door *peeled* away from the freezer with a long, metal squeal. Peeling away in a big U, like the goo and the ichor had welded the door to the unit behind it. The squeal went on forever until the door gave way, finally, flying backwards out of our hands, tumbling through the rest of the kitchen and kicking up locust shells where it landed.

A blast of coolish air came from behind the door, cool air and the stale smell of once-frozen food that was more warm than it should be. The first thing I saw were chickens and slabs of pork hanging from hooks in the ceiling of the fridge, and for a moment I panicked until I saw my friends on the floor below.

All of them were huddled together, packed on the bottom of the freezer like sardines. Jen and Sarah, Johnny and Nick. Nick held his Five-Fold blade. Zoe. And even the bartender was there, Renaldo.

All of them had been slashed and cut. Bitten. Each of them had little dried blood trails along their faces, locust bites and slashes. Jen was marked with them, though Nick was the worst, covered in slashes and cuts and green goo.

They all blinked at the sudden sunlight, holding hands in front of their faces. Each of them stirred, weakly, taking large breaths. They unpacked themselves from the center of the freezer floor, ducking to avoid the meat on the hooks above them.

I saw them all, but I saw Jen first. Her eyes fluttered a bit, then they focused on me. There were cuts along her face and arms; I noticed those and at the same time didn't really see them. All I could see was Jen. All I could feel was relief; it washed through me, tingled my skin with goosebumps.

Alive.

Jen smiled at me, the tiniest of her smiles, but also one of her best.

"Hey," she said. Her voice tiny.

"Hey." I grinned back and pulled her up. Jen let out a groan, as if she was stiff, but her arms wrapped themselves around my back and pulled me in, hugging me for all I was worth.

It felt good. My face nestled in her hair, taking breaths of honeysuckle. My arms holding her tight, feeling her heart beating in her chest. Feeling her body warm against mine. There's a safety there, being held by the person you loved. By someone who had your back, no matter what. There's a security, a feeling of home, of knowing that in that moment nothing could hurt you.

I hugged Jen tighter. She hugged me back, her arms pulling me into her. Creating a world that existed just between two people who loved each other and would always be there for one another.

Just good.

CHAPTER SIX

M y friends were starving.

Hell, I was starving.

And there was nothing to eat, anywhere.

And worse, nothing to drink. Anything perishable had, well, perished. And as important as food was, water was going to be more critical. Looking at the sink in the bar's kitchen, or what was left of it, that was going to be tough to come by. The sink was full of dead locusts; the stainless-steel sides dripped in green goo, the knobs on the hot and cold taps had been eaten off, hell even the faucet was missing.

We'd have to figure that out. Soon.

But first, introductions.

Michael nodded as I introduced him to the group. The angel stood in the corner, tall, imposing, a big, commanding figure. It struck me that there was something in Michael that reminded me of my father. Definitely not the language, but something in his size, in the way he stood. Something inside?

If my friends had issues meeting a real angel, they passed over it quickly. Nick nodded back in a *no big deal* kind of way. Sarah gave a wave. Johnny looked a bit lost. Zoe was the one person who had a thousand questions.

Jen shook Michael's hand with a firm grasp. Looked the angel up and down. As if measuring him. And then, quite distinctly, stepped close to me. Placing her hip next to mine. Still looking at Michael with a steady, even gaze.

We caught up quickly, exchanging stories of the night before. Nick started theirs with the search for Johnny, the gathering black cloud in the sky, the pelting of insect hail against the windows. He got to the part where they had gotten into the alley and were getting bombarded by locusts. He was talking about it seriously and thoughtfully, in the Nick fashion. Taking it step by step.

"We got out there, and the bugs were all over us. Tiny sharp bites all over my skin. A few of the things had gotten under my shirt, and they were crawling around my chest, and I kept smacking them..."

Nick gestured to his shirt. There were dried splotches all over it. "I had this thought, I couldn't believe I was going to get eaten by bugs, swatting the things in my shirt, wondering if the outdoor companies even made a locust repellant."

He smiled a grim smile. Shook his head once. Like part of him still couldn't believe it.

That was when Jen had called lightning. A cool breath of air had blown through the alley before whipping through the group. Then bolts had struck everywhere, striking with big booming sounds, echoing away in long rumbles, leaving shattered cracks in the ground around them.

The pressure of the locusts had eased then. The insects flew around, burst around, were tossed around by the lightning and the wind. They seemed to have lost their minds, flying in every which way. Trying to escape the death from above.

Nick finished the story. Jen leaned partly against me, her back warm against my chest, and my hand was over hers, my thumb in her palm. Jen's head was turned some, her lips curved in a smile. She whispered to me that if the locusts wanted a storm, she would be the storm.

I squeezed Jen's hand.

There *were* a lot of black marks zig-zagging around us on all the walls.

It would have been a hell of a storm.

I kept my story short. Just gave the highlights. Didn't go into the whole armor of faith thing, and I watched Michael watching me as I glossed over that part, and the angel's small curve of his lips. I finished up with Tabitha sealing us in the vault, under the earth, keeping the locusts out.

"We did your freezer thing," I said. "Just a little larger freezer."

Nick raised his eyebrow. "Well, without the freezing, too."

I laughed, feeling good to be around my friends. Feeling good about all of us being close to death and coming through. Sabnock had took his shot and missed. And now it would be our turn. "Yeah," I agreed. "Without the freezing."

Still, it wasn't all happy thoughts and jokes and laughs. During the conversation, Johnny's head kept turning to look back at the freezer. His mouth moved some, as if he was swallowing something imaginary down, slaking an unknowing thirst. His eyes pressed together, and he would turn away, but then he would turn back again, moments later.

The laughter died off. We were all hungry. Johnny, for multiple reasons. We needed to find food, find water, and find transportation. And while we looked for all that, we needed to keep an eye out for Sabnock. I brought up what Michael had said to Gabrielle before we left. That Sabnock wouldn't leave something halfway done.

"This is halfway?" Zoe waved her hand around the bar. At the tens of thousands of dead locusts lying around in piles.

"This is just the beginning," Michael said. "I think we angered him. I think I angered him, showing up, and saving Grimm. I think Sabnock released the plague before he wanted to. It was too much work, for too little reward."

"Too little?" I asked. There were very few people who could stand up to the demons now, in their dead zones. No army, nothing in the world, had won any battle.

I was the only person who had killed a demon recently. My friends and I seemed to be the only people who could stand up to the demons. Stand and survive, at least. I mean, even the Templar army was missing.

If Sabnock could take us out, I thought the demon would sacrifice any amount of work to kill me. To kill us, the Wolverines.

"You misunderstand," Michael said. "Azazel has a plan, something he put together thousands of years ago. Something he and the demons want. You weren't a part of that plan now. So whatever resources they use now against you, those are resources they pull from their plan."

They could waste whatever they wanted on me. I would survive it. "Sounds like a win, then."

Michael nodded. "For now."

Jen seemed worried, though. "Can he send more locusts?"

"Not like last night," Michael said. "I would guess he depleted his plague. He will have to make more."

"You would guess?" Jen asked. Not looking happy with the answer.

"If you are asking for certainty, I have none." Michael said. "So yes, I would guess. The plague ran its course. But Sabnock still has his Ushabti. He still has his army of vampires and whatever humans are under his command."

"So," Nick said. "To sum up. We need food and water. We need transportation to get to Cuernavaca. We actually need weapons, because whatever is around was eaten or ruined by the locusts. And we have to do all of that while watching for Sabnock's army to come out here and finish us off, and hope that he's out of locusts, since we don't really have a safe place to hide from them now."

"That sounds… accurate," Michael said.

Jen's hand tightened around mine. There was something about the locusts that really bothered her. I could feel the fear along the bond.

"Well, not much we can do standing around," I said. "So let's start with the basics and work from there. Food and water first. A place to bunker down from the locusts next. Then transportation."

Nick looked at the locusts. We all had seen the outside of the town. The rubble. The buildings, slumped and eaten. The few square-shaped things in the streets that used to be cars and trucks.

"Going to be hard to find enough vehicles," Nick said.

"That's why it's last," I said. "Food and water first."

My stomach rumbled at the thought as if backing up my point. I was thirsty; we all were, but water was hard to find. The bar had a sink, but we wouldn't be drinking out of that anytime soon. We might be able to get more water from it by turning some valve somewhere, but it wasn't water I wanted to drink. Not in its current state. So we broke up into groups. Fernando mentioned the grocery store had a freezer like his, so Nick and Sarah were going to go there.

Jen and Zoe were going to walk the other way, to the gas station. To see if it had a freezer too. Even though it looked like the tank underneath the station had blown up, it was something to check.

Michael was going to fly around. Take overwatch. Keep an eye on the town and the road heading into the town from Mexico City.

Which left Fernando, Johnny, and me to clean up the bar. While the locusts and the lightning and Jen's fight with Sabnock had taken something out of the place, at least it was still standing. Even if there were holes in the roof and a freezer full of thawing chicken and pork.

The bartender had found a broom somewhere, something not nibbled on, and was busy cleaning out his bar. Sweeping out the shells. Johnny was either helping him, or looking for a bottle of beer or liquor that hadn't been eaten by the locusts.

Which left me and the freezer.

I smiled to myself. This whole thing had been done subtly. Everyone volunteering to do a task here, or wander away there, until the freezer was left, and I was the only person without a task. The freezer full of slimy, dripping chickens and slabs of pork hanging from hooks.

I gave Jen the eye, when I realized what had happened.

She smiled at me and gave me a little wink.

So an hour after landing, that's what I was doing. Carrying large, thawing slimy hunks of pork a few blocks away, tossing them in a half-eaten dumpster there. Doing the same thing with the chickens, a little nausea in my stomach as the rubbery birds swung loosely from my hands.

It was nasty work, the meat was slimy, hard where it was frozen, slick on the outside. I held my breath as I entered the freezer; it smelled funky, the very beginning of a sweet, rancid smell that always came from bad chicken and pork. I found a few pieces of cloth in the dumpster, a couple of rags, and started using them to carry the meat.

There were still some locusts inside. Most of the insects dead. But some struggled to walk around still. Moving slowly as if they were cold. Some hanging from the meat, wings twitching.

I grabbed a hunk of pork, working it off the hook and wincing at the feel of it in my hands. I watched one locust, hanging onto a dead, plucked chicken. The locust fell off the chicken and dropped to the floor. It hit the ground and lay there a moment, then fluttered its wings. As if waking from some deep hibernation.

The thought froze me.

Not literally. But figuratively.

There was something there. An understanding. The last little bit of chill in the freezer. The frozen meat. And the slowly moving locust.

The realization fully hit me.

I knew what the tractor-trailers were carrying now. I knew what the demons planned. I even knew why Michael had said Sabnock had released the plague before he had wanted to. I even knew how the locusts were being created.

All those refrigerated carriers, all those people being led to the stadium. The people listless in their lines. Being herded by the knights. The huge swirl of ethereal energy, the hundreds of thousands of ghosts, in the center of the field.

Sabnock was building an army. An army of locusts. He was building a world-ending plague and shipping it out to the rest of the dead zones.

They were like bombs. Bombs of insects, built of refrigerated containers. Building his nests of locusts in each, and keeping the locusts in hibernation, as he sent them to the other demons. He was building a swarm that would cover the world. A plague to wipe us all out. Across the Earth. Any person, building, dog or cat would be gone.

Maybe there was a clock running; maybe the demon was keeping all his bugs on ice so that they would release at the same time. Each dead zone would have its own hive, be the epicenter of their own plague; all the locusts would spread out from each. Eating everything and everyone in their path.

Did locusts even have hives?

I stood there, looking into the freezer, holding a piece of meat in my hands. Frozen in thought. Johnny walked in, a broom in his hand, his eyes taking it all in. The open fridge. The crawling locust. To my hands, wrapped in a ragged, eaten cloth, holding thawing, slimy meat.

His head shook, left and right, in little motions. His eyes looked torn, tormented. Maybe the locusts had taken little bites of all of us, but something else was eating him up inside.

Maybe literally.

"Johnny, you good?"

His voice was rough. "Hungry Grimm. I'm hungry."

I knew he wasn't talking about hunger for a good steak. But I didn't know what I could do for him. Or what he could do for himself. I was holding out hope for Johnny, but I realized that I didn't have a plan, or an answer, or anything to really help my friend with.

All I had was hope that he could keep the hunger at bay. "You holding on?"

He barked out a laugh. "What choice do I have?"

And with that, he walked back out to the main part of the bar. Holding the broom tightly in his hands but not doing any sweeping with it.

I kept hauling the meat out. Until the freezer was mostly empty. I used the rags to clean out the few locusts left. It wasn't clean, but it was the best I could do.

Jen and Zoe came back empty-handed, as I finished. The timing seemed about right, and I didn't mention to Jen that the two of them only got back after I got done hauling all the slimy meat from the freezer. And she didn't mention it either, even if there was a little twinkle in her eye as she reported that the gas station was just an empty shell.

While we waited, I told Jen about the locusts, and the tractor-trailers, and what Sabnock was doing with them. My thoughts of how the demon was creating the locusts, and why. Sabnock's overall plan, and maybe even *the* plan, how the demons were going to rid the Earth of the human race.

"These locusts then, they used to be, people..." Jen said. Looking at what we all stood in, with a sad, disgusted kind of grimace.

I thought so, but the swirl of ethereal energy in the picture had been too strong to really see. The ethereal sun in the center of what Sabnock called the Zatar. The bright blue ball in the middle of the Crown of Bones, Aztec Stadium. The concentration of ghosts there, so many spirits that everything else in the picture had been masked by the radiance.

And Sabnock was creating them. Creating the spirits by killing humans. He was Anubis, the gatherer of souls, the guardian of the gateway to the underworld. In some way he took them, took their souls maybe, took their deaths and grabbed their souls and created monsters out of them. Locusts. The crabs. The Ushabti. All of those being created and shipped, weapons, armies in the making. From one of the countries that had held the largest populations across the Earth over the longest period of time.

There was a reason Mexico felt empty, now.

It made sense to me. We had pictures of people going in, but no one coming out. The things I believed were going on seemed possible. I had witnessed, personally, Hector in the golem's body. He was tapping into the afterlife through the pentagram, through the Zatar, and using the power that had created the dead zones to do it.

Don't quote me on any of that. It wasn't like I was an exorcist. Or some book of supernatural knowledge. Or had slept in a Holiday Inn Express last night.

The theory worked though, in my mind. Even if I couldn't

understand the math. The evil spirits, flocking to Sabnock's version of the afterlife. Being granted life again in the golems. The humans being led there, killed, becoming insects and other creatures.

How many locusts could be made from one person?

I didn't know. But the pentagram definitely held the power to do it. And that realization had me shift my priorities. Had our group shift their priorities.

"This might be about more than killing Sabnock," I finally said.

Jen got it. And smiled. I loved that about her. She got me and backed me up like we were two halves of the same person.

Whatever we did, Sabnock wasn't on the top of our list anymore. We weren't down here just to kill him and exorcise the dead zone. We needed to purge the dead zone, at any cost. Keep the plague of locusts from being made, being shipped out over the world.

And hopefully do it in time to save the Earth.

"We can still kill him though," Jen said, her smile a little less smiley. More serious. "Right?"

I loved that about her, too.

CHAPTER SEVEN

Nick and Sarah had come back bearing gifts.

Not incense and myrrh. But packaged food. Boxes of candy bars, boxes of the protein bars that were just candy bars in different wrappers, and some bottles of warm water. Some six-packs of soda, just as warm.

The grocery had a room that had made it safely through the plague. Not a fridge, but a good-sized room with a thick door stocked with food. The room held shelves of chips, dried packages of meat, shelves of bottled water, and a safe.

No storekeeper though. I remember the lady there; I had bought stuff from her before. A nice older lady, hunched over, maybe because of arthritis or just age. Nick said he hadn't seen her, though there had been a mound of shells behind the register, covering a large mound of meat and bone.

Nick's face didn't look good, talking about it.

The room had survived through the plague. The walls had been thick, and maybe the room had been built strong enough to withstand the locusts because of the safe. The door to the room had thunked like it was made of steel.

We couldn't wait to eat and put most of the food on the kitchen table. My fingers brushed over the black zigzag along the stainless steel; the surface felt rough there. Bubbly. Scarred. As if the bolt had skittered over the surface before exploding into the far wall.

My stomach rumbled again as we were setting the food out. Jen laughed at it, and then her stomach rumbled too, which had all of us laughing. My throat was dry. Parched. My tongue seemed larger than normal.

We tore into the food and the water. We were all starving and probably ate too fast. I know I had never eaten a peanut butter cup faster. Or multiple peanut butter cups. Jen rolled her eyes as I grabbed another package.

It felt good, to eat. To eat with friends. At least, it felt good until Johnny started throwing what he ate back up. The rest of us paused, I had a candy bar half in my mouth, not knowing what to do. Jen's eyes were worried. Johnny waved at us, trying a second bite of the protein bar, forcing it down with a swig of the warm water, and threw that up as well.

He retched a few more times, then looked at us with a horrible face, something sad and resigned and self-loathing, before moving away with a couple of the candy bars and a bottle of water.

Peanut butter cups aren't candy bars, right?

Dammit.

I sat my half-eaten bar down and followed him. He saw me and shuffled faster through the locusts. Out into the bar, with its ceiling half-open to the sky. Then out into the street.

"Stay away, Grimm," he said.

I stopped. Johnny stopped. He was so lean now, not actually lean, but *thin*. Cadaverously so. The shirt he wore hung loose around his frame, like a tent; a quick burst of wind might blow Johnny away.

"Brother," I said.

Johnny faced away from me. Bowed. His shoulders huddled around himself. His voice tiny and frustrated and lost.

"I'm so hungry."

Those three words cut me to the core. I felt the loathing and the pity and the shame in them. How much Johnny hated himself now.

It made me hate myself, too. After Red Rock, after Azazel in Charleston, we had put the dead zone and Sabnock at the top of our list. I had focused on them and had just kind of depended on Johnny to take care of himself.

I hadn't really tried to help. Maybe I hadn't had the time. Maybe there was a lot on my shoulders anyway. In either case, in *any* case, I still hadn't tried.

And now look at him.

Johnny's hands opened, and the candy bars and the soda fell to the street.

"The drinking helped," he said. I couldn't see his face, but his voice was strangely muted. "Maybe not with the hunger, but with helping me forget about it. It was all I had, and now that's gone. *Gone.*"

His fists tightened. "I can't tell you how hungry I am. How much it *hurts* not to eat. It overwhelms me with it, it's all I can think of... Sometimes I think it drives me to hallucinate. I imagine myself biting someone and the relief I would feel. The god-blessed *relief*, man."

"We're going to—" I let the rest of the sentence fall silent. The one I had said plenty of times. *Figure it out.*

What were we going to do? What could I do?

"Yeah, I know," he said. Still not facing me. Not saying the three words, either. "How, Grimm? Fucking how? Sometimes I think I hear you and Jen talking, but when I look, you just are looking at each other, and both of your mouths are closed. Sometimes you're not even there."

He barked a laugh. "All the time now, I'm feeling things. Seeing things. Hearing things. All the fucking time. All night, in the fridge, I kept feeling like I was getting bit. I kept slapping my skin, but nothing was there. *Nothing.* I had to hold my hands tight to my side and keep from screaming."

His laugh cut the air. Dark and sinister and angry. "Even my screams in my head felt different. Old. I screamed like an old woman, and I kept feeling locusts dig into my skin. I could have sworn I was getting bit."

His back shivered with a deep exhale. "It was like I was living a different life. Like I was a different person. Part of me wanted to go check on a fucking cat I don't even have."

Those words stunned me. Johnny had mentioned, a long time ago, that he had glimpsed some of the ghosts I tapped.

Way back in Red Rock, after our last fight. I hadn't thought anything of them then. I had filed it away in the interesting-but-not-important folder. He hadn't shared anything further since, keeping quiet about the pain, drinking it away when he could. Maybe it had been ego, Johnny's silence. Or maybe Johnny hadn't wanted us to worry about him, with bigger fish to fry.

We both had been wrong. I wished he had mentioned it further. I wished I had taken the time to ask about it. I wished I had remembered his comments, enough to ask about them. Enough to figure out what my friend was going through. Because what Johnny was talking about seemed very important now.

I reached out on my ethereal radar.

Felt the ghosts surrounding us in the little town. Not many, but more than I would have thought, having lived here the past few weeks. All of the spirits recent.

And one new ghost in the alley. Right behind the bar. Behind the kitchen and the walk-in freezer.

I cautiously tapped that ghost. Just a little. The spirit radiated pain. Fear. Mixed with a need to be home. To get home. An older lady carrying a tiny bag of groceries. The bag held some bread, a grapefruit, and a single can of cat food.

The spirit seemed familiar. I had seen her once or twice when the ghost had been alive. When the *person* had been alive. An older lady. An old woman, walking back and forth to the grocery every day, walking the same path. As if every day she went to the grocery to buy her groceries and one can of cat food.

Maybe it was her time to get out, to see people. Maybe all her children were gone, and the grocery store was her way of talking to a real person each day. Maybe she didn't have any money, at least, enough to buy food for the week. Her spirit was still driven by the need to get home. Driven by the need to get back for her cat.

I dove too far. The part of me observing the lady's ghost merged with the spirit, became the old lady. The things I had felt biting her were now biting me. My hands jerked to swat the things, I dropped my groceries, began screaming. We needed to get home to make sure her cat was safe, but the air was thick with these *things*, and now these things were biting us, and she needed to get home and get her cat fed and *now these things were biting her…*

Like I said, not the first spirit I had lived that day with those memories this past day.

Something slapped my face.

Johnny. He had a strange look on his face. My hands were high in the air like I had been swatting something invisible.

I swallowed. "A cat, Johnny?"

"Yeah." His look didn't change. "You living a ghost?"

"Yeah." I echoed. "One with an older lady, wanting to get home to feed her cat. Right behind the bar."

Johnny glanced behind me. Towards the bar. His eyes became unfocused, as if he was trying to see through the building. See something he should never be able to see. His gaze stayed unfocused, but he looked around him, up and down the street, pausing in places.

Places I knew—from my ethereal radar—held a ghost.

"Huh." His voice was surprised.

I unlocked the sheath on my leg. Pulled out the Five-Fold blade. Saw again the tiny whirl of ethereal blue, the slowing spin of the whirlpool of energy in the middle of the etched symbol on the hilt. "Hold this."

Johnny stayed lost. Gazing around. I repeated my words, and at the same time folded his hand over the hilt of the Five-Fold blade.

His body went rigid. Like an electric shock had hit him. His eyes opened far wider than they should have. His fingers spasmed over the hilt of the knife. And, after a long, long moment, he exhaled.

The breath seemed to go on forever.

Johnny blinked a couple of times. Came back to the real world. Took a large breath and smiled. One of the Johnny specials, white teeth bright against his dark skin.

Hell, he even looked… thicker? More solid? Less cadaverous?

I blinked on my ethereal vision, saw the usual blue-white energy racing from the hilt of the blade and spreading through Johnny's body, as if every vein and artery of Johnny carried the energy to every cell, to every bone and ligament and muscle. Johnny himself blazed briefly in my vision, and then his ethereal blueness winked out.

Johnny had dropped the knife.

And he now looked at me. His voice shaky. But carrying less hunger. Less pain. Honestly, he sounded like the old Johnny, just surprised.

"What the fuck, Grimm?"

I bent down and picked up the knife. The swirl of energy in the hilt was barely moving. The tidepool of blue was almost transparent in its thinness. Johnny had sucked up a lot of what was left.

What the fuck, indeed.

CHAPTER EIGHT

A long moment of silence ran along the street. The wind picked up around us, tossing a few of the locust shells in circles, rattling the husks along the blacktop. A few shells kicked up in front of me, stumbling along the street like a loose tumbleweed down an abandoned town in the desert. One bounced off my too-tight shoe and stopped there, laying on top of the laces and fluttering at me as if waving hello.

The air was bitter and sweet at the same time, full of the gangrene sickly smell the locusts had brought with it. The smell of death that would only get stronger as the day passed along. The sun, high overhead, bore a hot clarity down over us that I felt like I should get.

But I didn't.

Johnny came closer. He even looked better. Harder. Thicker. Less cadaverous. Like his body had taken the ethereal energy and made more of itself, in that same moment. Instantaneously. Even his skin had healed. There were no scratches and bites left from the locust swarm.

His smile was back, too. The happy-go-lucky smile of a man who found a joke in every moment. The wiseass who was always up for anything.

"Is that?" he asked, looking at the blade. "Was that the energy you talk about? The ethereal stuff?"

"Yeah." I looked again at the blade. The slowly whirling tide-pool of energy on the blade.

"I could see it," he said. "Blue. White. It was kind of swirly."

"That's it," I said.

"Man." Johnny swallowed, looking at his arms, his hands. "What's it mean?"

I didn't have an answer. What's any of it mean? These blades I had created, the full set of armor that seemed to slide out of my body? Johnny, now seeming to absorb ethereal energy like other vampires drank blood?

I laughed. Just a couple of chuckles, really. "I wish I knew."

I had created the blades to help us fight Sabnock in the dead zone. A way for us to use our powers once we crossed that line. It seemed though that I had stumbled on other ways to use them. Other applications of the energy I tap into. Other people were able to use it, once I put the energy into a form or object they could access.

I wondered what more might be done with the Five-Fold blades. This might just be the beginning, with Tabitha sealing the vault. With the energy healing Johnny.

Was what the blade had done, could that even be called healing? Was it feeding instead? Did Johnny drink the energy like a vampire would drink blood? With Gabrielle biting Johnny in Denver, and with me trying to heal him, was Johnny now some weird bastard mix of vampire and angel?

"I feel so good, man," he said. "Like I could jump a tall building."

I got it. It was what ethereal energy did for me. Made me stronger. Faster. Harder. It healed any injury I took, as long as I was conscious enough to wield it.

I had first realized I could use that energy in the Hindu Kush, a long time ago. After fighting the scourge to a rooftop of a long-abandoned monastery. After an explosion had killed all my friends but me. For ten years after, I had used it in much the same fashion. To help me fight and to heal me.

I was starting to realize it could be more. That there were more applications of the energy. Things I hadn't seen or thought about.

Just like Johnny was *more*.

And, like always when that word came around, I thought of my mother.

The chuckle came out a little more bitter this time.

For us to be more, a price would have to be paid. There was always a cost. And I would pay it, if it kept my friends alive.

I closed my eyes. Found the cat lady ghost. Tapped her and pulled all her energy out, put her energy into the blade. Maybe I was kind of wanting to put her to rest, bury the spirit as a recompense for her help in finding a way to help Johnny.

I was unprepared for the axe murdering. The lady had had a kid, once upon a time. A little boy. His constant cries and nagging had worn the lady down, so the boy hadn't grown up, and that was all I'll say about that.

Funny, how you can think an old lady trying to get home to feed a cat was sweet.

"Jesus," Johnny said. He bent over, hands on his knees, like he was about to throw up. "Was that... did she... to her own kid?"

I looked at the blade. The symbol. The whirlpool of ethereal energy spun maybe a hair faster. Maybe. Her spirit had barely moved the needle.

Damn.

Johnny took a large breath, pulled his hands off his knees, stood up. "Was that what happens when you live a ghost? When you pull energy from them?"

"There are variations on the theme," I said. "But yeah. Murderers, rapists, pedophiles..." My smile held little humor. "That's what's out there."

"Brother," he said, his eyes looking sad. "I mean, I knew it, I knew that's what you said, but Grimm, man, no one should have to live that. No one. Not for anything."

"It's okay," I said, holding the knife out to Johnny.

Who didn't take it. "Don't you need that for Sabnock? In the dead zone?"

I did. But I also needed my friends alive and well. I had messed up, not being there for Johnny before. I wasn't going to make the same mistake again.

After this, I'd ask Gertrude for a few more knives. Or other objects, like pendants or bracelets. Maybe I could make ethereal batteries out of anything. Create something for Johnny that he could keep around, and then drink the energy when he needed it.

Until then, all I had were these two knives.

Well, the knives and the keystone. Three items that held ethereal energy.

We would have to share what we could. I would make more later, with Gertrude's help. Though I would dread making them. I would dread what I had to do, the ghosts I would encounter, but with Zoe around, with that safety net, it was something we could do.

"Take it, brother," I said.

But Johnny shook his head. "Grimm, I'm good. Trust me. For now, I'm good, I don't feel the thirst, I feel great."

I guess I looked doubtful.

Johnny's voice got serious. The swear-on-your-kids type of serious. "I promise Grimm, I'll tell you." His hand pushed the knife away. "We need you to fight Sabnock. We need you in the dead zone. Let's sort this out later, I held out months, I can hold out a few more measly days."

He made a little sense. He did look good, healthy. "Only if you tell me when you're hungry," I said.

"I will brother," he said. "Promise."

"Okay," I said, sheathing the blade. Snapping the strap that locked the knife in place along my leg. "The moment you feel like you need it, you tell me."

"Sure," he said, then saw my glance. His hand made a motion over his chest. "Cross my heart and hope to die."

Then he waggled his eyebrows, both of them, up and down. "Well, maybe not *hope* to die. That shit wasn't fun the first time."

I laughed. It was a good belly laugh, and it felt good, even in the middle of a town eating to nothing by a plague of locusts. Even with the busted goo-filed insects everywhere, with its sweet, sickly smell. Even with little mounds of meat up and down the street, all that was left of dogs, cats, and people.

We have to take the moments where we find them.

"I'm sorry, man," I said.

Johnny cocked his head at me. "For what?"

"For not helping you when I should have," I said. "I thought you were okay." That wasn't right. I hadn't thought he was okay, but I had thought he was handling it.

"Brother, maybe you let me take that blame," he said. "You got enough on your plate. I should have spoken up. I was so locked in on the vampire thing with Gabrielle." He shook his head. "It's love for me, you know. I mean, the sex was great in the beginning, and it still is great, but the biting, being *hers*, giving her blood, for me that was always love. It was something I could give her, something that I just wanted to be ours."

I could understand that, maybe. Like the bond I had with Jen. Something the two of us had that was just ours. Something we shared that I wouldn't want to share with anyone else.

His head turned so that he faced south. "And that's changed now. Or it will change, when I do. When I become a vampire and bite someone, the person isn't going to be Gabrielle. I'm going to lose the thing I loved with her. When I take blood, it's going to be some random person. When she bites someone, it's not going to be *me*. And I don't want that. I want what we shared. And that's going to be lost, forever."

He swallowed. "I should love Gabrielle for Gabrielle. And I do. But I also don't want to share her. I don't want to lose what I had with her. Sharing my blood was something I could give her. Something I loved giving her, and soon that's going to be gone."

There was a long moment.

"I should have asked for help," he said. "But how could I? Gabrielle thinks I hate being a vampire, and that part does scare me, but it scares me more that I'm going to lose the one thing I brought to our relationship. That's all there was for me, and I was so focused on that, and then so focused on the fight against the hunger that I lost myself. I mean, I kept thinking everyone was going to tell me the same thing. In my mind everyone was just going to tell me to give in and bite someone. Get it over with, and you'll be okay.

"And I couldn't. Because biting someone would change my relationship with Gabrielle forever. I would lose being her complement, the one thing I brought to our relationship, and I didn't think anyone else would understand it."

Johnny stopped talking. Turned to me. Laid a hand on my shoulder, and I knew that even though he didn't blame me for anything, he was telling me he also forgave me. "So maybe don't blame yourself for something I decided a long time ago."

It sounded like he still had something to work out. But that he was working it out. And that was all any of us can ask.

"Come on," he said. "Let's go tell the others the good news."

CHAPTER NINE

F ood and water—check.

A place to hide from the locusts—check.

Keeping watch for random vampires or stone golems from Mexico City—check.

Now we just needed to find a vehicle.

That was going to take some time. This town of a name I never knew had been utterly destroyed. Every vehicle left out in the open was now just an empty metal frame lying in the street. If there was a garage somewhere holding a car or truck, that garage was likely buried in a broken-down building, and it was going to be hard to find a vehicle in that, or even know if a car is there, buried under all the rubble.

So we took some of that time, hanging out together. Finishing a meal of jerky and chips and candy bars dressed up like protein bars, as well as candy bars that were actually candy bars. Drinking the flat, tepid bottles of water, sipped on the warm sodas with their warmer, carbonated bubbles. Talked about small things, had a few smaller laughs.

It was good to have Johnny back. The real Johnny, with the flashes of smiles and the wiggling eyebrows and the bad jokes. He even deliberately set aside a package of peanut butter cups for one of the candy bars.

"Your loss," I said, ripping open the package of mouth-watering cups.

Fernando did his best to clean out the sink in the bar. After that he opened up the valve underneath. The faucet was missing, but water at least bubbled out of the pipe and ran down into the sink. While none of us would drink it, the water gave us a place to clean up, at least.

Finally, we were done with eating and washing up, and so we divided the town into a grid-like pattern. Then we searched all the buildings and all the garages we could for any working vehicle. We needed to get back to Cuernavaca; we all knew it, even if getting there was going to be a problem. The city bordered the dead zone there; the rest of our few allies were there; it was the perfect place to launch a counterattack.

Well, it was the only place to launch a counterattack.

And Gabrielle said she was working on the Mad Max plan. I thought I had come up with a plan that was flexible enough to handle almost anything. Turns out, there had been a limit to that flexibility.

Now, we weren't going to go in all Mad Max so Nick could get in a sneak attack. Not anymore. We were going in for real, with as many people as we could, depending on what vehicles she could scrounge up. We would go in, get to the Crown of Bones, and fight it out there.

Us versus them.

Winner takes all.

Now, though, we walked the streets and alleys of this place. This little town in the middle of nowhere. Even if there was nothing left here. Even if it wasn't even a town but a collection of walls and collapsed homes, of eaten-up hulks of cars and trucks, of what was left of Tabitha's gray sedan and the beat-up Ranger Nick and I had used on our trips to outside Mexico City.

At some point me or Michael would have to head back and let Gabrielle know what was going on. None of the phones worked. Cell phones either. There was no power anywhere. No way to communicate other than one of us flying down there. Carrier angels, instead of pigeons.

We searched, half-heartedly, the rest of the day. Hoping to find a car that had escaped the plague. Every now and then we'd find an intact garage and would break into it with a little hope, and then, after seeing what was left of whatever car or truck had been stored there, move on to the next place.

Fernando stayed in his bar, the rest of us divided up in pairs. Me and Jen. Nick and Sarah. Johnny and Zoe. We searched, but everything anywhere around us was much like the town. Destroyed. Plague-ridden. Walls collapsed. Roofs broken in. Things like brick and iron and steel corroded. Things like cotton and electrical cables and any soft material just gone.

And vehicles? Well, just frames of trucks and cars and vans remained. Husks of metal littering the streets.

Part of me had to give it to Sabnock. It was a diabolical way to stop someone from attacking you. In a blink he had removed homes, warehouses, food supplies, vehicles. It would cut off any army at its knees.

Not that we were much of an army. Not me and my friends here in Mexico. But if enough containers of locusts had made it to the other dead zones, if enough of the plague could be spread from other centers of the world, well, it would be game over for those armies and navies and the air forces in play.

Then it would be game over for the human race.

I started to worry we would never find a vehicle to make it to Cuernavaca. I started to think about other plans. Nick could shadow-walk his way there. Michael and I could fly, and maybe each of us could carry someone that distance. Make several trips.

Angel Airlines, capacity of one. This is your captain speaking. Don't worry about the tray tables or keeping your seat belt on. There's no need to figure out how to put your oxygen mask on, and we won't have a steward around to call on.

Oh, and there will be no mid-flight snacks.

I moved that idea over to the when-we're-desperate pile. Whoever we took with us each trip, we'd be leaving others behind here, unprotected. Right now, after the plague, I didn't want to leave anyone, anywhere.

We gave up looking in the city somewhere in midafternoon. We found ourselves back at our apartment building. There hadn't been a building taller than four stories in the town, and our renovated from the seventies hideout had only had three floors. Jen had wanted to go back, see if we could get in and find anything of ours. It felt like more than that, along the bond. She needed to get in, it felt like.

I wasn't sure that was going to happen. All three floors of our hideout were still standing, though the faded yellow exterior walls were slathered in splotches of green ichor. The floor-to-ceiling windows had all collapsed under the roof, leaving no way to get in from there.

The floor-to-ceiling windows on the third floor had all been broken in. I jumped up there to see if I could get to our apartment that way, but the roof had collapsed in the hallway, and it would have taken a lot of digging.

The back door from the alley was filled in with the floors above it; there was no way we were getting in there without a lot of work. The effort was halfhearted, even if Jen kept pushing to get to our room. More of us were worried about getting a vehicle than finding a change of shirts.

We tried to build up the bar so it could withstand something more than a hard wind, but materials were in short supply. Jen spent some time with her sister, the two of them talking, maybe like sisters did. Occasionally she would glance at me, and I'd smile, and she'd give a tiny smile back.

When night really fell, Jen came over. I was sitting on the floor in the main room of the bar, my back against the wall, facing the open doorway. Looking at the twisted remains of the jukebox there and imagining a little music playing.

"Hey," she said.

"Hey," I said back, making space for her. Well, there was a lot of space along the wall; still, I scooted a little over in that motion people did when someone was going to sit next to them.

Jen sat down, and for a bit we just sat there. Her hip next to mine. Her head on my shoulder, her hand on my arm. I realized this was the first time the two of us were by ourselves, just the two of us.

"I was scared, Gus," she said.

"Scared?" I let her talk. Feeling the word along the bond. Feeling her memory of it.

"Not just the locusts," she said. "But the feeling of someone else out there. Someone wanting to kill me, hiding in the swarm. Someone specifically there to kill me."

Jen shivered. And repeated herself. Things that were repeated held meaning.

"So, I was scared."

I got it. It doesn't take being dead to be scared of death. I got her fear.

"Scared of the locusts," she said. "Scared of the sounds they made, zipping around. Scared of how much they sounded like bullets. Scared of them eating me," Jen let out a big breath; I felt it in her body. "I wonder if I'll ever not be afraid again."

I pulled her close and tried a joke. "I think we're always scared, right? Fear is just something telling us how stupid the thing is we're about to try."

She nudged me with an elbow. "I'm serious."

I took the nudge and sighed. "I want to tell you something. About Sabnock."

She looked up a bit at me, from where her head lay on my shoulder. Her chest against mine. I kept my arms around her and told her what the demon had told me. About Sabnock wanting to kill her and all our friends, because of what I had threatened Azazel with.

About his threat to take all my friends away, to kill her, before coming back for me.

"So that's why he came," Jen said. "That's why he came here."

"And why he came after you," I said.

Maybe it was a bad thing. If someone is scared, it might not be a good thing to add to their fears. But Jen was different. I knew she was different. And I thought, I *knew*, that if anyone could feel the added pressure and come out stronger, it would be Jen.

I was rolling the dice and betting on Jen.

I could tell exactly what she was thinking. I didn't need the bond for that; I knew her thoughts from knowing her. The same feel I had when looking out at the stars at night, knowing Jen was doing the same; the two of us had that bond long before we had the key.

Jen was going over our conversations. The one we had now, and the one we had over the phone after Michael had rescued me and we had fled Sabnock. She was reviewing it all to see if she could poke any holes in it.

And she couldn't. Or at least, didn't want to. Not anymore.

Didn't want to blame herself for what was going on.

Didn't want to be scared of something she was going to have to face anyway.

"It doesn't change anything," she finally said.

"No," I said.

It didn't change her fear. It could have added more. But it let her know I trusted her, and sometimes that would be enough. There was nothing else I could do, other than show Jen I believed in her.

I couldn't tell her to be less afraid. I couldn't make her less scared.

Jen would have to find that on her own.

"No," I said. Still holding her. Feeling her arms circle around me and pull me close. "But it lets you know."

We sat there a bit. Both of us understanding whatever our reasons for being here now, in Mexico, whatever we had thought to do before, whatever my threat to Azazel *had* been, taking out the dead zone was the priority now.

Whatever Sabnock planned, we'd have to handle. If he got in our way, we'd try to kill him. But the demons were planning to take out the human race, and the most important thing we could do to throw a wrench in their works was get rid of the dead zone here. Nullify it. Stop them from being able to make their plagues, their Ushabtis.

"Kink," Jen corrected.

"What?"

"Kink," she repeated. She must have been listening in the bond. "Not wrench."

She laughed then, into my chest. Small laughs, but real ones. "We're throwing a kink in their works. Remember?"

I did remember then. I had said the words over the phone. And I had stuck with them then.

"I did say it, didn't I?" I chuckled with her, and held her close.

"Yeah," she said. "You did." Her arms pulled tight around me. "And I'm holding you to it."

My eyes might have gotten a little misty then. Sitting there, holding Jen. Her holding me back. Feeling her in my arms, and the slight laughing in her body, the quiet shakes of a woman I loved very much.

"Deal."

CHAPTER TEN

We knew it might take some time, getting out of this town. But the waiting still wore on us. Most of us finally got some sleep that night, lying down on the floor of the bar between taking turns for standing watch. Michael kept up observation from on high, flying up in the air and doing circles.

Even though we understood it might take some time, we grew impatient. Then the impatience turned to worry. After the hours passed, after the stars changed overhead, after the big bright moon had rolled on by and slipped over the western horizon, the worry became something else. It became the thing worry did when the fear had been around too long, it had moved into that area where we were just exhausted from it.

The sun rose.

Night turned back into day, the deep purples of night lightened into the slate-blue, cloudless sky of the Mexico we lived in now. The sun rose, burning and angry, and the heat returned. All the decaying locusts and the eaten bodies of the town began to ripen, and the sweet sickly smell of death thickened into something more rank.

The morning passed, and boredom set in, harder. We needed something to do. Jen wanted to get into our apartment, the need from yesterday had swelled into something more urgent in her. So we went back into one of the ground-floor windows and tried again to dig our way up to the second floor.

None of us had anything better to do, so most of us went. Only Fernando stayed at the bar. Michael went back to circling the air, looking for Sabnock's creatures to the west, though there had been no sighting of any.

We made some headway. Everything on the first floor was a mess. We were able to clear enough of the rubble on the first floor to get to the hallway leading to the stairs, and we abandoned that when we saw how packed the stairwell was with the collapsed roof overhead. The roof and the third floor.

It was Jen that had the idea of digging up the ceiling of that first room we were in. We broke into the second floor that way, and it was a bit clearer there. A bit less collapsed, as if more of the rubble had fallen on past. After handing everyone up to the second floor, we made our way to the hallway.

While the stairwell and the roof had collapsed in on itself, most of the second floor seemed... whole. I mean, locust shells were everywhere. Everything was covered in their shells. And things were eaten and corroded, but the walls were still standing. All the apartments were at least standing.

Still, dead black things lay everywhere, like a heavy snowfall. Just of carapaces. The hallways, the floors, everything was covered in them, the shells crunched under our feet and seemed to give off a smell like old meat. Most of us used a sliding motion to walk, shuffling through shells like we were walking through snow.

Sarah and Nick went to their rooms. Zoe picked her way to

where she and her mom had stayed. Jen and I went right to our place and wandered through it. The locusts had eaten everything. Our apartment, our bedroom, all wrecked. All buried in bodies of locusts. The glass shattered inward from all the windows, tiny bits of it sparkling among the shells in the light of day.

They had attacked our place viciously. Like something had driven them there. Every curtain and every blanket eaten. Nothing was left of our couch, or our bed, just metal springs in mounds of shells and wooden feet, gnawed at their tops, leaving pointed splinters.

Our dresser was in pieces. It had been made of wood, a sturdy oak, and had six-drawers, three big drawers on the bottom with three thinner drawers above them. Jen hurried over to it, her feet scattering shells, trying to dig through what was left.

The sturdy oak lay in pieces. The sides, top, and back all had collapsed, looking like swiss cheese. Jen pushed the top aside, digging through a pile of clothes, T-shirts, pants and underwear. Tossing socks aside. All of it covered in the green snotty goo. Every piece of clothes chomped on and eaten through.

She looked frustrated. No, that was the wrong word. There was a manic franticness about her. A need. She kept throwing clothes aside until she found one of our towels, a blue one, folded around itself. Her face lit up; she smiled and fluttered the towel open.

A few locusts tumbled out, landing in the pile of clothes underneath. One of their wings buzzing a bit, like it was about to take off.

Jen gave a little shout in surprise. She dangled the towel some more. A few small pieces of something fell out. Her face colored with a dark anger, and in a second she was stomping on the locusts. Screaming at them.

I stopped her. Felt her trembling under my hand. Trembling in a fury.

"Hey," I said. "What's wrong?"

It took her a moment to calm down. Her chest heaved in and out in big breaths, before slowing down. She didn't look at me for a bit, and then, when she did, Jen looked a little shamefaced. "It was my gift."

Oh.

She had gotten me something. Even down here in Mexico. And I should have known Jen had, when she had brought up Christmas before. I should have known she had, with Nick driving me to get Jen something. "Oh."

Her eyes were surprisingly shimmery. Not crying. But angry enough to be. "I know it's silly. But I loved this gift. The idea of it, it came to me and I loved it. I wanted you to have it, I knew you had to have it." Her voice broke a bit. "And now it's gone."

Part of me wondered if she had needed this gift as much as me. There had been a hint of joy in her words, the happiness of finding the perfect gift for someone. The building excitement of wanting to see the face of the person opening your gift on Christmas Day.

And now, finding it gone, Jen was furious.

"It's okay," I said, pulling her close. Feeling her draw in a breath through her nose, a large wet sniff. "I hadn't gotten you anything, so we're even."

"You never get anything," she said. Correcting me.

"Well, yeah," I said. Trying for levity. "But it's kind of my thing, right? Tradition being what it is?"

"It was perfect." She talked into my shoulder, her voice muffled. "Gus... it was perfect."

I kept holding her. Kept telling her it was okay. Feeling her anger in the tightness of her body. I wondered what the gift had been, but I couldn't ask her. Not now.

"Christmas is just a few days away," she said.

"Yeah," I said again. With her words came the images, the way I always imagined Christmas, the way I first experienced the day for real. A tree with a bright star, circled in multicolored lights, blinking on and off in some random pattern. A cracking fire. Snow falling outside. And Frank Sinatra singing from a scratchy record.

"Not the Christmas I'd hoped it'd be." Her muffled voice carried a tone I usually didn't hear from her. Sadness. Something forlorn, regret. A something missing.

What had Jen's Christmases been like after I had left? Without her, I had never really celebrated it. This was the first one in ten years. Maybe a first for Jen as well, the first without her mother, the first away from Grafton, away from a home she had always lived in and a mother she would never see again.

It had to have been a big change for her. Bigger than I would have thought, since all my good memories of Christmas had been with her. The two of us wouldn't eat pepperoni rolls, sneak squares of fudge, snuggle on the couch under a blanket. There would be no mugs of hot chocolate, no Christmas tree, no Frank Sinatra singing with snow falling outside.

No gift from me.

It was a long moment, between us. A long quiet moment where I wondered how Jen really was. A long moment where I worried about her without trying to let that worry touch our bond. A long moment where I was kicking myself, because Nick had told me, he had *warned* me, and I had put it off.

I had messed up. Nick had warned me, he had told me, and still I had messed up. Jen's body was still tense. So obvious now, Nick keeping after it with me. Keeping after the gift. Sometimes our friends see things in our lives that we completely miss.

And I had really, really missed it. There was nothing I could do now. A lost gift would always be lost, for Jen. A gift never gotten could never be given, from me. It was a moment I could never recapture.

Dammit.

I had failed.

"It's okay Gus," she said. "I'll be okay."

I still felt bad. Even if it was my tradition. I had missed something with Jen, the same way I had missed something with Johnny.

We all have failures. We all miss things from time to time. It was those we loved who accepted those failures and stayed with us anyway. It was those we really loved who would sit next to us in some broken-down bar and love us anyway.

I knew Jen had forgiven me even as I knew I should have been better.

We stood there, in the ruined remains of a place that had briefly felt like home. In an odd way, the first place Jen and I could call our own. An abandoned apartment complex outside the edge of a dead zone.

A little sad, right?

The moment went on, with the both of us holding each other. Jen's chest pressed to mine, her head on my shoulder, our arms around each other. Her fingers occasionally gripped my back, as if Jen reassured herself I was there. For a while we stayed that way, feeling each other breathe deep, measured breaths that slowly synced with each other. Slow, methodical beats of our hearts, thumping in time.

It was nice.

While I had a lot of worries, a lot of concerns, and a lot of things I maybe should have spoken to Jen about, questions I perhaps might need to ask, I thought nice was enough, for now.

CHAPTER ELEVEN

We had run out of ideas. Of places to look. And, likely enough, time. So, as night fell outside, as the sky deepened into that dark purple that led into black, we had a dinner. A send-off of sorts. It was a quiet dinner, with the types of glances people had where everyone knew what was going on and what the chances were, but we were going to do it anyway.

We were going to give Nick a chance to find something. Sarah spent a lot of time around him, her hand on his arm. Even feeding him a peanut butter cup, stuffing it into his mouth with a giggle. Which led him to trying to feed her in return. And, like any good food war, it broke out over the table.

It took Jen to settle us down. Mentioning how low we were on supplies. After, somehow, smearing me with an iced cinnamon roll.

I raised my eyes. I did like the mischievous twinkle in her eyes. Something from the old Jen. A twinkling smile, with the glimmering of a little devil.

We all washed up the best we could, but a slow-running sink tap could only do so much. Most of us left that kitchen with the scent of the Battle of Peanut Butter Cups. And a smile.

There weren't many places to go, but Sarah and Nick disappeared. Michael fled the battle of candy and chips, resuming his flying overhead. Fernando started cleaning up, which just told me you can take the bar away from the bartender, but not the bartender from the bar.

Fernando had done a good job on the bar after the first day. He had gone back to the grocery store, to the back room there, and found more brooms and cleaning sprays, and had brushed as much of the locust shells out as he could. The green goo was harder to clean, and it wasn't like we had a lot of water and soap and rags lying around, so we scrubbed it away where we could and let it dry where we couldn't.

Zoe had been quiet during the dinner. She hadn't participated much in the food fight, and she hadn't really talked much since her rescue. Most of the time she stood in the background, watching me. Johnny was standing by her now, talking, joking, all of it in the usual Johnny way. Zoe gave an amused laugh once or twice, but for the most part she stared at me. Not overtly. Just glances. I had the feeling I wasn't being measured, not quite, but that I was part of a jigsaw puzzle she was trying to put together.

It grew to be time. All of us felt it. All of us gathered back in the kitchen. It had become our new center of operations, all of us standing around the pitted metal table with the smell of ozone and the lightning scar. The open ceiling was just a skylight. Everyone needs a place they feel safe in. And if not safe, at least known. Anything at all over the unknown.

Michael had helped me to put the door back on the walk-in freezer. He did something then to smooth out the door a bit. I don't know what it was, but the metal seemed... warm to the touch.

There wasn't much we could do about the smell, though.

We sat around the kitchen, the purple night peeking at us through the hole in the roof overhead. All of us in our places around the pockmarked, lightning-struck table, on half-eaten chairs and fragile stools. Night started to fall, and we had one last card to play.

Nick.

He could search faster, his way.

We gathered back at the bar, after the moon rose and the sky darkened from the grayish blue of day to the deep purples of night. Nick gave me a last fist bump. "I can cover a lot of ground, but depending on how far I go, it might take me a bit to get back."

"I got it," I said.

"I mean it," he said. Nick was going to head outward from this town, towards the Gulf of Mexico, and northward, hoping to find a place the plague hadn't touched. "I'll find something, but could take me a day or so to drive back. Depending on how far I have to go."

"I understand brother. I get it," I said again, smiling. "Just be careful."

Nick gave me the same look he always did when I said that.

Sarah hugged him tightly, and I thought that did a lot more than me telling him to be careful. At least, Nick's glance at her when he left told me he would do anything to make sure he got back.

We gave him a wave, and then he was gone. One moment there, the next nothing. A shadowless shadow.

The real waiting would begin now. Not the waiting and hoping of finding a vehicle. Not the waiting and hoping of finding some way to get south. But the waiting of hoping for someone you cared about staying alive.

Jen and I did our own disappear. Well, we at least found a quiet place in the front corner of the bar. Fernando had done a good job sweeping all the locust shells out. There were still stains on the floors, and on the walls, and the place smelled a little sickly, but beggars couldn't be choosers.

The ceiling there was mostly missing, just like all the other buildings. There were just the walls. There were no tables inside; the jukebox was a small pile of corroded metal. The two of us sat like we had in many places, laying our backs against the wall and staring up at the purpling night.

For the first time in decades, in maybe forever, Jen smelled differently. Not like honeysuckle, or a cool summer rain. More like chocolate, with a hint of sugary cinnamon, and a dab of peanut butter.

Time passed. Her arm was warm against mine. Her body had a rhythm, a feel to it. The slow lopping of her heart. The long, unhurried draw in of a breath, followed by the whisper-soft, leisurely release. Even her mind wandered, her eyes picking out the first star above us. Then the second.

We were on the floor now, but the feel of it all was much like the two of us, just kids, on top of the water tower back in Grafton. With both of us sitting on that walkway, our arms on the middle railing that ran around the walk, the flaky, rusty iron bar cold on our skin. With the town fading into sleep below our feet and the night sky opening with pinpricks of light above.

With Jen's shoulder next to mine, her foot swinging, just a bit, from the walkway.

Staring up into the night. Thinking my thoughts. Me thinking hers.

Before any of this happened. Before we were Grimm the half-angel, and Jen the storm witch. Before the two of us had grown up and seen the world we faced today, before we each had the fears and the worries that life brought.

Jen's voice reminded me very much of that little girl, and that time. It was soft, little, in the night. "It's nice, isn't it?"

"Yeah," I said, the word causing my chest to tremble, just a bit. A shuddering breath. "Yeah."

My thoughts went to the us back then, and the us now. Each of us facing different fears. Each of us there for the other, but not sure what to do in order to help.

There was Jen and her fear.

And then there was mine. Something that lay underneath the dead zones, the plague of locusts, Sabnock. Something outside of the Crown of Bones, but could be summed up in just one word.

Hector.

Not the maniacal evil spirits. Not the ones that fought me. Those I could handle, just like I had handled all the memories I had lived. Even ones like the grandma in Lewiston, like Jo, like the Aztec warrior, those were evil, and they left stains, but I was stained already. Theirs were just a bit darker.

Not Sabnock either. I was scared of him like I was scared of any of the demons. But fear also fueled me. It stirred an anger. I had used that anger to kill other demons, and I would with Sabnock too.

Hector though, Hector…

"Why him?" Jen asked aloud.

Because he had been the first one to leave his ethereal tap. Because he had stared at me, knowing what he was doing, *knowing* what I was doing, before wresting that tap away. Because he had left his spot, where he was mired on the ethereal plane, and found a new body.

Because there was some part of him that was darker than the others. Some part of him wanted me more than others. Some part of him that believed deeply in the *recompensa del rey del inframundo*.

"I don't know," I said.

Jen got it. Understood it. The fear of unknown fears. The worry of unknowable worries.

"It worries me some," I admitted, aloud.

Then quiet. The night purpling some more. One or two more pinpricks of stars appearing. A slight whistling in the air, something soft, but mournful, an echo, like the far-away cry of a locomotive, hundreds of miles away.

"Just him?" Jen asked. "Really?"

"Yes," I said. Then changed my mind. "No. Maybe. Maybe it's everything. Maybe he's just the face of it."

"Yeah," Jen said, leaning her head over onto my shoulder. "I get that too."

The night was black now. Jen's breath warmed the skin under the thin cotton sleeve of my shirt. I wondered how far Nick had gotten. If he was already headed back.

Doubtful.

My thoughts went back to Zoe. The wisps of her hair, sticking out like a crazy librarian. Her glasses, somehow found, cleaned and back on her face. Even now she watched me, her and Johnny, across the front room. Laughing a bit with Johnny. But staring at me.

Unwavering.

That was the word Zoe had used. That there were spirits that wavered. And then there were the ones like Hector, the ones who went after me because of some weird bounty. Or went after me because I was trying to do right in a world where all they wanted to do was wrong.

Well, I wasn't going to be someone who wavered.

That was for damn sure.

CHAPTER TWELVE

The sun rose.

Night turned back into day, the deep purples of night lightening into the slate-blue, cloudless sky of the Mexico we lived in now. The sun rose, burning and angry, and the heat returned. All the decaying locusts and the eaten bodies of the town ripened, and the sweet, sickly smell of death thickened into something more rank.

Waiting became a four-letter word. And it still wore on us. Most of us had slept some, but all of us were waiting. Waiting and worrying. Waiting and doing the thing that worry did to us when it lasted way too long. All of us snapped at others occasionally; then we were too quiet for too long after. When Sarah slept, it was fitful. When she awakened, her eyes would flutter open and look to the east. Her fingers always fingering the cylinder-shaped locket hanging around her neck.

Zoe slept as well. Johnny's jokes may have finally fallen flat, even as he tried one after the other, as if making up for lost time. A time I prayed fervently would end.

Jen snorted next to me, as if she had been thinking the same thing. We both lay back against our section of wall, and she was nestled against me. My arm tucked around her back, her body warm against mine. Her hair light against my cheek; her scent, the honey-suckle and spring rain, back again, overpowering the sickly-sweet smell of the locusts.

Each day both Michael and I would fly around a bit, scouting; the angel spent more time up there, I thought maybe giving me more time with Jen, although he hadn't said anything.

He was circling now. A tiny dot high above the town. In the moment I found Michael headed northeast, looking for Nick. Maybe there was a chance he would catch Nick driving back.

We could hope.

He hadn't though.

And we all looked for something to do.

We dug through buildings, hoping to find things we could use. Not things like a bed or a chair, but even simple things like cups or dishes. We found more things that used to be alive and now weren't, and ended up turning away more often than not.

After a while, we just stopped looking.

Jen and I ended up together most of the time. Now we were down the street from the bar, east, near the burned-out gas station. The tanks underneath had gone up under the plague, and I was trying to figure out why. It's not like the locusts carried matches.

I was down in the hole. It was deep and almost star-like. There was the round center with furrows radiating out like sharp, pointed fingers. There was clay mixed with dark earth mixed with twisted pieces of blackened metal, and the air carried the sharp, sweet scent of gasoline mixed with the loamy, wet scent that deep earth had, like a fresh-dug grave.

"Done?" Jen asked, her face turned north. Her skin was darkened in places by dirt and dusted with rubble, and her hair, loose, drifted in a slow, unseen breeze.

I had a piece of metal in one hand. It was thick and twisted, dark, and might once have been part of the shell of the gas tank underground. I couldn't catch any scent of accelerant, and there was no locust standing around with a lighter in its foreleg, like it was at a concert.

"I guess," I said, and started climbing out. It took a minute. While the ground at the bottom of the hole was still damp, the earth was drying up quickly, and the sides crumbled as I tried to pull myself up.

I ended up on my ass back in the hole, a piece of broken blacktop in my hand, my jeans soaking in the wetness of the grave.

I swore loudly. Then tried to get my ass out of the ground. I felt like a turtle, flipped over backwards, arms and legs all splayed out, as I tried to find a way to pull myself up.

Jen burst out laughing. It was a moment of pure joy; her eyes lit up, and she bent over trying to catch her breath.

Of course, that's when the attack came.

Something buzzed in the air. For a quick moment I thought it was the zipping of a locust. It took a moment before I heard the ricochet, the quick thwack of a bullet against something hard before the sound wound down into something like a ringing of a bell.

Jen's reaction was immediate; her laughter cut off, and her face paled to something ghost-like. Her eyes wide with fear. Her panic streaking across the bond.

The lightning shield formed in place. Crackling blue-white energy sizzling around her. Right as more bullets struck her—struck the shield—and sizzled into nothingness.

I reacted almost as fast. As scared as Jen was, I was just as scared to lose her again. Without a real thought, I was tapping into a ghost and leaping out of the pit.

I was nowhere near as fast as Jen.

I landed as thunder rumbled along the street, a low, growling thunder, the kind accompanied by the promise of heavy rain.

Although there was no rain.

Landing, I almost missed a step. Jen had started pulling from me, pulling in a panic, stealing the ethereal energy faster than I could pull from the ghost. Her lightning shield swelled, and I almost lost her in the sight of it. The crackling blue-white blinded me.

And then lightning started pouring down. West of us. Past the bar.

Large forks of it struck the earth. Even from here I saw the damage, rubble blasting in the sky after each strike. The bolts tattooed the earth, one after the next, starting on the west end of town and then going... further.

More bullets struck around us. They evaporated with a sizzle against the lightning shield. One flattened itself on my shoulder, knocking me back like I had been hit by a boulder. It stung like I had been hit by a tank.

It was time to join the fight.

I jumped into the air, pulling on ethereal energy, letting my wings form as I flew west. A small form ducked into the bar below me, maybe Zoe, with Sarah following her in. Then I lost them both in a blast of lightning.

I shielded my eyes with my hand. Kept flying west. Trying to pick out the snipers through the after-image glow of lightning that continued to stream down from the skies. Flying high over the rubbled buildings. Watching tufts of earth and road fly up in a pattern that reminded me of artillery shells pounding the ground in some old war movie.

There.

A mound that might once have been a three-story building. A

semi-flat roof, still holding, on the top. With a couple of figures lying there.

I called my ethereal sword and dropped from the sky, hoping Jen had enough control of the lightning that no bolt would strike me. As I neared, each of the figures coalesced into the prone forms of snipers, both of them lying on the flattish roof of the ruined building, cheeks pressed against scopes.

Another group of people huddled behind the building. Hiding. One was pretty big, though he was tough to make out after a particularly brutal flash of lightning.

I landed on the roof first. Well, kind of landed. With the plague, the building was barely standing, and the roof was just as weak as the rest of it. So I landed—I'm still saying I landed—my sword in front of me, ready to pounce on the snipers.

The roof collapsed under me.

And the snipers.

I didn't even really get a chance to see them. The roof fell inwards, opening like a giant mouth, swallowing the three of us whole. Like that pit monster in Star Wars, the one in the sand with all the teeth.

The monster swallowed us, the walls of the building toppling inward, the roof breaking into pieces, those pieces of rock and shingles and locusts falling in with us. There was dust and gravel and pieces of locust that blinded me, and I fell, only really knowing I was falling from the gravity-type feeling of getting pulled down. And then I hit bottom.

At least, I was pretty sure it was the bottom. It was hard to tell with all the dust and rock and pieces of drywall. It was dark, hard to breathe, and it was all I could do to keep my skin hard and try to dig my way out.

It was slow going. Less of a dig, and more like trying to swim out from under an avalanche. It was all I could do to move an arm, push whatever held it enough to move the arm further, and then do the same with the other arm.

Then the legs.

Then my head. Like a blind fish, I tried to swim to the edge of the rubble. Tried to find my way out by feel. Pushing hard against larger rock and plaster. Grunting as I found myself navigating past a large broken section of what seemed to be floor.

Then my hand broke free.

And someone helped me out.

With a large hand. Attached to a large forearm. A large, stone-like forearm.

Hector.

The Ushabti tugged me out. The side of the building came with me. Rocks and pebble and drywall, all blown out of the side of the building like I was a man-sized bullet blowing through it.

Hector let go, and I tumbled over the earth. Hitting the occasional thing, bouncing off a rock, until I hit something that shook and creaked like the old suspension of a car.

Looking back, it was a car. Or what the locusts had left of it. A metal frame perched on rims.

Things flattened into me. Things accompanied by the rat-tatting, pelting sound of gunfire. Each of the bullets stung; I closed my eyes as they struck my cheek and grabbed more ghost.

Which was a good thing.

Hector grabbed me again. Keeping a hand on each of my wrists, tugging me up off the air and waiting until I opened my eyes.

Stone-like skin. Boulder-like muscles. Gigantic frame.

But the same eyes. Mad. Insane. The eyes of someone who was broken and furious about it.

I hung from Hector's arms. The creature laughed. And said something in Spanish. At least, I thought he said something. The words came out echoey, like from a deep cavern, and growled like Hector's vocal cords were made of rock.

I summoned my sword, but the golem held my wrists tight, and the blade just waved in the air above the creature. I tried moving my hands, twisting them, until a sound came from them that suspiciously sounded like matchsticks breaking.

The pain hit. Both wrists were broken. I healed them fast enough, but I couldn't bring my sword to bear. I could only hang there like a rag doll. A rag doll trying not to scream.

Hector laughed. The sound like a rockfall. Echoing from deep within his chest. He leaned forward, maybe thinking he was whispering, his mad eyes on me, unwavering.

His words bellowed over me. "Tú eres mi recompensa, mío."

Was it just me, or could someone made of rock have rancid breath? Like breath from a rotting corpse?

His eyes caught mine, a rock-like tongue licked the side of his rock-like lips, and suddenly I wanted to be elsewhere. "*Mío.*"

I kicked him in the chest as hard as I could with an ethereal-energy-powered foot. Hector barely moved, still holding me high by my wrists. But the force of the kick almost yanked my arms out of my socket.

I pulled more energy, hanging there, healing. Swinging from the golem's arms. Wondering how I was going to get out of this. Even as Hector's grin grew larger and larger.

I was scraping the bottom of the barrel. I couldn't use my sword. I couldn't overpower the Ushabti. I had no tricks, so I tried to pull my ethereal energy from Hector. Hoping that, since he was a ghost in a golem's body, maybe I still could banish him that way. Like I banished all the other ghosts. Like I had almost banished Hector before.

I came up with nothing. There was nothing to pull. The ethereal energy was still there, still in that spiritual plane that ghosts were tied to. But Hector was different now.

His ghost didn't have a tap.

He felt like the wights back in Grafton. The corpses stuffed with the spirits of dead animals. He had a body; I could sense it ethereally, but his spirit, his ghost, wasn't something I could reach anymore. He was almost alive; I could see his spirit in the middle of his stone body, glowing blue and red, almost like I could see any other spirit in any other person, or demon, or vampire.

But I couldn't pull from it. I couldn't access the ethereal plane. I couldn't live Hector's memories and access the plane's power through his tap.

Which left me out of options. Left me hanging there, staring at the mad, smiling face of Hector in rock form. Left me wondering how the hell I was going to get out of this.

If anything, the rock-grin grew larger.

Blue-white flared around us. Flashed so bright that Hector darkened in that instant. Like a bolt of lightning, like a thick, ground-pounding lightning bolt, had struck him in the back.

Which, of course, it had.

The force of it tumbled the golem through the air. Hector hit me like a truck, but I didn't mind because he had let go of my arms. Thankfully. The two of us tangled in the air until we came apart, me falling quickly to the ground.

And the Ushabti still flying. Blue sparks racing over his granite form until I lost him in another blast of lightning. And another.

Jen strode around the corner of the building like a gunman, firing bolt after bolt. The group of soldiers with Hector fired back, but the stream of bullets hit the shield and evaporated in metallic puffs of fog. The sizzling and crackling of the shield sounded like a thousand bags of popcorn popping.

And Jen stood among all the popcorn sounds, throwing lightning from each hand, dealing it like she was at a casino, one hand after the next, pulling and tugging on more energy from me, from the bond. Pulling more and more, enough that I had to find another ghost to keep up.

Then it all went quiet.

The lightning shield disappeared. There was just Jen, her face still pale. Her eyes wide open, but wide open with anger. With fury. Her chest still heaving in large breaths.

I was still sitting there on my ass. Which might have been fitting. It was the place I had started from when this fight began. Carefully, I pulled a little more ghost and healed up my wrist. Then my foot.

Then I turned around.

The ground had been hit so many times it smoked in dozens of places. I had never smelled burned earth before, but I could say I had now. The scent was both wet and charcoaly. Like trying to fire up a really wet log.

Pieces of people were everywhere. Some of them smoked, too. Bones poked up, white leg bones with spots of black, skin flaked off from where it had been burned to a crisp, hands and arms lay strewn about, heads, even a kneecap.

Of the golem though, there was no sign. No bits of rock lying around. No hand of granite pointed back at me, middle finger raised. Hector had gotten away. There was no sign of the Ushabti.

He moved fast for someone so big and, you know, made of rock.

A bit further away I saw something I had missed flying in. A couple of pickups lay a few buildings back. Pickups that looked like they had once been in working order, because they did not look like they had seen the plague.

Probably how the soldiers had gotten here. Quietly rolling in from the west. Maybe one of the trucks riding low to the ground, with the weight of a Ushabti in its bed.

No one would be taking those trucks back. We wouldn't be borrowing them either. While the plague hadn't hit them, both vehicles lay in tatters now. Hoods twisted and blown off. Engines exploded by strikes of lightning.

I looked back at Jen. She realized it the same time I had. Her face twisted up in frustration, though her face was still pale. Her eyes maybe a bit too wide.

I felt the same way. Probably for different reasons.

CHAPTER THIRTEEN

We gathered back at the bar, back at the kitchen, Jen and I washing ourselves off with the tiny stream of water trickling out of the pitted sink. The water was warm, and though I was thirsty, another part of me took a whiff of it. The liquid smelled both peppery and eggy, so I put my thirst aside and finished washing with a quick flick of my fingers.

Jen was there with a water bottle in her cleaned hands and a tiny smile. Not a happy smile, but what was left after the frustration burned out and regret set in. I took it; we both felt each other through the bond, and I gave her a quick kiss on her forehead.

Night was coming. Again. It felt like it was always oncoming, the purpling black, the weak white moon, the tiny pokes of stars. But it was just the third night after Nick had left.

Our supplies were low. Maybe another day for the food. Well, the packets of jerky and crackers and candy bars. A few more days for the water.

I looked back at the sink with a wince.

Michael had landed not long after the fight. The two of us spoke for a bit, acknowledging it was past time that someone flew back to Cuernavaca. Someone had to let Gabrielle know we were alive and trying to make it back down her way.

I mentioned Hector to him. How the Ushabti had quickly disappeared from the fight. The angel just smiled.

Then he left.

Everyone looked tired. Jen and Sarah spent some time together. Johnny was out still, looking for more food. I thought maybe trying to make up for something he didn't need to make up for.

Fernando was already tucked against his corner of the wall. Zoe wasn't far away from him, staring into her globe. Her face intent.

I stopped by, kneeling next to her. Waiting for her to pull away from the misty fog under the glass ball in her hand. Her eyes tracked something in the fog.

The mist caught me. It swirled and glowed in spots, fading away as soon as the brightness caught my eye. Almost like something was alive in there.

Or the globe itself was alive.

An interesting thought. I didn't know much about witches in general. Witches or warlocks or wizards, people born to use magic. I had rarely encountered any of them after I had left Grafton, though witches were prevalent in my life now.

The winking continued. I got the sense there was something inside. Not a person, but a thing.

A thing with a life, or a place, or a time all its own. I remembered being in there, briefly, as Hector and his friends surrounded me. I remembered the uncommiteds, the hundreds of spirits surrounding that group. I remembered the pit of darkness Hector was pulling me into, and I remember it all pausing with a word from Zoe.

And me pausing with it.

Pausing inside that mist. Pausing inside the world of the globe. Wherever, whatever, whenever that had been.

The globe winked out. Zoe looked up, one brow poking up behind her glasses, asking the question.

"He said it again," I said. "Hector."

"Recompensa del ray del inframundo?"

"Not quite like that." I wasn't sure how she remembered the saying, what all the spirits were thinking back in Hector's ghost world. I thought back to hanging in front of the golem formally known as an enraged spirit, and Hector's insane eyes boring into me. "Tú eres mi recompensa, mío, I think."

Her brow turned into a frown. "You are my reward?"

"Is that what it means?" I said. "He said the mío word twice."

"Mine," Zoe said. "Mine."

Someone had offered a bounty. The reward of the diablo, or something like that. Something had been promised Hector.

"You think about him a lot," Zoe said. Her face unreadable. "Don't you?"

I had found him here. Here in the grave, surrounded by the thugs he had captained. Surrounded by those he had killed. An evil spirit like many others I had lived, like many others I had banished.

Like them, and also not.

I nodded.

"Yeah," she said, her gaze lingering on me another moment before turning back to the globe. "Me too."

Hector had come back here. He was from here. And La Familia Diablo was from the area. They were the clan that had tried to wipe out Alejandro and his family. Could La Familia Diablo be offering the reward? The reward of the devil?

I didn't know. What could Hector want from here? With Maria

dead and buried next to him, after he had killed her, and everyone else with her, in some church.

What else could he want? Life? Is that what the golem thing was about for him? I felt lost wondering about it, like I was walking through a field full of mines. With no map, with no idea of what was going on, any step I took could be my last.

I left Zoe and went to the front room to think. To the spot Jen and I had taken as our own. In the corner of the room, the ruined jukebox not far away, the front door to our right. What was left of the bar to our left. A little corner in the front of the bar that was ours alone.

I could think about Hector all day, but he was a distraction from what I was here to do. A distraction from purging the dead zone. A distraction from Sabnock, who was trying to kill me, kill my friends. Kill Jen.

I couldn't afford distractions.

And Hector was certainly that.

I would have to focus on something else. Anything else.

I felt, more than heard, Jen snort. From our bond. Then she appeared in the doorway to the kitchen, alone. As always, it felt good just to see her. Just to have her here. Just to be with her.

Something everyone should have.

She came around and lay next to me, so that both our backs were against the wall. Our usual pose. We lay back, her nestled against me, my arm tucked around her back, her body warm against mine. Her hair light against my cheek, her scent, the honeysuckle and spring rain, overpowering the sweet, sickly smell of the locusts.

Johnny walked past. He winked at the two of us and shook something in his hand. A bag that rattled the way plastic wrappers do.

More food.

Johnny smiled, and I nodded back to my friend. Then he disappeared into the kitchen.

"He looks so much better," Jen said. We both spoke quietly, in low voices. It still seemed too loud. The town was empty, quiet; there was no chirping of crickets or croaking of frogs in the night. Nothing in the background. There was no occasional rumble of a truck heading down the street. "Fuller."

Johnny did. Bigger. As if his body had drunk the ethereal energy in, and all his cells had gone to work, dividing and dividing, over and over, rebuilding him from the feet up. From his bones to his muscles to his hair.

I had let him go on too long, alone. I had thought Johnny was handling it, and now I could see that he had just been putting on a brave face as he sank deeper and deeper into a hole he couldn't get out of.

He wasn't the only Wolverine in a hole. He wasn't the only one struggling to find a way out. He wasn't the only one I had missed helping when they had needed it.

The thing was, I didn't know how to help this person.

Jen knew what I was thinking. I could sense her follow my thoughts along our bond. I could feel the reluctance in her. An avoidance of the talk, *this* talk, a fear of looking at the thing inside of Jen bothering her. As if she didn't really want to know.

Some knowledge is always to be feared.

Mortality is the greatest of that. When you are young, you never think of it. As you get older, it becomes the thing you think about the most.

Our thoughts both ran along those lines. Fear. Avoidance. Mortality.

Jen spoke, without me having to ask.

"I was dead, Gus," she said, again. Like she had before. Like we were picking up the same conversation, just on another day. "How many people can I talk to about that? Who understand what I went through? It's not like there's some Dead Persons Anonymous group I can go to on Wednesdays and talk this out."

Sometimes letting people talk about it was enough. She was right, though as much as I couldn't understand it, I could understand the anxiety it brought. The fear. I could understand how those things overcome a person and color every decision they made forever after.

After all, fear had colored my choices. Had made me run for ten years. Until Jen had brought me back to the life I should never have left.

"There's something missing, I think," she said. "Some part of me I had once, it's gone now. And I don't know how to replace it. I don't know if I *can* replace it. Part of me worries I'll be this way forever, this person who worries and fears and doubts."

I tried a Johnny. Raised an eyebrow. My whisper was light. Fun. "Welcome to the group."

She punched me in the ribs. Lightly. Well, somewhat lightly. I pretended to be hurt, rubbing my chest. Her hand met mine, and our fingers entwined, her fingers clenching maybe harder than they needed to, and I just held her hand there.

She had been the strongest person I had known. Had ever known. There had been a purity of thought, of purpose, of *existence*, in Jen that now seemed tarnished. Taken. Eaten away in tiny pieces until what was left of her was just the bones of the house she had once been.

Just like the town around us.

I could tell her she'd get it back. That she'd be okay. But those would be just words. Jen would know that, and I did know that, so I let those words pass unsaid.

As much as I could. Jen felt the trail of my thoughts; this close together it was easy, through the bond. Her fingers stayed tightly threaded through mine. They spasmed, once, as if some feeling of anger washed through her.

I let myself wander down a different path. Something I had been contemplating a lot lately. "There's something to what my mother told me," I said. "Something to this good and evil thing. Something to how Evil grows, and how good responds to it. To how good becomes *more*."

I paused, not trying to order my thoughts, but allow them to come out naturally. Without guidance.

"The thing is, good doesn't just grow on trees," I said. "It's not something that we can plant and water and allow to grow. It doesn't work that way. Good doesn't grow on its own. It can't become more by itself."

My mother had told me I would be more. That the good side was finally responding to centuries, to thousands, of years of Evil. That the tide of darkness swallowing the world had come up against a bastion of light.

But that light had to start somewhere. Someone had to light it. From there, others would come. They would be drawn to it. That single light would become two. Three. It would start with someone standing against Evil and screaming, *Enough*.

For us, it all started back in Grafton. With Jen calling me. With me saving Jen. And then making a decision, to stand and fight with my friends.

Maybe then it had just been us, the Wolverines, in some little town in West Virginia. It had just been some small place in the middle of nowhere. But that's where the light, my light, our light, had been lit.

And look where we were now.

Good is never good on its own. It sees Evil with the capital E and stands against it. It sees wrong and tries to right it. If it did anything else, it wouldn't be good. It wouldn't grow. It wouldn't become something *more*.

I held her hand, and hoped she got it. Hope Jen felt what I was feeling, the Grimm I had been before, running from Azazel, and the Grimm I was now.

"It starts with a decision. With making a stand. With knowing, even though you are flawed and scared and maybe a little lost, a little broken, that you're going to do the right thing. That right thing becomes another. The good you do, it multiplies. It makes you stronger, and you come up against more things that are wrong, and you go through the process again. Just on a larger scale."

I squeezed her hand, then. Not tightly, not hard, but comforting. My thumb circling the inside of her palm, her skin warm, soft.

"The doubts, the fear, the worry," I told her. "It's all part of it. Part of growing. Part of life."

It was always part of it. I lived with it all. With the fear of not being enough. With doubts and fears and running from it all. With telling myself people were safer when I wasn't around. With telling myself I was protecting the world, keeping it safe, by just keeping the key from Azazel.

I hadn't grown then. I had now. And though I had my own doubts about that, I didn't doubt that I was stronger. That I would be stronger still in the future. Understanding that strength might come at a costly price. That it might come at the cost of my friends.

The largest fear. Which maybe caused my largest growth. The fear of failing them, of not being able to protect them, drove me more than anything else. Had always driven me, maybe.

That kind of person, who I was now, had begun with Jen. She had been that light for me, a brightness that had illuminated my world. It all had begun with a little girl, coming into class and telling me my face would look better if I smiled more.

I tried one now. I was battered, and I had my scars, but the core of me would always be that kid. Would always be that person who wanted Jen to be proud of me. The person who reminded me of this very topic.

"You taught me that, Jen. You taught me being good isn't good enough," I finally said. "Being good without fear is meaningless. It's *easy*. Growth only comes from standing strong, despite the fear overwhelming you. Courage only means something when you stand toe-to-toe with Evil, even when you doubt you can win."

My thumb drifted from Jen's palm to her chest. I rubbed a tiny circle right above her breast. Her T-shirt was thin, and I could feel the beat of her heart thumping softly in her chest. "Even if you doubt your friends can win without you. The fears and the doubts and the worries, that thing that's missing inside you, it's all necessary. Because anyone can face Evil if they didn't fear. If they didn't doubt. If they didn't worry. Anyone."

"But facing it when you doubt yourself? Facing it full of worry and fear and still resolving to make your stand? That's when you fill that gap inside you. That's when the something missing is filled with something too vast to comprehend. When you become something greater. Something more."

My fingers relaxed. Hers too. Her thumb played a little with mine. I could tell she was thinking, so I stayed away from the bond. Let her thoughts be hers alone.

Then she kissed me. It was light, her lips warm and soft and oh-to-brief against my chin. "You're pretty smart sometimes, Gus."

I smiled and did the full-on Johnny impression. His bad one, including the Bogart voice. "Don't let it get around, kid."

It struck me that we were back in the garage in Alabama. Hiding from Kimaris and the cops. We were having the talk Jen had had with me, but in reverse.

It was a strange feeling. She had been my rock for so long. As much as I wanted, as I needed that rock back, I would have to be hers, for now. For as long as it took.

Jen nestled harder against me. I tightened my arm around her back, feeling how Jen fit perfectly against me. The press of her body against mine. The warmth and the light and the everything that was good in my world.

The reason I was greater. The reason I could be more.

Hoping I would be her reason, too.

CHAPTER FOURTEEN

I may have heard the sound first. My eyes opened, fitfully. Blinking their way to adjustment. The sky had lightened above us, and through the eaten-away roof of the bar, a light gray stretched from the east to overtake the dark purple of night in the west.

Jen snored lightly against me. Her cheek on my chest. Her breaths long and slow and peaceful.

Sarah was awake. I caught her eyes, and they looked hopeful.

That's when I heard it again. A weak rumble of an engine. A vehicle.

Nick had found one.

I gently woke Jen. Enjoyed watching her eyes open and find mine. Felt a little thrill at her tiny smile.

I kissed her on the lips.

"Ewwww." Johnny grinned and made one long kissing noise. The sound with the high-pitched smack at the end.

Sarah laughed. I did too. I couldn't help it. It felt good to have Johnny back. Even if we all weren't fully healed, even if there were things to deal with. Even if there was a demon to kill and a dead zone to nullify.

The group of us walked out. A van puttered down the street. A large blue van, square-shaped, with windows circling in and something painted in big white letters down the side.

Basilica de Guadalupe?

Nick pulled up in front of us and switched the van off. The vehicle died off in little coughs and sputters. Like something way past its prime. It looked like it was from the nineteen eighties. It had a short nose, and the windshield was sharply angled right above it. Windows circled the van, square bubbled things that wouldn't roll down, but would pop out at the bottom slightly by means of a little latch. Except for the front doors by the front seats. Those would have the old manual window cranks.

The top of the van had a couple of plastic gas jugs tied to it. The big square red ones. A black strap was wrapped tightly through the handles of the jugs; the strap circled down the sides of the van, over the white letters, and ended up somewhere underneath the rear fender.

The big white letters stood out. There was a cross in the background on either side. I thought the letters meant something like church of Guadalupe. Or the church in the city of Guadalupe.

"You found us a church van?" I asked.

"Hey." Nick shrugged. "Beggars can't be choosers."

He wasn't wrong.

He walked behind the van and opened the back door. It was like a big blue gate and swung out on two big hinges. The back of the van was full of water and food. Bottles of water, forty-eight of them, wrapped tightly in the hard plastic wrap that stores have. Packages of bread and peanut butter and jelly. And small, rectangle-shaped packages colored in a reddish-orange…

Johnny grabbed one first. "Gimme."

I laughed. "I thought peanut butter cups weren't candy bars."

"Who cares?" He tore into the package. "They're delicious."

It was good to see him eating. Good to have the gang together. We made some quick sandwiches there and ate them, standing at the back of the van. I put too much peanut butter on mine, and all of it —bread, jelly, and peanut butter—stuck to the roof of my mouth. Jen laughed, watching my face as I tried to work it down with my tongue and some water.

A lot of water.

It was a good time.

We piled into the van. Inside, everything was blue. Just like the outside. Blue carpet, blue vinyl over the seats. Not the same blue; the carpet was fuzzy and a bit darker in color than the vinyl.

Johnny got into the driver's seat. Zoe took the navigator's position. Their chairs were like captain's chairs, big and tall inside the van. The rest of the seats were benches, three of them. Nick and Sarah took the front bench, Fernando the middle. Jen and I took the back row, the one where the loudest kids usually sat.

"That's the problem child seat," Nick said, grinning, as we worked our way down the little aisle on the side of the van.

Jen hip-bumped me along. "He knows."

I collapsed onto the seat. The blue vinyl cushion was worn, and I sunk into it. Placed my back against the window. Leaning against the side of the van. Jen collapsed right next to me, putting her back against my chest. Her hair lay right under my chin. I wrapped one arm around her; she grabbed it with both of hers, doing that thing women do, where they hug the arm to them.

I took a deep breath of honeysuckle and cool rain.

These moments, of Jen and I, of the Wolverines, of peanut butter cups and sandwiches stuck to the roof of our mouths and of laughs, they were too few and far between.

Johnny fired up the van. Well, he turned the switch; the engine coughed its way back to life. Then he took off, slowly, the van feeling a little loose on the road. As if the suspension was soft. We picked up speed, the van feeling like a plane rolling down a long runway. At least, it did until we hit a pothole and the entire van bounced hard into the air, hard enough my ass lifted off my seat.

It wasn't all bad. Jen grabbed my arm a little tighter.

"First-time driver?" Nick asked. Sarah smiling and kissing the side of Nick's face. The motion reminded me so much of Jen and me, and I knew Jen felt the same. I felt her gaze on me, her thoughts on me, through the bond.

"Seatbelts, everyone," Johnny said, ignoring Nick. Grinning at us through the rearview mirror.

That was our drive.

Johnny knew the route. He had driven it many times in the past few weeks. I knew the route almost as well, having driven it plenty in the past few days. I had been doing a lot of back and forth lately, a lot of being in one place, then the next. It felt like my life was like a game of whack-a-mole; there was no clear direction or order to it. I was just looking for the next mole to pop its head up so I could bang it with the rubbery mallet.

Part of me wondered about that. There was a feeling to the thought, a truth I perhaps needed to iron out. Something about my friends. Something about us growing. About the need for me to be everywhere, to protect them.

Maybe it was just the evil we faced now. Not just Raphael back in Grafton. Not just Azazel in New Orleans. Not even a conclave of vampires in Colorado.

This evil was vast. It encircled all of Mexico City. It may even be half of Mexico. The dead zone was larger than any one of us could tackle on our own. Throw in Sabnock, the knight army he was building, the plague he was shipping out, and I guess maybe it was natural to feel a bit overwhelmed.

Maybe it was just me.

My fingers rubbed the hilt of the Five-Fold blade. Empty. Or almost. So as Johnny drove, I reached out and tapped what ghosts I could. Keeping my eyes closed. Living the memories they passed on to me as fast as I could. Sucking up spirit after spirit, as if the church van was a vacuum, scooping up the ghosts as we rode by.

Maybe I filled the knife some. It seemed like I wouldn't find anything like the power of that night. Of being out at the graveyard, of Hector and those he had killed, and those that had haunted him in return.

I took a deep breath. Let it out. Wondered how much I would have to pull, to fill the knife again. Wondering if I could. The last time I had, Zoe had to pull me back out of the ghostly world I had been sucked into.

Still, Sabnock was waiting. The dead zone was waiting. And my friends—Johnny in particular—now could use the blade in ways I hadn't imagined when I created them.

Just a few days ago.

We got to the town with the crabs. The town by the shore of the Gulf of Mexico. The dead crabs were gone, the large shells the size of trucks perhaps eaten by the locusts. Maybe they had been eaten by other things. The vehicles that had been shot up were still there, parked in the street where we had left them, and the van picked its way through them.

The homes and houses here didn't look as bad as Cuernavaca, or the small town we had our hideout in, as if the plague had blown itself mostly out by the time it reached the gulf. There were fewer husks around, less of the green glops of goo everywhere. The walls of the homes and the storefronts were still pockmarked with bites, but most of the roofs were still standing. The cars and trucks were still recognizable as such.

Jen stirred against me. She had felt me living the memories of the ghosts. Her hand, the whole time, tight in mine. Allowing me to do what I needed to do. Understanding. Giving me strength. "Penny for your thoughts."

Her voice was low. I felt her words reverberate in her body. It reminded me of all the times we had spent at her house, as kids, on her living room couch. The television on, maybe Saturday morning cartoons, and the two of us tucked up under a blanket.

"Just wondering where all this is going," I said.

Jen gave an *hmmm*. Then settled back into me. She knew, like I did, where it was going. She also knew, just like me, that while the end destination was known, the journey was unfathomable.

Johnny stopped the van in a place where we could see the ocean. The sunlight glittered across the waves. The water seemed peaceful, with tiny white crests scattered across its surface. We all got out. It was midday, the sun was high in the sky, and though it was warm it wasn't the humid heat of the past month. A nice breeze blew inland from the water. The gulf was close by, and the beach was a nice white sand, marred only by the occasional dead locust.

The waves were large enough to bring the crashing sound all waves had, the breaking of the crest, the tumble of water over itself as it raced towards shore. The group of us stood there for a bit, watching the waves rush up the sand, watching the foamy edge sink into the sand, watching the water draw slightly back along the beach, back into itself, the sea readying itself for the next wave. The motion had a nice rhythm, soothing, peaceful.

The salt air was welcome. I took big breaths of it. The air of the sea made me think of explorers, sailors piling into tiny wooden ships and heading out to the unknown. I wondered what had made them look out over the ocean, that large expanse of blue, and want to see what was on the other side of it. I wondered what it had taken for a people to move from canoes to longships to those sailing vessels, what had driven them to search for the other end of the horizon.

The stay at the beach was far too short. But, again, like the feeling I had in the van, needed. The feel of us together. The wind whipped over all of us. Sarah danced barefoot in the surf, and for a time it was just our group in this tiny part of the world. Just us, and no one else.

Thoughts like those kept popping up, and I wondered why my subconscious felt it was so important for me to know them. I wondered what it was trying to tell me. Or why.

After too short a time, we left the shore. I stopped for a minute at the edge of the street, looking back down the pavement. The haphazard location of cars and trucks that just days ago were part of a gunfight in the street. A gunfight and a crabfight.

The street there had stores on both sides. Or, storefronts. Most of the stores had been boarded up, but there was one off to the side. The one Nick had broken into to get that pink butterfly clip for Sarah.

All that stuff was gone now. The gift he had gotten for Sarah was buried somewhere in that apartment building. Likely we would never find it. Never even get the guitar, or any of our other stuff.

I guess I felt lucky that I hadn't found a gift yet for Jen. Everything we had brought down with us had been there, in that building. Most of it had been temporary, like plastic plates and bowls, but there had been other things. A favorite quilt that Jen had found that we both had liked, something light blue and with thick threads. A tiny succulent in the window that had been there when we arrived, that both of us, for some reason, had named Hairy. With an 'i.' The pair of toothbrushes on the bathroom sink, hers pink, mine blue.

Little things, maybe, but things that had started feeling like a home to me.

And I hadn't had a home in a while.

Johnny and Nick came up. Nick caught where I was standing, and where I was looking. Put it all together in the way friends do, with everything I was feeling. With everything he knew about Jen, and about her gift being eaten by the plague, and how she had been feeling.

"Maybe it's not too late."

My smile was maybe a little lost. "You think?"

He shrugged and gave his little Nick smile. The one where the corner of his lip turned up a touch. "It's the season for miracles."

My laugh barked out of me. Brittle. Sharp.

Maybe Christmas was important in ways I hadn't thought. I wished I had a gift for Jen, but that time was gone now. There was nothing to get. There was nothing left to give, not in the home we had built. Not in the store Nick had gotten his butterfly guitar thing at. Not in all of Mexico.

It was just us.

Johnny slapped my shoulder. We headed back to the van. I ate another peanut butter and jelly sandwich there, putting enough of both on the bread that the jelly squirted out onto the street. Jen smiled when I offered her a bite, shaking her head at the mess. Nick took a moment and filled the gas tank, unstrapping a gas jug from the top of the van.

Well, he tried to fill it. It ended up taking everything from both of the jugs. I guess big blue vans from the nineteen eighties didn't have gas mileage as their top selling point. Even after Nick finished, Johnny kind of gave a shrug from his driver's seat.

"We'll at least get close," he said, after starting the van with its weak coughing putter. Then he flicked the gas gauge with his finger a couple of times. As if hoping the needle would rise a little higher on its own.

We piled in. All in the same positions as before. Jen looked at me and rolled her eyes. Then she licked her thumb and wiped my cheek with it. Her thumb came away with a tiny spot of jelly and peanut butter.

I grinned. A man has to get his calories.

The rest of the ride was the same type of peaceful as back at the beach. The road lulled me to a half-sleep. Maybe church vans weren't a bad way to travel.

There ended up being enough gas for us to get closer to close. We actually got all the way there. To Cuernavaca.

Where Gabrielle had a surprise waiting.

It was a doozy.

CHAPTER FIFTEEN

I t was night when we arrived. Shocker, since it always felt that way now. But it had been a long drive that got longer at the end, slower in the city, there being no streetlights illuminating the way. There was nothing but crumpled, high-reaching ruins of buildings to navigate through. No stoplights or the big glaring poles highlighting the names of cities on green signs. Just the white and yellow strips that occasionally glittered in the weak headlights of the van.

Johnny pulled us into the building formerly known as Alejandro's compound. He whistled, low, as he did so, having known what the place looked like before. Slowly the van made its way into the little semi-circle, maneuvering the van a bit when the headlights picked up the large blocks of eaten metal that used to be the blue Camaro and the sport utility trucks.

Then he shut it off.

The entire city was dark; there was no power anywhere. No window was lit. No door opened with a warm yellow light behind it. We all pulled ourselves off the benches with the groans of people who had been sitting for too long, climbing out from between the side doors of the van and stretching.

They had people waiting. Vampires, from the tactical gear. As we climbed out, more people came out to greet us. Among the first was Tabitha, who rushed down and hugged Zoe. Gertrude was next, the tall Valkyrie easy to pick out in the crowd.

Johnny stood off to the side. A little hunched in. Waiting.

Alejandro came out. With Millie. He invited us all back down to the vault. Explaining, with a grimace, that it was still the cleanest place around. He also said Michael had let them know we were coming but couldn't tell them when.

Then the angel had disappeared. Explaining that he would be back.

Finally, Gabrielle came out. She held herself tight, as if still in some pain, even if I had seen all her scars healed. I watched her look over the crowd. Her eyes widened a bit in surprise.

The two of them stood there a moment. Hunched-in Johnny. Too-brittle Gabrielle. Then Johnny shook himself, straightened up, and went to Gabrielle. Stood too close to the vampire. I watched them, past Alejandro, and saw Gabrielle turn her head aside. Johnny's head moved, as if his words were, well, not urgent, but words that needed to be said.

Gabrielle nodded, once. Then wiped the side of her cheek with her hand. She took a breath and let it all go.

She caught me watching them. Her cheek twitched. Her gaze went back to Johnny and to me. Then the vampire said something to him, and maybe Johnny's shoulders slumped a little, I hoped not in defeat, before Gabrielle made her way to me.

Her voice was the same clipped elegance I had gotten from her when we had first met, way back in Grafton. "Grimm."

I made small talk. "Nice place you have here."

"It is," she said, her face twisting a little. "Clean."

I guessed it would be. Cleaner than anything else.

"Come," Gabrielle said.

We didn't go back to the vault. Gabrielle walked us down the street, southwest. Away from the dead zone. Johnny stayed beside her, firmly beside her, even as he made sure to keep the slightest distance between them.

He had always been a casual guy. I remembered him leaning back against his car, jean jacket loose around his frame like he was auditioning for the cover of an E-Street band release. Always smiling. I remembered us talking that night, in Raphael's club, where he was the one relaxed human in the midst of hundreds of vampires drinking that damn drink. Relaxed because he trusted in Gabrielle.

I hoped the two of them made it back to that.

The city was quiet. Eerily so. There were no sounds of a neighborhood. No televisions playing. No people shouting. No kids screaming. No dogs barking or cats howling.

There was no comforting rumble of thousands of engines as vehicles made their way through stoplight after stoplight. No occasional beep of an angry horn. Not even the chirping of crickets.

There was just us. Our feet crunching through an occasional shell of a locust. Sometimes a quiet voice, as someone spoke in hushed tones. As if afraid a normal tone would be too loud.

I got it.

I felt it.

Gabrielle walked next to me. "We walk this, more often than not," she explained. "We have a few vehicles, but save them for scouting trips. And for ferrying." Her eyes glimmered in the light, dark glittering things. "We found the police station. And we were able to get into their armory."

"Fifty-cals," Alejandro said.

Gabrielle nodded. Just so. "All their Humvees had them. The

turrets mounted with the guns. But none of those were salvageable. They had replacements, though, in the armory."

"So we've found enough for a convoy?" I asked, hoping the Mad Max plan still held.

The vampire smiled. It was evil and delighted. "Something better."

It took some time, it was a few blocks away, but we made it back to the package station I had first found Alejandro's people at. The train station. It looked much like everywhere else: eaten, smeared with goo, crackling with husks.

The thing I noticed was the roll-up doors on the side. The large ones that had been over the tracks. The doors were missing now, leaving a large dark gap open to the air.

"We had to pull them down," Gabrielle explained. Motioning to the side of the depot, where a couple of piles of metal lay. I guess a little locust-eating had destroyed the mechanism that raised and lowered the doors.

We walked into the bay. Everything was still dark there, though I could sense the shapes of things. Toolboxes, I thought. Pallets of metal. I bumped into something that might have been a welding machine; it was square and short, and I felt a tank on its backside.

Alexandro disappeared for a moment. By disappeared I meant stepped out into the darkness. There was the sound of a cord being yanked. Once. Twice. And then the puttering sound of a motor running.

"Cover your eyes," the man said.

He waited the obligatory moment. I closed my eyes, hearing a switch or breaker flip. Immediately after that a yellow light warmed my eyelids.

I slowly opened them. Keeping my eyes squinted as I got used to the light.

In front of me was the train. The one Gabrielle had been looking at when I had first found her. As the plague was descending on Cuernavaca.

The locomotive was the same. It hadn't been eaten. Maybe the building itself had protected most of it. The engine was a glistening white and held a couple of horizontal streaks of red. The same couple of cabs lay behind it.

Machine guns lay on the floor around the train. One was mounted on swing arms that had been placed along the sides of the cabs. One of the larger guns, a Browning .50 cal, mounted on top of the engine itself. With thick plates of metal surrounding a small area where soldiers would fire the guns from.

Well.

Well, well.

"We've walked some of the tracks," Gabrielle said. "The angel checked as far as the dead zone. They lead right into Mexico City, and they are clean. Unbroken."

We all waited a moment, staring at the war machine.

"I believe," Alejandro said, "that some of those tracks lead pretty much to the stadium."

Gabrielle's smile was delightedly evil. Her tiny scars, the ones left from the locusts, stood out starkly in the warm light of the bay. Her eyes still glittered as if she was some dark angel of vengeance.

I took it all in. Someone had painted the words *Grimm Express* on the side of the locomotive that faced us. It wasn't half-bad; large, cursive blue letters had been painted evenly between the horizontal red streaks.

These locomotives weigh hundreds of tons. I imagined the metal beast barreling its way into the dead zone, into the heart of Mexico City, with its machine guns dealing death. Picking up speed. Thundering through whatever Sabnock would pitch against us.

Maybe I always had known it would come to this. Maybe my

subconscious knew something I hadn't, and that's why I had heard that forlorn cry of a train whistle, way back when. The cry of a locomotive at full speed, rumbling down the tracks.

The grin on my face grew large. The imaginary horn blaring through my mind. It was going to be a hell of a ride.

Gabrielle's voice was flat. Deadly, in its lack of tone. Wolverin-ish, in its elegance.

"Is this Mad Max enough for you?"

You know, I kind of thought it was.

CHAPTER SIXTEEN

I t took another few days to get the Grimm Express ready for its maiden trip.

We worked in shifts, mounting the rest of the machine guns onto the train. Getting ready for battle. There were three of the Browning .50 cals, and four of the M240Bs. The Brownings would be for some of the heavier work, like tanks, or those weird knights. The M240Bs would be more crowd-control. People-shredders.

I went with the team back to the police station; we brought back the rest of what we could. Cases of ammunition, including belts and belts of the .50 caliber rounds. More tactical gear and vests. Walkie-talkies. We found another generator and even small barrels of gasoline. A motorcycle was tucked away in the armory, an old Harley Davidson Fat Boy. White with a large front-mounted plexiglass shield, like on the old cop shows.

And more good stuff in a tucked-away back room in storage. Grenades and C4. Some RPGs, and a box of cinnamon pasty rolls. The sticky ones that always left white icing in their plastic wrappers, that Jen somehow always got on my face.

At the time I wondered what kind of person stuck a box of cinnamon rolls with RPGs. And I couldn't decide which made me happier.

The group of us working on the train slept there, for the most part. The humming of the generators became constant, a background noise we all forgot about. The vampires were careful to avoid sunrise, either by staying in the vault during each morning or —for the few working on the train—hiding away in the back cargo room behind the counter. That room was windowless.

We built short walls in the two flatcars, building thick plates of metal forts on each. Each car had two machine gun nests. Tabitha kept working on strengthening the metals in the locomotive. Every plate, every wheel, every block. The transmission, cylinders, the pistons, everything in the engine and out. The drive shaft, the wheels. The cowcatcher, the cabin, the controls in the cabin. The walls on of the forts on the flatcars. The machine gun nests. The earth witch barely slept. She looked more and more pale over the days, and I thought it wasn't because of the lack of sun.

Someone had topped off the diesel in the engine. Maybe recently, maybe before the dead zone had appeared. I hoped the fuel was still good. The pumps holding the fuel in the rail yard had been eaten down to little nubby pieces of metal.

We didn't have an engineer, but Millie's father had worked as a conductor, and she had some knowledge of them. He had taken her on plenty of trips when she was a kid. When I asked her if she could do it, the vampire had replied, "It's not like we're going to stop anywhere. It's point-and-click."

She pulled her forefinger like she was pulling the trigger of a gun.

And that had been that.

I finished up mounting the last Browning. The metal of the gun was cold in my hand. It felt lighter than a machine gun should be but also much, much heavier. Dense. It brought back memories of my time in the army. The thundering of the gun would sound much like Joe's MK. The same rhythm of death, if a bit thumpier.

Gorilla, I thought, rubbing one hand down the barrel of the huge M2. The metal cold in my hand. Dormant, for now. But very much alive as well.

It's been a while. I left my hand on the barrel, thinking of Joe and the last time I had seen him. The last time I had seen my team, in the Hindu Kush. Not the fondest of memories. Part of me would always blame myself for living when they had died.

Everywhere I go, people die.

Well, that thought came from nowhere. And everywhere. I knew it well. People always died around me. They would always die. I hadn't understood that before; I thought by running I was saving those that might die, but they always did. Running just prolonged the death. And, like Parker, like Miss Tammie, like Miss Cooper, it could even make it worse.

I recognized it now. And I understood everything I could do about it. I could get up and make the promise. I could do everything in my power to save those I loved. I would do everything I could to protect those I cared about. To keep as many as I could alive.

And that was what I could do.

There were limits, after all.

"Hey." Gabrielle's voice surprised me out of my thoughts. She frowned at my hand, which still loosely cupped the barrel of the M2. Hanging onto it.

Her eyes were flat. She looked tired. But sharp. Like a knife hiding a brittle flaw. Something that would make the metal snap at the moment you needed it most. The tiny scars, the thin lines marking her face, her arms, her hands, still stood out against her skin. The scars seemed angry, thin dark lines. They made it hard to see her freckles, the light dusting of them around her nose and cheeks.

Right now Johnny was out with Nick. Nick had been shadow walking the tracks to see where they led. He had found a train station, not far from the stadium. It had been full of other tracks and abandoned trains, but he thought there was a path north through all that, to the place where the tracks passed closest to the stadium.

Nick was going one last time to make sure he understood it all, after talking to Millie and figuring out what he could about how to operate the tracks. Johnny was going with him to keep him company. They would get to the dead zone and Nick would go on, doing his shadow-walker thing, while Johnny waited.

I had told Nick to be careful. He had given me his Nick face. We both had shrugged. I knew he was going to take a peek at the stadium, at Sabnock. I couldn't very well tell him not to. The two had left before dark, aiming to get to the edge of the dead zone right as day transitioned to night.

For the past few days, for the most part, Johnny and Gabrielle had been back together. Though not in the same way as before. He stood close to her, she stood close to him, but neither leaned on the other. Neither laughed or held each other. They stayed together, but also a little apart.

"What's up?"

"I wanted to thank you," Gabrielle said. "For Johnny."

"Sure," I said. Wishing I had figured out how to help earlier. "It was more accidental than anything."

"Still," she said. "Thanks should be given."

The two of us stood there. I got the feeling Gabrielle wasn't done. She looked like she wanted to say something, and her lips moved, then stopped. Her eyes glistened; I wanted to look away but couldn't.

"How," she said. "How can I trust him?"

I wanted to laugh. I wasn't the king of any relationship. This was more Jen's type of thing. But Gabrielle was serious, deadly serious, her voice cracking.

"He broke my heart," she said. "I'm a vampire. He knows it. He *knew* it."

What could I tell her? Was there something to fix what had broken between them? Some way to fix a trust broken? A love perhaps ending? The gap opening where they had once depended on one another? I didn't know.

I didn't think so.

But then, broken things shouldn't be fixed easily. They shouldn't be fixed with words. They shouldn't be patched with duct tape and rolled back out. Something broken between two people could only be repaired with time. Effort. That was the only thing that could build back up what had fallen between them.

"You still love him?"

"Gods." her voice was a tiny whisper. "Yes."

"That's got to be enough," I said.

You could see Gabrielle got it, but also didn't.

"How?"

I looked at the corner of the large cargo bay. Where I knew, without seeing, Jen was. Standing at a little table we had set up in the corner. A clean enough table holding a silver coffee canister, one of the tall ones that held a thousand cups, and the box of packaged cinnamon rolls.

Jen was eating a roll, and whether she felt my glance or something through the bond, her head turned back and looked at me. There was a bit of icing on the corner of her mouth. She winked at me, mouthed the word *hey*, and smiled.

I felt a little taller.

I mouthed *hey* back to her.

And I knew what to say to Gabrielle. It came to me. In that blink of a word. That quick connection, between Jen and I.

I caught Gabrielle's eyes. "Look," I said. "I might be the worst person to ask something like this. I had *her*, and still I ran away. I don't know what it is about her, but she waited. She understood that whatever I needed, I had to find."

Jen and I had never talked about that. About the day I had run and the reason why. About why I had been gone so long. We just accepted that we were.

I wondered now if I would have ever come back, if she hadn't called me in the parking lot of that cheap motel. I wondered how long I might have run before realizing what I was missing in my life. I wondered if I would have been able to realize it without her nudge, or if I would have always run from everything, smaller inside than I should have been, knowing that I was missing something but not understanding what that something was.

Standing where I was now, feeling a little taller, basking in the happiness Jen's smile had just given me, how could I have not come back?

I didn't know.

"I was scared," I said. "I ran from Grafton scared. I didn't know some things then that I know now. It took time for me to understand that. Hell, I'm still understanding some of that."

Gabrielle's eyes were focused. Taking all this in. Trying to apply it to her and Johnny. Maybe not getting it yet.

"What I'm getting at is this takes time," I said. "There's something you both have to understand about the other. Maybe you'll know in a year. Maybe it'll be tomorrow. All I can say is, don't let the understanding, the lack of knowing, don't let that get in the way like I did. Don't run from it. Run towards it."

"Grimm, losing him hurts," she said. "It hurts more than I can take. I don't know… I don't know if I can go through that again."

I smiled then, a gentle smile. An understanding smile. I had suffered that loss. "I get that. That fear is always there." I had it when I had lost Jen in New Orleans. I lived with it daily now. "It's what makes having the person you love with you important. It's what makes your time together special."

I slapped the M2's barrel. Lightly. "Johnny's good people. You are too. So trust yourself. Trust who you love," I said. "That kind of pain, that kind of loss, the fear of loss, it's what makes us alive. It's what makes the relationship important. It's what makes you more."

I put it in words she might understand. "If you give up, if you don't fight for something like that, then you might as well walk away. You might as well turn away from the dead zone too. From Sabnock. From going after your father. Because you've already given up the fight. You've given up your *ability* to fight. You're living in fear because you've already decided the cost isn't worth it."

I saw the vampire's eyes open a bit. In shock? Realization? Anger? I didn't know.

The cost was always going to be worth it for me. I had made that decision. I had jumped in with both feet. I would be with Jen until the end of this, or the end of me.

Jen was still eating her cinnamon roll. I could almost taste the sweetness of the icing along our bond. I felt, more than saw Millie walk up to join her, the vampire sipping on a white styrofoam cup of coffee. Jen laughing at something the woman had just said.

I could feel Jen know I was sensing her. I felt her awareness through the bond. And I sat there, embracing Jen's laugh, the way her hair trailed down over her shoulders, the motion of her hand as she replied to whatever Millie had said.

God I loved that woman. Whatever it took, I would be with her. Forever.

"Love will see you through a lot of things," I said, quietly. As if speaking to myself. "It's hard to live without it, so hang onto it however hard you can. However much fear you have about it breaking you. Because without it, what are we?"

I don't know how long Gabrielle was quiet. I don't know how long I stood there. But when I turned back, her eyes had gone from flat to contemplative.

She even offered a tiny smile.

"Thank you, Grimm," Gabrielle said. "Again."

For what I just said? For Johnny? Either or both. I nodded and gave her a fist bump. "Wolverines, right?"

Her smile relaxed a bit. The vampire softened before me. The brittleness of before maybe still there, just hidden. Maybe the hardened metal had melted some. Become more malleable.

I could hope.

Gabrielle nodded. Once more the elegant vampire. "Wolverines."

CHAPTER SEVENTEEN

The night passed much like that. With a few quiet talks among everyone working on the train. A few cinnamon rolls. A lot of coffee.

The feel of the city was too quiet. The night too dark. A wrench clattering on the concrete floor of the cargo bay sounded like a gunshot. We all went on high alert every time a truck came back from the police station. The nerves got to us all.

The work on the Grimm Express finished quickly. That night. All five machine guns were mounted. A Browning .50 cal on top of the locomotive, and one on either side of the last flatbed car. The pair of M240s, the crowd-thinners, on either side of the middle car. Each platform would swivel to cover a nice arc of fire, and each gun had witch-strengthened plates protecting whoever was firing it.

The middle car held the RPGs, too. Grenades, other guns. I had packaged the C4 on both of the cars and the engine and set everything up to a remote with a button. Making the Grimm Express a five-hundred-ton thundering bomb.

I didn't really have a plan for that, but I thought it was a good idea. If we made it close enough to the Crown of Bones, maybe the explosion could take out part of the stadium. And if we didn't, if the army of monsters and knights slowed us down too much, if Sabnock had us surrounded and stopped on the tracks...

Well, it'd be a hell of an ending.

Alejandro's family—vampires and the humans—drew straws from a group of volunteers. The vampire was coming, and Millie *had* to come, but the rest of the Express would take only those who were willing to fight, and willing to not come back.

There were no illusions anymore after the plague. No hope that this would be a decoy run while Nick snuck in through the back door. Nick was still going to try his thing, but the train was going to be the main thrust of our attack. It would work or it wouldn't, but Nick was the backup plan now. Humanity wasn't giving up Mexico without a fight.

Michael appeared. Out of nowhere. The angel looked haggard. I guess he did have a world to look after.

He brought bad news. About the other dead zones. A few of them had high-rises like Mexico City, tinged with the greenish-rusty rot that we now knew were homes to swarms of locusts. Nothing like the ones here, where every tall building held its own nest, but enough to be worrisome.

Michael had sunk a cargo ship in the Pacific. One carrying a lot of the containers like the ones we had seen in Aztec Stadium. Apparently the ship had hit a major storm and capsized.

I wondered how big a storm would have to be to sink a cargo ship. Those things were like a floating city. The storm, the waves underneath, almost would have to be tidal.

Angel of Death, I could believe it.

There were more ships in Manzanillo, Michael said. There was no internet to search, so I had no idea where that was. Apparently, it was a port city on the West Coast of Mexico. The cargo ships there were being loaded up, though everything seemed to be paused at the moment. As if the people doing the loading were waiting for more containers.

Which made sense after the plague. Sabnock had run low on his locust stock and would have to build more. Maybe we had interrupted his plans enough to delay the whole end-of-the-world thing. I could hope. I had been a thorn in many a demon's side.

Everything finished up with a few hours of nightlight left. It was early dawn, or late night, whatever time that was in between midnight and three in the morning. We were waiting for Nick and Johnny to get back, and we would have one last day of sleep before heading out.

I found myself with Jen. We shared one of the last cinnamon rolls, the two of us leaning back against the far wall of the cargo bay. Just us. Her side was against mine, and I laid back there enjoying the feel of her, the way her leg was both soft and hard, the way her foot played with mine.

She still had a few scars, too. A few of the locust bites. Though they were healing better than Gabrielle's were. Or maybe Jen had less.

"I figured something out," she said, licking her fingers from the last bite of sticky-sweet cinnamon. Looking at me with a devilish smile.

"Cinnamon rolls are better not shared?"

The smile grew wider. "No, silly."

"Care to share, then?"

"The roll? Or the thing I've figured out?"

"Both."

She answered by tearing a small bit off the roll and thumbing it into my mouth. There was a burst of sweet and cinnamon on my tongue, and a little bit of soft, sticky bread. I kissed the tip of her thumb before Jen pulled it out.

"So tell me," I said.

"I needed something to happen, like the locusts," she said. "I needed something I could take care of. Something I could beat. It felt good, calling lightning down on the locusts. It felt good, protecting Sarah and Nick and Johnny and Zoe."

"I get it," I said. And I did. There was power in being able to stand up and do something, to protect those you cared about. "There's something you can do. Something you can fight."

Jen nodded. "Something I could beat." She tore and plopped another piece of roll into her mouth. She was eating the sweet slowly, something I could never do. I always wolfed them down.

Which Jen knew. She watched me watch her, eyebrows raised. Tore off another piece of roll. A very small piece of roll. Tiny, even. And then plopped that itsy piece into my mouth with a grin.

"Maybe even something I could control," she said.

I got that. Death would do that to a person. It *should* do that. However we struggle against death; it always wins. Life is the thing we fail at.

I had never felt that fear in Jen. Not from her, and not through our bond, but maybe she was just good at hiding it. Jen was always the person I leaned on most; she was my foundation, something I counted on, depended on.

Her fear made sense. Even if I felt Jen had always been the strongest one between us. Even if she was my rock.

I had always feared I wasn't enough. I always feared I wouldn't be everywhere I was needed. Why wouldn't Jen, after coming back from being dead?

The same fears I once had, Jen would have too. About all of them. Sarah, Nick, Johnny, Gabrielle, everyone.

I had thought a lot about the garage talk the two of us had back when we were running from Kimaris. Right before New Orleans and the dead zones. About how Jen had told me I had to let my friends try, let them grow. Let them fail and possibly die.

It was funny, and possibly ironic, but I wasn't going to point that out now. I could understand the feeling of loss, of not being enough, if Jen had tried to face down death and lost. I could understand needing to get some knowledge back, something of her younger self, some feeling of being invulnerable. Of being able to handle anything. Or at least not having the fear of *not being enough* hanging in the background of her brain.

"I am," Jen said, nodding at me.

We were doing this conversation in reverse. I looked a question at her.

"I am that good," she said.

Oh. She had been reading my thoughts.

"Exactly." She finished the last bite of roll with a laugh. "And I'm aware of the irony."

I thought something else.

She laughed some more and slapped me. Lightly on the chest. And gave me her wicked grin. The one with all kinds of mischievousness to it.

It was as Jen as Jen got. And I loved her for it, even as I wondered how I could possibly help her overcome that kind of fear.

CHAPTER EIGHTEEN

The day was closing. The shadows grew long as the sun set in the west; the light coming through the cargo bay door grew shorter and shorter. There were a few tinks of someone working with a hammer and the slight muttering of people talking to one another around the train over the background noise of the generator outside.

There were fewer people here than even a day or two ago. Nick had taken to long shadow walks at night. Johnny went out on patrols. Some of Alejandro's family went back to the vault; some stayed here.

There was very little left to do on the Grimm Express. I stood looking at it, the shiny white locomotive, the thick red lines streaking horizontally down the side, the blue, cursive words naming the train as mine. The two flatcars on the back, hip-high steel walls welded around each, machine guns mounted on either side.

The big machine gun on top of the train itself.

People kept working on it, but the train was ready. Ready enough. It was only scheduled for a one-way trip, after all.

Millie was in the cab of the locomotive. Familiarizing herself with the controls. Reaching back in time to where she sat with the conductor, when she took trips with her father. She looked young, too young, the scar on her face still thick and still red, and I realized the trips might not have been as far back in time as I imagined.

Alejandro was with her; I watched him appear through the front windshield occasionally. Walking back and forth. Other vampires climbed across the flatcars, testing connections, placing ammo boxes, swinging the machine guns. A squeal echoed in the room from the gun mounted furthest away from me, across the second flatcar. A vampire there from Alejandro's family was working it back and forth on its hastily constructed mount, a grease gun in his hand. The man was leaning over to place the nozzle of the gun in some place I couldn't see.

"Think we're ready," Nick said, standing next to me.

"Yeah," I said. I wasn't going to say the other thing.

Nick said it instead. "Christmas is tomorrow."

"Yeah," I said again.

He waited a moment. "That makes today Christmas Eve."

"I get it."

I did get it. But I didn't want to take the day off. I didn't want to waste another day. I didn't want to sit around with my friends, with Alejandro and his family, and laugh and play with people who could likely die the next day. That would likely die.

But I also was beginning to understand the importance of something like Christmas.

I wasn't sure where Nick was going. And I could feel Jen in the bond, I didn't think she put him up to this. I didn't know—and couldn't believe—anyone had a gift to give to anyone else. And I wasn't sure who wanted what, whether it was a gift, a day to celebrate, or just time with friends.

Thankfully, right then I didn't have to make a choice.

The throbbing exhaust of a motorcycle echoed from down the street. Johnny, back from patrol. Most of us stopped what we were doing, walking to the large roll-up door opening. Johnny brought the Fatboy there, slowing the bike to a stop before shutting it off with a final chugging glop or two.

He stayed on the bike, kicking the kickstand down, leaning a bit to his left with the bike before the Fatboy settled against the blacktop. A pair of binoculars hung across the front of his T-shirt, no helmet on his head, a grin on his face. Not a happy grin, but a down-to-business one.

Johnny flicked his eyes behind me a moment. To Jen. Then back. "We got company."

"Company?"

"Looks like a scouting group. A dozen men. One of them looks like a golem." His face harder to read now, obscure. Composed.

A scouting group? La Familia Diablos? Coming back to see if they could retake their territory? If there was anything left to retake? Did Johnny feel an attachment there, a need to prove himself to Gabrielle? Against a group of thugs and their Ushabti?

My hands tightened a bit. It could be Hector. Maybe he could sense me like I could sense other spirits on my ethereal radar. Maybe the two of us had been tied together back in that grave, and while I couldn't see Hector on my radar, with the golem-spirit not really being a ghost anymore, maybe he could see me. Maybe I was all he could see, a big blue Fergus Grimm dot blinking *here I am, here I am, here I am…*

Zoe was tucked away into the corner. Her face unreadable. Her mother next to her, an arm around her daughter. Gertrude is behind them.

Faces looked at me; I became aware of all of them. Alejandro and Millie and his family of vampires and humans. Gabrielle. Michael. Sarah and Nick and Jen.

Hector could have found me up north. He could have brought the snipers there. And he could be bringing them here.

If he wanted to find me, then I'd make it easy on him. Hell, I'd prefer it to making a decision about Christmas. I was almost happy to have that taken away from me. I hid it as best as I could from the bond, but I was definitely relieved.

Then I caught Nick rolling his eyes. His tiny shake of his head at my arched eyebrow. When did he get so good at reading me?

Jen stepped close to me. Like me, she hid her feelings in the bond. I hoped she was not feeling my relief at the whole Christmas thing, and at the same time I wondered if she was hiding her anger, her frustration, at losing my gift. It had just been a few days ago I had seen her screaming in our destroyed apartment, shaking out a rag of locust shells, shaking in her anger.

That still worried me. Jen had been something I had never seen in her before. Anger like I had never seen. Frustration and anger that had mixed almost into madness. I would have said madness in any other person other than Jen.

Something I had never really seen in her before.

Something I never wanted to see again.

Her fingers on my arm were light, but the squeeze of her hand was firm.

"Be safe." Was all she said.

"Hey," I said, giving her a wink. "It's me."

Michael already stood outside, by Johnny. Who leaned a little on his handlebars, giving me directions.

"I barely caught them before they ducked around a building. They're right on the northeastern edge of the city," he said. "Like they are circling around to the east. There's a gas station there, looks like the roof had been painted green once. Green with white letters."

Johnny paused. "You want me to come, show you where?"

I looked at Michael. The angel, like most times, was unreadable. He gave a slight shake of his head.

"I think we can find them," I said.

The serious moment lightened then, Johnny giving a big Johnny-grin. He slapped my arm. "Well, don't take it easy on them, okay?"

I grinned back. "Deal."

Michael leapt into the air, his wings bursting out behind him. I did the same. Even though the Five-Fold blade was strapped to my leg, I reached out and tapped into one of the hundreds of ghosts around the depot, feeling my ethereal wings mimic the angel.

The air seemed heavy, hard to fly through, and I pulled a little more energy. Pushing the memories aside. Another spirit dying a painful locusty death.

We both headed north, the blackened rubble of buildings zooming by underneath us. We flew fast and low, curving east once the buildings underneath us stopped being muddled ruins of city blocks and became more looping ruins of suburbs and thin, spider-like streets. I hoped the speed helped and that if Hector could sense me in some way, that I was moving too fast for the golem to get a bead on me.

Soon we came upon the gas station. It was hard to miss by itself. A long rectangular roof still stood above the pumps, and it did look like a bit of green paint remained around the edges of the roof, along with a white horizontal line and maybe some white letters.

I punched through the roof of the station, summoning my sword. Landing in a pounding of the earth, feeling the thunk of it in my knees. Ready to fight.

There was no one there.

Michael landed next to me. His sword still in his sheathe. At my glance he lifted one shoulder, briefly, and let it drop.

So we searched. All the homes and buildings around. All the ruined streets. I punched through them all, pulling ethereal energy as needed. Ready to fight at a moment's notice.

And found no one.

It got to me. I wondered where they were hiding. *How* they were hiding. I looked for them on my ethereal radar, seeing nothing. Nothing but bright and faded dots of blue, with an occasional bluish-red hue to a ghost here and there.

An hour passed. Maybe another. I looked for them in my ethereal sight. I could see humans and vampires and other creatures that way. Vampires had a purple spark inside them, humans a blazing white.

I saw nothing that way.

And it got to me more. If Hector was here, if he had brought another sniper team to take us out, to take Jen out...

Michael finally stopped me, with a hand on my shoulder. The two of us hovering over yet another building. "Whatever was here is gone, Fergus Grimm."

"Yeah," I said. My hands in fists. Wondering what kind of plan Sabnock had now. "Yeah."

I blazed up then. High into the air. Circling back north to the edge of Cuernavaca. To the edge of the dead zone.

I rose high, using ethereal energy to power my sight, looking as far north as I could. North through the purpling backs of early evening. Hovering, looking, seeing the Crown of Bones in the distance, nestled in the city center among towers of high-rises, the towers with the nests of locusts at their top.

Thick red lines dug through the earth, thick lines of power in the shape of a pentagram the size of Mexico City. In the center of the pentagram was another star-like shape, traced with the same thick lines, forming another pentagram with another star-like shape inside, over and over, until we got to the Crown of Bones.

The nexus of it all.

The lines ducked underneath the stadium, while the white bones of concrete of the structure circled above, much like the skeleton fingers of a hand, spread outward, ringed with steel and glass, topped with tall metal panels on its roof, all angled in.

The roof bubbled up slightly, much like a head, the crown sitting squarely on the ground. Inside, I imagined, was the bright red sun of ethereal energy, ethereal energy created by sacrificing millions of people, people made into golems and crabs and locusts and whatever else Sabnock had in store.

My face tingled a bit, and I realized I was drifting north in my hovering. Drifting towards the crown.

It would be so easy, I thought, to end it now. To take the Five-Fold blade and fly right to the Crown of Bones, to descend through the hole in the roof, and take on Sabnock and whatever he had in store.

No more Ushabti. No more locusts. No more Hector and vampires and whatever army Sabnock had waiting. Just him and me.

I took a big breath.

Let it go.

And drifted back.

Michael waited there. Watching me. His wings spread out, holding him in the air. His serious face a mix of compassion and contemplation behind the smallest of smiles.

"You have good friends, Fergus Grimm," he finally said.

I did. But I didn't know where he was going with this.

"It's not something I've had," Michael said. His face cracking just a bit, the smile letting go into something like regret. "Not for a long time. When I look at you and your friends, and I've seen how you've grown, well, I look back at myself and wonder how much I've changed. If I've changed. Or if I should have changed, perhaps differently."

Michael had always seemed in control, from the moment I met him. He was, after all, the leader of the forces of heaven. But for the smallest of moments, I got a look at the real angel. The sadness there. The fear. The loss.

The loneliness.

The rage.

He went on, his gaze going north. To the same place I stared at, the Crown of Bones. To Sabnock, the stadium, and the plan the demons had concocted. "I wonder if, without those who were once my friends, if I had stopped growing. Stopped evolving... If I merely have been fighting the same fight, doing the same thing, stagnant, for thousands of years."

His expression slowly returned. As if Michael had trouble putting it back into place, slowly putting block after block back, the control, the compassion, the smallest of smiles.

"It is a tough thing to regret."

I stood there a moment, watching him compose himself. Watching the commanding mask slide back over. The angel of death, flying beside me, the two of us hovering over the dead zone and staring at the Crown of Bones in the distance.

"You have good friends," he said again, turning back. Taking me with him. "Let us return to them."

CHAPTER NINETEEN

I t was night by the time we returned. The moon pale in the east above us. It was well into evening, and apparently, everyone had gone to bed.

The lights were off inside the depot, the big cargo doorway a darker black in the darkening night. The faded moon just gave me impressions of the edge of the doorway, the thick corners of the large building.

A tiny fear ran through me, a fear I dismissed as soon as it came to me. If Hector had gotten here, if the golem and his team had gotten to the depot, I would have felt something in the bond. I would have felt Jen, fighting.

I thought.

Michael landed next to me. The dark of the depot didn't seem to bother the angel, and he took a couple of steps before stopping and glancing back at me. While his face was in its normally unreadable state, I felt his gaze was questioning.

For some reason I hesitated. Something didn't feel right. Something felt off. The darkness and the quiet. The not being able to find the scouting team. The unknown of Sabnock's plan, the fear of Hector... some fear remained in me even as logic dismissed it.

And I got it then. I couldn't hear the generator.

My heart beat a little faster.

I couldn't hear *anything*. Not an echo, not a tinking of a wrench or hammer, not a pin drop. Nothing.

I found myself taking a step, my hand curling up to hold the hilt of the sword I was about to summon. The other hand touching the hilt of the Five-Fold blade in its sheathe around my leg. At the same time I reached for Jen through the bond, reached deep into the darkness inside the depot, reaching for her location, feeling her hiding...

Lights blazed out from the train station's bay.

Not the bright fluorescent lights that regularly hung overhead in the depot, but warm lights. The warming yellows of a spreading illumination, blazing as if from a fire. The light flickered even as it strengthened, as if someone was dialing in the brightness, throwing shadows out from the building and behind me. It all happened so quickly. I blinked at the light and hid my eyes with my hands, shading them so I could see.

The train, cleaned up before me. The Grimm Express. With a large pine tree in the middle of the last flatcar. A pine tree decorated in tiny globes of red and green and blue, a pine tree with a tiny, piercing white light at its top.

All the lights twinkling in their own pattern. As if each bulb pulsed with its own breath. With their own heartbeats.

And my friends there, standing around and before the tree. Laughing. Nick and Sarah right in front, Sarah sitting on the edge of the flatcar, a new guitar somehow in her lap. Nick's lips curved in the slightest smile, which for him said volumes.

Johnny there, standing by the car. Leaning against it, one arm around Gabrielle who was tucked against his side. He had a big "we got you grin" on his face and gave me a long wink.

It had been a setup.

The report of the scouting group and the golem. Nick's late-night shadow walking. Even Alejandro's group, his family, always shuffling back and forth from the vault. There was a long array of food and drinks on the counter hub with his clan behind it.

All my friends had done this over the past couple of days. Done this and kept it hidden. Done this and had given no sign.

My eye found Jen. Beside Sarah, her hands clasped in front of her. Jen's eyes shimmered with mixed emotions, with hope and worry, and her lips moved, just for me.

Merry Christmas.

My eyes narrowed, looking at the angel. Michael stood off to the side, and even he was smiling. He had been a part of this as much as any of them.

"You have good friends," he said, one more time. I caught the edge of emotion from him from above the dead zone, a mix of wistfulness and unknowing and maybe regret.

And even then, I was frozen. I found it hard, incredibly hard, to transition from who I had been to the now. From someone hunting a scouting group, from hunting Hector, from hovering above Mexico City and *wanting so badly* to fly to the Crown of Bones, to face Sabnock and end it all right then.

From someone who had returned from that, to *this*.

It was so quiet in there. Still.

Then there was a pluck of a guitar. A single note, slowly strummed. The note became a chord. Then another. The beat of the song picked up, until I could recognize it. Until I could hear, ever so slightly, Sarah's fragile voice hum an accompaniment. Hear her hum until others joined her, the humming breaking through the quiet of the depot. A humming that swelled louder and became words. Words to a song, whispered by some, spoken by others, sang by a few...

. . .

Have yourself a merry little Christmas,
Let your heart be light,
Next year all our troubles, will be out of sight…

My first step felt shaky. It was like my leg, my foot, like they had no strength in them. Like they couldn't hold me up, even as I carefully placed it in front of me.

But I took a step in, then another. Slow steps. Shaking my head. My gaze locked with Jen's. The bond trilling with something strong between us.

Once again, as in olden days,
Happy golden days of yore,
Faithful friends who are dear to us,
Will be near to us once more…

I started mouthing the words too. Not really knowing them, never really having learned the song, but from memory. From Christmas after Christmas with Jen. From listening to Sinatra sing them softly from a scratchy record playing in the corner. A crackling fire in the fireplace, radiating a toasty kind of warmth through the Cooper's living room.

Feelings washed over me. Sitting with Jen on the couch, her hip pressed to mine. Covered in a blanket. Warm mugs of hot chocolate wrapped with our hands, maybe, just possibly, a glob of melted marshmallow on my chin. The Christmas tree, her Christmas tree, sitting in the corner. Blinking blue and green and red, gifts wrapped and tucked under the boughs.

I neared Jen. A smile broke from me. A hand, my hand, wiped something away from my eyes. She took a step; I took another, and all of a sudden she was in my arms. I held her tight and swung her around, around and around, her familiar scent of honeysuckle and rain almost hidden under the strong scent of pine.

And still people were singing. Sarah's playing grew stronger, the plucking of the strings weaving around their words, echoing them here, accenting them there.

Someday soon we will all be together
  If the fates allow,
  Until then, we'll have to muddle through somehow
  So have yourself a merry little Christmas now

Jen laughed in my ear, and something in me let go.

And then the party started.

There weren't any gifts. Not of the physical variety. There was just celebration, and laughing, and Christmas song after Christmas song. People telling stories of their favorite Christmases. Me finding out Alejandro's first Christmas gift had been a car from his father, a Lexus something or other that the vampire went out and promptly wrecked.

His next car had been an old Dodge Colt. Something from the eighties with a hatchback. The passenger door frame bent a bit, so the door wouldn't shut right. Which Alejandro drove carefully the entire next year.

I stood a moment, admiring the tree. The lights on it were real Christmas lights, bulbs on a string. Nick had found them and brought them back, and even though the string wasn't plugged in, Tabitha had lit each with her magic. Earth magic, bringing out the colors of the bulbs. More of a radiance than a glow, and I watched as each bulb, whether red, blue, or green, swelled in illumination and then released, every bulb different in its interval, irregular, as if each was breathing color with long breaths. Pulsing, like the slow crashing of waves along a shore.

"Magical, isn't it?" Jen said.

I grinned at the words. They were magical, but that wasn't what either she or I meant. Looking at her, feeling the feeling only Christmas can bring, that special feeling of being with someone you love, someone you always loved, someone you would always love.

Johnny came up and stood next to us a moment. It struck me again how much more solid he seemed, bigger. More capable. I knew if I looked at him with my ethereal vision I would see that ethereal energy running through his veins.

He had a cup of the punch in his hands, wincing a little after each sip. Gabrielle next to him, quiet, her eyes for once not the eyes of an intense, elegant vampire. She even gave me a small smile.

Wonders will never cease.

"You know, hundreds of years ago they used to take trains and set them up to run into each other," Johnny said.

Both Jen and I looked at him.

"Really," he said. "In Texas. They set them up miles apart, pointed them at each other, fired up the boilers and let them go."

"It sounds like a demolition derby," I finally said. Looking at the locomotive, the white sides, the horizontal red streaks, the blue-painted words, *Grimm Express*. "Just with trains."

Johnny laughed. "Exactly." He slapped the side of the car. "So whatever we do with this thing, it's only going to be the second stupidest thing people have done with a train."

Jen laughed first, but I wasn't long after. The two of us went to find the punch bowl; Renaldo was there, pouring the drinks. He poured each of us one, a dark liquid spilling into white coffee mugs, before handing them over.

Jen held hers carefully. The mug was warm in my hand. I took a quick sniff, smelling a thick, dark chocolate, and some kind of alcohol. I took a sip. Tequila.

I must have made a face.

"Mexican hot chocolate," the bartender said. "You don't like?"

I grinned a bit and took another. It was chocolatey and sugary with a weird agave kick. It was weird, but when in Rome.

We ate some of the food there. Mostly Mexican, but there was something resembling a sausage roll that I ate a few of. Almost a sausage roll, but with some kind of chile in it. Something a little spicy and a little smoky.

It wasn't the same thing as the rolls at the Coopers, but it reminded me of something from my youth. Something from where I had ground up. Tabitha and Zoe were there, eating them as well, and we exchanged knowing glances, having come from the same area, where sausage and pepperoni rolls were the meals of Christmas morning.

People stood there talking. Other stories came out. Other tales. They seemed to get longer as the punch bowel got emptier. It grew cooler outside. At least that was my sense of it, as people huddled closer and closer together. I happened to glance at Gertrude over by the depot door, and I put two and two together. It wasn't like the ice witch could make it snow. Not this far south. Not with this heat, even though in December.

But there were points for trying. Someone found a metal barrel and was burning some wood in it. Maybe more pine, by the scent of the smoke. More singing came from the group there, more singing and humming, though I couldn't make out the words.

At some point, Jen and I found ourselves back with her sister.

Sarah stopped playing; we brought her the Cuernavaca version of sausage rolls and a cup of Mexican hot chocolate. Nick grimaced when he ate one.

The four of us sat there in front of the tree, our legs dangling off the side of the flatcar, the machine gun nest to my left. The hip-high walls that would be welded to the side lying on the floor in front of us. The smell of a pine tree everywhere. We sat and drank and nibbled and looked over the group of people in front of us. Vampires and humans and witches, an angel and whoever and whatever else. All singing and telling stories, illuminated by the soft firelight glow Tabitha had rigged above us.

Nick got up to get more drinks. Jen patted me on the shoulder and followed him.

"It's nice, isn't it?" Sarah said, Nick's arm around her. Her voice was soft; her gaze lingered a bit over Jen. Which was where I happened to be looking, too. Jen had happened upon Zoe. The two of them were laughing, Zoe holding her globe up between them, the globe flickering as if playing some kind of show.

"It is." I agreed.

A little moment passed. "I figured it out," she said.

"Figured what out?"

"You know, my question," she said. "What I asked you, back when Grumpy was sleeping."

Ah. The time back in the apartment, in the town up north whose name I would never know. The question about why her powers worked in the dead zone. The Good and Evil question. The one asking if the powers you had defined you as a person. The one I wrestled with sometimes, too.

"And?"

Her shoulders shrugged in a delicate manner. Her smile, though, was stronger, more forceful. As strong a feeling as I had ever gotten from her. "I've decided it doesn't matter. As long as I'm protecting those I care about."

A memory broke in. Sarah sitting in the back of a car. Telling me to leave Grafton. Telling me to find Jen and leave her.

That memory would never leave me. The window rolling up between us. The feeling from Sarah that she was not worth saving. Me seeing my reflection in the mirror and not liking what I had found.

What a long journey we had all had since then.

Sarah might understand the powers I wielded better than most. The taint of something dark and evil, for me the memories of evil spirit's lives; for her the fear of not being able to control her power, a power that would kill in an instant, with the tiniest slip of control.

I threw an arm around her, pulled her close in a quick hug. Felt her let go and become the little sister again, and for once she didn't feel slight and fragile, but more solid. More Sarah.

"Good," I said. "Good."

And we left it at that.

After a while the singing slowed. The cold remained, and the darkness grew longer. The bulbs on the Christmas tree took longer and longer breaths, dying off one after another. The fireside yellows Tabitha had set up in the depot doing the same. The last of the punch being drunk. The last sausage roll gone.

People began settling down in places, mostly in pairs, tucking themselves on the hard floor with a blanket around them. Tomorrow was Christmas, and tomorrow we would be unwrapping the gift that was the Grimm Express, and giving that gift to Sabnock.

It grew dimmer, and dimmer, and the star at the top of the Christmas tree began its long, last breath, its light flickering smaller and smaller.

Jen came back, smiling at her sister, pulling me away. Tugging me over to a section of the wall she had built a little nest in, a mound of blankets and even a pillow. We slipped underneath one blanket, the cold concrete of the floor still present on my back, and Jen lifted my arm and snuggled against my side.

Her breath, warm on my chest. The bond between us full of peace and happiness and the best of wills. Her hair under my nose, with its scent of honeysuckle and rain, with the tiniest breath of Christmas pine in each breath.

One loose golden strand tickled my cheek.

I blew it away from the side of my mouth.

It came back.

Jen laughed softly against me.

And soon, we were both asleep.

CHAPTER TWENTY

It may have still been early Christmas morning. I may have just woken up. It was hard to tell, other than the muscles knotted up in my back. My sleep had been hard and deep and rejuvenating, even though I might have woken a time or two, quickly, before falling back into a dreamless slumber.

Now though, I lay on the floor, my head to the side, my eyes looking across the bay, across the Grimm Express, to the open depot doors in the east. To the darkness of the fading night, to an almost early morning, with maybe the tiniest yellow sliver of the morning sun in the east.

Morning-ish.

Jen lay still across me. Her body using my chest as a pillow. Her head over my chest. Her arm wrapped tight around me, her leg wrapped around mine. The tiniest of snores coming from her deep sleep. Her head was using my thighs as a pillow, and her arm was wrapped around my calves. Some of her hair lay strewn across my T-shirt, a black one this time, a Journey shirt with the words Don't Stop Believin' scrawled across the top above the band.

It was an appropriate shirt, I thought. Maybe a little fortuitous, with the battle ahead. I could believe in luck, or fate; I could believe in the power of belief... it was that time of year.

Last night had been good for Jen. Good for all of us. Had it fixed everything? No. We all had stood around and lived past Christmases; we had enjoyed good company and pretended we weren't about to go on a crazy kind of suicide train run, and there had been healing of sorts.

But there was still a darkness in Sarah. A worry between Johnny and Gabrielle. A dread in Tabitha. And Jen...

There was still an anger in Jen, tucked deeply inside of her. A pulsing anger, mixing with an unknown fear, desperate in its reach. She had masked it well, but nothing can be masked fully between us, even without our bond. I felt it, and caught it sometimes in her eyes as she looked at her sister, or Johnny, or someone else, but still, it had been nice to see her laugh again. To see the smile again, occasionally, the one that made me feel a little taller.

Last night hadn't healed anyone. But it had been nice. It had helped push back the bleak rush of the tidal wave of demons, and self-doubts, and worry for a brief moment in all our lives. And if for nothing else, that was what Christmas did to those who celebrated it.

The sky was still dark outside, though it lightened to the east. Near dawn. If we had slept it hadn't been for an hour. My brain felt murky; it struggled to wake, and I wondered what had prompted me to open my eyes.

There. I saw it now. A tiny shadow by the cargo bay roll-up door. The door that wouldn't roll up or down anymore because it was gone. I blinked a few times, and the shadow resolved into Nick.

Leave it to him to keep up patrolling, even on Christmas Eve.

There were more shadows. Johnny and Gabrielle. The three of them talking before both looking my way.

Nick's face looked the same as always. Johnny's had his usual grin, though without any humor. Gabrielle's might have been a little wistful. As if the fun and games were all over now.

"I guess we're waking up," Jen's voice came, a little muffled, speaking into my pants. Grumpy, but smiling. I guess she had woken a short time after I had. I felt, along our bond, a deep desire in her to pull a heavy blanket over her head and tuck the world away, and the thought had me smiling.

That thought had Jen pull herself up. A small groan escaped her, which she quickly cut off with a grunt. Her hair spilled over her face, so all I could see was her jaw, her smooth cheeks, the reddish-pink of her lips. Jen gave me a hand after I struggled to stand. My legs were numb, and as soon as I moved them I got that pins-and-needles sensation lighting up everything. All my nerves fired with it, so I pulled the tiniest amount of ethereal energy from the Five-Fold blade.

Jen smiled. "That's cheating."

"Cheating'll work," I said, still trying to stretch my legs and back out. The pins-and-needles were gone, but the muscles still ached a bit. I felt like I was a hundred years old. "I'll take it."

She laughed. Then went serious. Because Johnny's face was. We both could see it as he walked over. Alone. Without Nick.

"Grimm," he said. "We got trouble."

Behind him, Gabrielle was already getting the volunteers to the train. Not shouting at them, but commanding. I saw her get Millie and point towards the Express.

"That kind of trouble?" I said.

"Is there any other kind?" Johnny asked.

"Where's Nick?"

"Already on his way back to the stadium." Johnny pointed to the train. "We need to get that thing moving."

The sky was brightening, even now. There was a grayness to the air past the large depot doors. Sunrise and true daylight was right around the corner.

Sunrise.

Oh shit.

The vampires had gotten around the past week by staying in the vault during sunrise. Or staying in the back cargo room. I wasn't sure if they could survive sunrise in their tactical gear. Their clothes were thick and made to protect them from bullets and sunlight. Even their helmets were heavily polarized.

I hated to ask. But we needed them.

"They can," Johnny said. "But we don't have enough. And, if their suit gets punctured, or it tears during the actual sunrise..." He made a motion with his hands. "They're just gone."

He shook his head.

I needed to get a better idea of what was going on.

"There's an army mobilizing," Johnny said. "Headed this way."

"An army?"

"Thousands of people, as far as I could see with the glasses," he said. "Tens of thousands? Hell, there's a shit ton. People, monsters... a bunch of those knights."

Hector would be a part of that group. He could even be leading the charge. I knew it as well as I knew anything. I had escaped him, and his memories had shown me he didn't like people escaping him.

"They find Nick?"

Johnny shook his head. "Nick saw it, or they saw him," he said. "He wasn't sure which. He got back to me and told me to get moving. And told me to tell you he was going to look at the switch-yard and make sure the tracks are lined up right. He's got the radio, but..."

It was a big but. He'd be able to contact us if we got close enough, but not until then. We were a long way from the stadium.

And even then, I wouldn't want to buzz him over the air. We wouldn't know exactly where he was hiding. We wouldn't know if buzzing him over the air at the wrong moment might give Nick away.

We'd have to depend on him to reach out to us. To let us know the pathway was clear and the Express could roll its way through.

Sarah stepped out from the front of the locomotive. Her eyes fearful, worried. She saw Jen and I felt Jen's worry in the bond. Her fear and love for her sister. Jen's wondering, cut short, about her sister maybe not even getting a chance to say goodbye.

All of those feelings cut me. Not just my feelings, not only my worry about Nick and Sarah; the pain was tangible through the bond. Jen looked at me, grabbed my hand and squeezed it.

Speaking of moments.

"Sounds like we need to get moving," I said.

Plopping sounds came from above the bay. Louder than the thrumming of the generator powering the lights in the bay. They were accompanied by pings of metal, followed by that kind of sound you hear when a sheet of metal reverberates after something hits it. Like hail was hitting the roof, followed by rolls of hollow thunder.

People started yelling outside the station. Vampire and humans alike raced in. Little things blurred in the air, one or two insects spinning through the air in lazy circles, heading towards the big lights.

The hail wasn't hail; it was locusts.

Again.

Not as many as the plague this time. More of a light rain of locusts instead of the storm of a few days ago. As if Sabnock didn't have a lot of the insects, and the demon was just sending those creatures he had recently made.

The plopping increased above us, like the wind had picked up and thrown more locusts against us. A few insects struck the ground outside and burst open in the green goo that had become so familiar. The ones that survived moved slowly, as if dazed. Some of those even took wing in circling, drunken flights.

Less a plague of locusts, and more of a light cold of them, then.

Still scary though, for those of us who had survived before.

We went over to Gabrielle. She was suiting up. The plops and pings and little thundering sounds of thin metal happened all around us. Her scars stood out stark against her skin, which seemed pale, which seemed odd for a vampire. Unless you had seen what she had endured before.

"You don't have to go," I said.

She gave me a look.

"Just saying."

The vampire tugged the tight tactical suit up from her legs. Johnny had already moved behind her, zipping it up. The tight, thick material hugged Gabrielle's form, made the curves more pronounced.

The rest of the bay seemed crazy. The light rain of locusts continued outside. Everyone inside the bay moved in spurts, in hectic motions. Everyone knew what we were doing, but no one was organized.

There was a little bit of a panic. Which I understood. No one here had been in a real war. In a real battle, where bullets could kill anyone from thousands of feet away.

Everyone here had been in street fights. Maybe tiny battles. But not a war. Not like the one that would happen today. If there was an army coming, no one here would be safe. No one on the Grimm Express would be safe. There would be no safety anywhere. Not today.

I had a promise to keep.

"Get everyone on the train," I told Jen. "Everyone who's going."

I left her to handle that. I went to find Gertrude. The Valkyrie was behind the counter. She had just come out of the package area in the back, the place the vampires slept in. Gertrude looked almost as tired as Tabitha, but then, all of us probably looked like that.

"It's time," I said.

Her eyes questioned me, and then she nodded. Understanding.

"There's an army coming," I said, loudly. The thumps had gotten louder, the insects bouncing off the roof above in heavier and heavier waves. "Appreciate your help."

The tall witch looked past me, over the train. Maybe imagining the battle ahead. "There's nowhere safe, is there?"

I knew what she was saying. There wasn't a place here that was safe. There was no place safe around Mexico City. Likely in all of Mexico.

But there was no place safe in the world. A person could go hide somewhere. Maybe in the mountains in Montana. Maybe in the wilds, up in Canada. There would be safety there, for a while.

But only for a while.

"Probably not," I said.

Gertrude looked back. Tabitha and Zoe were both coming out of the package area behind the counter. Tabitha leaned on her daughter and looked worn, worried, but also happy.

"It's not in me to avoid a battle," the Valkyrie finally said, in a quiet voice between us. "It's not in me to not fight."

A memory fluttered through my brain of a long time ago. A time before Grafton. It made me smile, not a happy or sad smile, just one of recognition. "It used to be not in me to not run."

Her eyes narrowed in thought. Maybe puzzling on what I meant. She stood as if a burden weighed her down. "These two cannot fight."

My smile disappeared. I knew where her promises had led her, just like I knew where mine had led me. I understood she had people she was responsible for. I did, too. "I get it."

There was a long pause. Then she nodded, as if understanding that I did get it.

"There are a few trucks around," I said. "Take one and run south as far as you can."

Tabitha and Zoe were close enough to hear that. And while Tabitha said nothing, Zoe immediately jumped in.

"No," she looked at Gertrude, then her mother. "We're staying with them, right? With Grimm?"

The two witches looked at each other. A knowing look. One Zoe recognized.

"You're doing this for me, aren't you?" the young witch said, "Because you think I can't fight."

Zoe's powers ran towards the spirits and ghosts. More of *séancey* things. She could talk to ghosts and spirits, but that was about it. Not the type of power to take into battle.

"Hey, look," I said. "Someone has to make it out of here. Someone has to tell the others what's going on with the plague and the dead zones and the demons."

Zoe snorted. "You think they'll believe us? Why?"

Well, I couldn't answer that. I didn't think anyone would believe them. Hell, the president of the United States was actively negotiating with Azazel. They likely were having nice dinners in the capitol, pretending to laugh at each other's jokes.

Well, Azazel was probably really laughing.

I put a hand on Zoe's shoulder. Caught her eyes. Waved my hand towards everyone around us, the vampires and humans suiting up in body armor. Watching as one person slipped some armor plates in the back of another. Listening to the clicks and clacks of people checking the magazines in their assault rifles.

"Somebody has to survive," I told Zoe. "I hope it's going to be us. But it needs to be someone."

There was a long pause. Zoe's face went through a lot of little expressions, as if she were thinking. Then they all washed away, vanished with some realization. Zoe finally nodded. Though she looked the least happy about it of all of us.

Out of the corner of my eyes, I saw Tabitha let out a breath.

Gertrude inclined her head as well, in thanks. Though her smile wasn't a happy one. "If you survive this, call me up for the next one."

"I'll say the same." I wasn't sure how many of us would survive this day. But I was planning on being one of them. And if I survived, I was bringing as many people as I could with me. "It's a deal."

"Not a deal," Gertrude said, finally grinning. "A promise."

I grinned back, shook the Valkyrie's hand. "You got it."

The panic around us got heavier, but it also seemed more organized. The running around under the light hail of locusts were not people running from the insects, but were people hurrying to their stations. Jen and Johnny and Gabrielle were getting the train loaded up. I watched Millie climb into the engine. She was in a tactical suit, and I only recognized her from her slight, short form.

A few of the locusts spun lazily through the air as if lost. I ran over, swatting a few of the insects out of the air as I ran. There was a ladder on the side of the engine; I climbed it. Millie's helmet looked over at me. I tossed her the remote to the explosives I had wired. "C4," I explained. "Wired through the train. Blow it if you need to."

That would happen in two cases. One, if they made it all the way to the stadium and were close enough to maybe destroy the pentagram's center.

Two, if they were surrounded and wanted a quick ending.

The vampire nodded. Understanding both cases.

Alejandro climbed up past me on the ladder. He had his helmet off, which is why I recognized him. Both he and Millie wore body armor, and there was also an M4 strapped to his back, the barrel black. His face was serious; he didn't say a word; he just started helping Millie get the engine started.

It would take a little time to get the locomotive running. It was a large engine and needed a few steps before it was warmed up and ready to go. Then we all would have to help Millie navigate the tracks, get the train and its cabs maneuvered around and situated on the right set. The tracks heading north.

"Twenty minutes," Millie told me.

I looked outside. It was that time in the morning right before sunrise, where the sky was black enough to fool us all into it being in the middle of the night. But our time was running short. Not just for sunrise, but for Nick.

He needed darkness for his moment. Hell, we needed darkness for Nick to have his moment. We were rolling the dice here with the Grimm Express, with rolling the train right up to Aztec Stadium; it was a Hail Mary type of pass to demolish the Crown of Bones and hopefully destroy the pentagram in its center.

Twenty minutes was a lot of time to get all that rolling. Plus, getting it set up on the right track. Not to mention the running battle the train might have to fight to make it into the dead zone.

And beyond.

Maybe I could help some with that.

The plopping got louder above. Everyone stopped and looked up in the same moment, as the plops became huge, roof-shuddering booms in the beat of a heart. Not the heavy waves of locusts. But big cannonballs of thunder.

Someone screamed as a section of the roof broke inwards. Metal and concrete dropped down to the bay floor, behind the train and the cabs. Something else hit the concrete floor with the pieces of roof and exploded outward.

I swore as a large shard of a red and white shell hit my face.

I couldn't believe it.

More screams started outside. Real screams. The piercing cries of people dying. The cries were accompanied by more of the thunder-ball-sounding explosions of car-sized creatures impacting the pavement.

All hell broke loose.

It was raining crabs.

CHAPTER TWENTY-ONE

The darkness outside the bay hid a lot of what was going on outside. A scream came, the voice cutting off in mid-yell, leaving just the sounds of people running around inside the bay, the booms of crabs hitting the roof, and the low, low thrumming of the generator.

A large claw appeared in the dim light outside the depot, right outside the cargo bay door. It was large and red and white and stained with crimson. It snapped quickly, once, twice, and disappeared.

I did my thing. Reached out on the radar and pulled a ghost—

Felt my fists punching something small. Something that might be a kid. Might be a woman. The hair was black and thick, and I couldn't see the face. All I felt was the anger and the pain of my knuckles as I beat my fists into their skull. Fuck her. Fuck what she said about me. Fuck her and her high-and-mighty—

I pushed the memories away, filtered them and got to the ethereal energy.

Gunfire erupted outside. Time slowed down for me. I heard the automatic firing of the assault rifles as individual bursts. A quick scream became a long, drawn-out cry. The thrum of the generator, something subsonic, too low to hear.

I raced over to the section of roof that had collapsed, avoiding the mess of broken shells, white meat, and viscous liquid that had once been a truck-sized crab. Piles of concrete lie around, puffs of white dust, a long torn sheet of metal, and a long piece of rebar.

Perfect.

I grabbed the rebar and broke it off with a twist. The long, thick piece of steel weighed fifty pounds or more, but it was light in my ethereal-assisted grip. The rebar was thick, hard, longer than the Five-Fold blade, and more real than my sword.

Perfect for stabbing crabs.

The gunfire sped up some as more rifles joined in. There was a unit of vampires kneeling by the doors, facing outward, tiny bursts of light echoing out from the barrels of the M4s. It gave an eerie strobe-like effect to the crabs showing themselves at the cargo bay.

I hardened my skin, raced past the vampires to wade through the crabs. Dodging the snipping of the person-sized claws. Feeling a few bullets strike me in the back and bounce off. I ducked a second claw and stabbed the piece of rebar deep into the center of the crab's shell. A little wiggle of the steel, and then I pulled it out.

The crab went dead.

I kicked it aside and went after the next. Blinking on my ethereal sight, out in the dark. Seeing the glowing shapes of the monsters in the darkness. Seeing more fall to the ground around us and burst open.

Sabnock must be digging deep into his bag of tricks.

I kept up the stabbing. The wiggling of the rebar, mixing up whatever tiny brain the crabs had in their centers. A few of them survived the initial poke of rebar; some had to be stabbed a few more times. One particular crab, the largest I'd seen, the size of a Dually truck, took seven stabs. And the final stab bent the rebar in half.

Dammit.

I went to the next thing I had handy. What had worked before, in the small coastal town. I pulled more energy from the ghosts, picked up a car and started flattening the crabs.

I could do this all day.

The problem was, I might have to. The sky wasn't letting up in its reign of crustaceans. Big glowy shapes kept dropping around me; a few times I had to step aside at the last moment as a crab burst on the road next to me.

I ran out of ethereal energy. The ghost popped with a silent scream. I tapped another, and then another. Went through the memories of a dog-kicker. Another pedophile. And, for some odd reason, the ghost of someone who had kept stealing packs of gum from the local store.

The crabs kept falling, still. The gunfire had quieted down behind me. My shirt was slick with crab fluid and sweat. I swung cars on crabs, I threw crabs onto other crabs. In some places I threw them against the locust-eaten building, watching their bodies crash through walls and disappear.

Maybe I couldn't do this all day.

Then the skies opened up. Really opened up. Not with crabs, but with lightning.

Bolts streaked to the ground. Slammed all around me. The horizon echoed with the thunder of a storm never seen before in Mexico. Forks of electric blue danced up and down the street in a staccato rhythm.

I paused and watched the beauty of it. The sizzling dance of electric blue on the pavement. The explosion of crab after crab after crab.

Then the depot was empty. At least, of crabs. A few locusts spun around. One tried to bite me; my skin was still hard from the energy, and it tried a couple of times before I smacked it with a bare hand.

Jen walked up next to me. Her hand glowed with tiny streaks of electricity, tiny threads of blue-white raced around her fingers.

I smiled. "Show off."

She winked back. The lightning rolled outwards from us, dancing further and further away as the bolts picked out targets in the distance. Thunder reverberated back, the echoes smaller and smaller until the booms became faint rumbles, and then silence.

Then it was us. And the quiet of after the fight. Deep breaths, tiny cries of pain, deep breaths of exhaustion, and in the middle of all that the powerful rumbling of a locomotive.

We were a go.

"I'm going to take a truck," I said. A few trucks of ours had escaped the rain of crabs. "Make sure the road is clear."

"I'll come with you," Jen said. And, at my questioning look. "I'm a little better at the whole destruction thing."

Well, I couldn't argue that.

I raced back to the train. Millie was in the engine with Alejandro. Gabrielle was up behind the fifty-cal on the roof. Johnny and Sarah were in the second car, one of the flatcars we had built up. They all were suited up in the body armor as well, the camouflage of the suits looking weird behind the steel walls we had built on the flatcars. Johnny stood behind one of the people-shredder machine guns there.

"You going?" I asked Sarah, surprised.

She just nodded, an assault rifle loose in her hands, the battle suit loose on her shoulders. The gun was heavy, but Sarah held it well. She didn't look scared, just sad. It was her usual look; something in me told me she worried Nick was already dead.

I had been there before. She understood that I understood. The best I could do was pat her on the shoulder and tell her it would be fine. We both knew those words didn't have to be true, but I felt like they were, and I hoped that came across.

The battle had come to us quick. Quicker than we wanted. But it was still something we were ready for. Well, ready enough.

There was my group of friends. Johnny and Sarah. Gabrielle. The rest of those who had volunteered. Alejandro and Millie, and the vampires and humans with them. All told, thirty of us going in. The rest of the people left were going to hide and hope in the vault.

"I'm taking a truck," I told everyone there. "We're going to make sure the way is clear."

"Aren't you going in?" Johnny asked.

"Yeah," I said, grabbing one of the walkie-talkies by the train and waving it at him. "I'll meet you all at the dead zone."

I'd jump on then. Once the way was clear, and the Express was making its way inside. "I figure you have a few minutes now to get on the right track."

"Got it," Alejandro said.

I waved the radio at him. "We'll keep in touch." The train had a radio on it. We were all tuned to the same channel.

"Got it," the vampire repeated.

That was about it. I thought maybe there was something more I should say, some inspirational quote, or something moving. But nothing came up, no win one for the Gipper; no he who continues the attacks wins; no we shall defend our island, our Earth, whatever the cost.

To be honest, I wasn't really that kind of guy. All I had was a last wave. "See you guys there."

"Or in Hell," Johnny said.

I looked at him.

He waggled his eyebrows. "That probably sounds better in the movies."

I laughed. So did the others. Even Sarah.

It did sound better in the movies.

Still, *Mad Max*, here we come.

CHAPTER TWENTY-TWO

I raced back outside. Jen was waiting in one of the sports utility trucks. It was a four-door truck, dark blue, and to my surprise it came with a nice tan leather interior that still carried a new car smell. I was surprised in two ways, that the truck had survived the plague, and that we had found it.

"Nice," I said, slamming the door shut, hard enough the truck rocked a bit.

Jen smiled. "It's nice to ride in something clean for once."

She was teasing. I thought.

When I had rescued her back in Grafton, my car had fast food bags and empty energy drink cans scattered around the back seat. It had been me and the Camaro on the run for a long time together, and I had lived in it, slept in it, fled Azazel in it. So it hadn't been the cleanest thing to put the love of your life in.

I had kept it clean later. Tabitha had worked some magic on it, too, so that it almost always appeared new. So I missed it, but the truck would do. The fob was on the center console; I pushed the start button and the truck fired up with a healthy rumble and a radio turned all the way up.

Immediately country music started playing, loud and blaring, some song about some girl leaving some guy and taking his winning lottery ticket with her. There was a twang to the guitar and long, drawn-out vocals. I quickly pushed the mute button on the steering wheel. Who needed that kind of song before going into battle?

And who played country on the radio in Mexico? That must be one hell of a signal. Especially with the plague. "How is that station even on?" I asked, looking at it.

"It's satellite, silly," Jen said.

Satellite? There wasn't a dish on the truck.

"Satellite radio," Jen laughed. "Trust me, it's a thing most cars have." She arched her eyebrow. "You know, cars built after the nineteen-sixties."

Oh. I had no idea.

I guess being on the run for a decade, you miss things like that.

I still liked my Camaro.

I pushed down on the truck's gas, and we took off with a nice low-thrumming rumble. The navigation unit in the middle of the dash was large; the map on the screen showed us as a tiny blue square cartoon truck in the middle of Cuernavaca. A little number on the bottom corner of the map showed our speed.

At least GPS still worked.

Yeah, I knew about GPS.

The truck vibrated a bit on the road, the rubber of the tires catching shattered shells and crab guts and also, thankfully, pavement. I accelerated after pulling away from the depot; we shot down the street and headed north. Both of us were quiet, focused on the fight ahead, the thrumming of the truck a soothing background sound.

Jen worried. It was hard to miss in the bond. I couldn't tell if it was the worry I had sensed from her down here in Mexico, what we had talked about a bit, or something new. Fear was like that, fear and worry; once it took a bite of you, it kept taking.

It felt like the wrong time to ask about it. We had done this before. Riding into battle. Before it was in the Camaro, in Grafton. Heading into a town full of vampires, the two of us armed with water balloons full of a drug they were addicted to. We had driven in and drawn all the vampires out, Jen throwing balloons behind us, like some kind of *Fast and the Furious* version of *Hansel and Gretel*.

Since we both were thinking about it…

"Remember Grafton?"

Jen smiled. A real, worry-lifting smile. The memory eased her a bit. Something I felt through our bond. "I remember… You said I threw like a girl."

I gave her the Johnny look with the waggling eyebrows. "You *are* a girl."

She smiled at me, a knowing smile, and held up her opposite hand, making a fist. For a brief moment my eyes watched tiny electrical blue lines wind their way around her fingers. Like a cat's cradle of lightning.

Then it disappeared.

"I can throw better now."

I remembered the first time I had seen her do it. Call lightning. It had been at Raphael's mansion up at Grafton. She had walked up his driveway, her fists electric blue, throwing bolts of lightning like in the movies. I had seen it and thought it beautiful and destructive and for one crazy moment Jen had swung the fight in our favor.

Since then, I had seen her do crazier things. More powerful things. There had been a storm of lightning bolts when the two of us had fought Kimaris and his clones. In that fight, I had seen Jen create a lightning shield, a globe of lightning that circled her, a bubble of electricity that sparked as bullets struck it.

Then there had been Red Rock, where she had pulled ethereal energy from me through our bond and started throwing lightning down on the thousands of vampires there. The storm then had been unrivaled in its power. I thought now the very beginning of the idea of the Five-Fold blade had come from that. The idea that other people could use the energy I accessed.

But in the beginning, in that very first fight at Raphael's, Jen had just thrown a few lightning bolts. Mostly from her fists. Sizzling sparks had flown from her hands with just the occasional blue bolt streaking down from the clouds.

And now, or at least a few moments ago, I had just seen her throw dozens of bolts at the same time, a storm of lightning spreading out in a wave away from the train depot, a hammering of electricity that rolled through the city and into the land beyond.

My bones could almost still feel the thunder. The pounding rhythm of bolts. The rumbling along the skies. The booming explosions of earth.

"Are you stronger?" I asked.

There was a small moment. I could feel her toss the idea around in her head. I wasn't sure she had thought about it before. I know I hadn't.

Her answer wasn't quite what I expected. "Aren't you?"

Huh.

I hadn't thought about that either.

I guessed I was.

Things like the sword, the wings, even the armor of faith, those had just been things that came when I needed them. I hadn't thought of them as power. But now, thinking about it, had they just come because of the situation I had been in? Because I had needed them? Or had things like the sword, like the armor, like flying, were those things that had come because I had grown stronger? Because I had grown into them?

It was a real chicken-and-egg thing.

The road bounced under the truck. Or maybe the truck bounced over the road. It was pitted, eaten, worn away from the plague. Spiderweb cracks ran everywhere across the road, black chunks of tar poked up in spots, and instead of driving the truck around, I just plowed through.

The worry was a background to the rumbling of the truck. It radiated from Jen. The cab was thick with it, as much as she tried to push it down. She was stronger. I was stronger. But I felt her wondering if she was enough. If she could be enough.

We all needed that, maybe. The knowledge of who we are. Who we can be. Our ability to grow. The chance to become more.

And that growth came with pain. The pain of battle. The pain of worry, of loss, of taking those feelings and working to become stronger, become more.

I grabbed her hand and squeezed it. "We're going to be fine."

The worry swelled along the bond. "I know," Jen said. Then a moment later, said the words again. Quietly. As if to herself.

"I mean it," I said. "All of us."

Jen's eyes shone a bit. "I know you mean it Gus." She squeezed my hand back, and I felt her try to rid herself of her worry. I felt her try to fight it back down. The feeling came with a swelling of anger from across the bond.

She whispered those words one last time. Her hand clenched mine now. Maybe we did need some country music playing.

Our hands stayed tied together. I drove one-handed, hammering down on the gas pedal, holding the steering wheel tightly in my left hand as the truck surged ahead, bouncing across the breaks in the road.

The map of Cuernavaca on the navigation unit moved south one mile at a time. There was a red number on the bottom corner, telling me I was exceeding the street's speed limit. I was okay with that.

Had I ever carried worries like Jen did now? I had been afraid, but I had only been afraid of not being enough. Of not being able to protect those I loved.

Jen carried that fear, too, and she usually carried it well. Death had changed her perspective. She had to worry about protecting those she loved; in order to do that, she had to stay alive.

There was a chink in her armor now. An Achilles heel. A part of her too fragile to protect. Too weak to build upon. A sliver of a crack a few weeks ago had widened into a canyon. No matter how much Jen fought it.

I had no idea how to help her with that. I could protect her as much as I was able. I could save her. I could march into Hell and bring her back into the living.

But I couldn't make her strong again.

That was something she had to do herself.

I hadn't ever worried about my own death. Not when Raphael had almost killed me. Not in the Hindu Kush, among all the scourge, in that horde of the undead. Not when Dominic had ordered my mother to kill me. Not in all my fights with Azazel, not against Kimaris or Buné or the geas or even among thousands of vampires in Red Rock.

Hell, I had spent a good part of my time in the army *trying* to die.

The truck bounced along the road. I had a hard time steering it across the pitted surface. The wheel kept jerking in tiny bits, and I fought it constantly.

"It felt good, you know," Jen said, out of the blue.

"It?" I swung the truck around a few cars that had been left in the middle of the road. Well, not cars anymore, but car-like shapes after the plague. "What felt good?"

"Calling the storm," Jen said. I had the feeling she wasn't talking about just now. But about before.

The feeling came from the bond. The feeling and the memory. Jen's mind was still on the little town up north, about their flight into the freezer. About barely making it, but surviving. About calling down lightning and protecting those she loved. About being enough to take care of our friends.

There was power in that, too. About facing something you *could* fight. And beating it.

The truck jerked. I swore at the wheel, letting go of Jen's hand. As I did something caught my eye far in the distance. Ahead of us. Tiny trails of smoke came up from the road there, just visible in the early morning dusk.

I stopped the truck. Placed it in park and focused in the distance with my ethereal sight. We were on the slightest of elevations, just outside of Cuernavaca, and the edge of the dead zone was maybe a mile away.

Not a surprise, but the smoke came from vehicles, tearing along the road ahead of us. Trucks and cars of all different sizes and colors. Colors tinged in my ethereal sight with the red of the dead zone. There were sedans and trucks, tractor-trailers, and even a couple Volkswagen Beetles.

My fingers drummed the steering wheel. I wanted to swear. Not because of the fight but because it had come too soon. Too soon, with how Jen was feeling.

But that was a battle for you. They weren't ever convenient in timing or place. Still, I felt it was inconsiderate of Sabnock.

"What is it?" Jen asked, squinting her eyes.

"Them."

The very first cars and trucks left the dead zone. Like horses of different colors, the vehicles seemed to morph in my ethereal sight as they exited. An orange Charger left the red tinge behind and transformed into a bright yellow. A purple Beetle became blue. A brown minivan with a black windshield left the dead zone green, with heavily tinted windows.

They left in ones and twos, then threes and fours, the main pack of cars not too far behind. There must have been a hundred vehicles or more. Dust blew up behind from the convoy. Some of the larger trucks had smoke streaming from stacks and exhaust pipes, and the whole image looked right from a movie.

Mad Max, indeed.

A reverse Mad Max, actually. Sabnock had stolen my plan. What an architect, right? I bet the Pandemonium looked a lot like the Sistine Chapel. I'd say great minds think alike, but I didn't like what that said about me. Or him.

We had maybe a mile or more between us and the convoy. According to the navigation unit, the train tracks were slightly west of us, parallel to the road and heading north. In front of us was a long stretch of highway, sloping downward until it hit flat ground. The rest of the land was flat, with scattered munched-upon agave plants, some loose, dead brush, and an occasional lone desert willow standing against the horizon.

The area felt like a graveyard of sorts. The brush and trees and plants withered and eaten, various tombstones of a dying land. A deathly landscape that would hold one terrifyingly large battle.

And then become a graveyard again.

"I think this is us," I said.

We would have to hold off the army here. Or the advance force. Whichever the convey was. We were going to have to draw everyone in along the road and wear them down. We would have to fight and strike and kill, take out as many as we could, as the Grimm Express came rolling through.

The first vehicles, dots in the distance without my ethereal sight, appeared. Jen could see them too. And feel what I had seen along the bond.

"Eh," she said. "We've fought worse odds."

A laugh escaped me. We had. Grafton. New Orleans. Red Rock. Each time the odds had grown, and we had beaten them.

Even if some of those fights hadn't gone the way I wanted.

We radioed the Express. Gave them the situation. Letting the convoy get closer and closer. Imagining, more than feeling, the rumbling of the oncoming cars and trucks and tractor-trailers. Imagining the screaming and the yelling and the blood lust of all those headed towards us.

A few thoughts tried to escape me. I clamped down hard on them, making sure they never touched our bond. Hoping Jen never sensed them. Never sensed that I wished we had more time. That I could fix the fragile thing inside her. That if there was anything I could do for her, anyone I could kill, any fight I could take, I would do it.

None of those thoughts honored who Jen was. She was tough. She deserved a chance to see this through. To build herself back up.

So I waited as the cars came at us. Waited as the convoy rushed down the road. I turned on the radio, it was still country, and I sang the wrong words to whatever new song was playing. They included an empty bottle of beer, a missing dog, and a lost lottery ticket.

It got a smile from Jen.

I winked.

Flashed the truck's high beams a couple of times. Challenging the oncoming vehicles, like a matador facing a bull. Grabbed the steering wheel in both hands.

Jen gripped the handle above her door.

I let the emergency brake out.

Hammered the gas.

And spun off.

CHAPTER TWENTY-THREE

The matador expression was wrong.

We weren't the matador.

We were the bull. Thundering down the road. Into an army of bullfighters. All waiting for us to run into them.

Lucky for us, we took our thundering seriously around these parts.

These parts. I snorted. See how quickly country music can get a hold of you?

Jen rolled down her window. Maybe just to be safe. Stuck one hand out, a hand colored in sparkling white-blue electricity.

The first boom scared me enough I almost ran off the road.

The second and third I could barely hear, after the first.

The eighth, twelfth, twentieth, those I didn't hear at all. But I sure did see them.

Lightning bolts struck down from a cloudless sky. Big forks of lightning. Each bringing its own thunderclap. Afterimages of brilliant electric power burned in my eyes, I pulled a little ghost just to keep my sight, well, *sighting*.

I had to drive, after all.

Air rushed into the truck, whipping through the cab, carrying a dry desert smell. Blue electricity spread up Jen's arm, a bright blue glow enveloping her skin up to her shoulder. She screamed. I screamed. And lightning pounded the earth again and again and again.

Cars and trucks and anything else on wheels blew up in front of us. Three and four and eight-ton vehicles tumbled through the air, undercarriage over cab, crunching across the barren landscape. The first I passed, the yellow Charger, lay with its roof crushed in, all four tires spinning and no one moving inside.

Then the Beetle. The minivan. Trucks and cars of different colors now were different things. No long vehicles, nothing but burned and blackened remains of various twisted metals, of peeling melted metals. And occasional pieces of what might have been people. What might have been vampires of the La Familia Diablo clan. What might have been those Ushabti.

We rushed through most of the convoy on our first pass. The thunderclaps that I heard came slower; the rumbling echoed longer. We bounced along hard after I had swerved to avoid a tumbling truck, and I glanced over at Jen.

She was pale from the effort. But smiling. A deadly, *don't fuck with me* kind of smile.

Not one I'd seen on her much, but I liked it.

Ghosts littered the landscape. I pulled from them. From the murderers and thieves. I felt them claw at me and I pushed them away. Fought them down, and passed the energy into Jen, along the bond.

It was something we had done at Red Rock. Back when Jen was in the key. We hadn't done it since, but Johnny, Tabitha, the Five-Fold blades, all of that gave me some hope.

So, I was more happy than surprised to see it work.

Jen took the ethereal energy. Color flooded back into her skin. She maybe even glowed. And her grin got a little nasty.

I spun the truck around. Most of the convoy was slowing down. There had been a dozen of the large tractor-trailers; now there were ten. Two lay on their sides, exploded, the rigs on their sides and their containers shattered and twisted and jack-knifed.

Big figures, the Ushabti, were climbing out of the containers. Smaller figures crawled out too, maybe vampires, maybe thralls. Maybe something else. Some were pulling themselves out of the broken wrecks that once had been minivans and beetles and trucks.

My heart raced. The battle was still beginning. The fight was still in its infancy. At some point, I would be needed. And my body was ramping itself up for that need.

Lightning began dancing in front of us, picking on the little figures. Some blew apart. Some just evaporated. I hammered down on the gas again. The truck lurched forward. Some kind of noise was coming from Jen, though my ears still weren't hearing things normally.

I thought she was singing that country song. Or some country song.

And laughing.

We sped down the road. The fifty or so vehicles that had made it away from our first pass started circling back around. Lightning kept striking the lead cars there, even as single bolts struck the wreckage around us.

I laughed. Thinking just a couple more passes and we could follow the Express into the dead zone. There wouldn't be a need to keep anyone's attention. I started thinking Sabnock hadn't sent enough, that Jen and I could easily handle this, and from there, we could all meet at the stadium and end him.

Yeah, I jinxed it.

The bolts were blinding me. I kept healing them, but somehow between blinks and heals I missed a Ushabti standing in the middle of the road. The knight stood there, arms outstretched, waiting for the truck to hit him.

Which we did.

The Ushabti went one way.

Our truck another.

I didn't know how fast we were going, but we tumbled a lot. Glass shattered and the engine whined and then blew itself quiet with a loud metal-snapping sound. I threw one arm against the roof of the truck, the second around Jen and held her against the seat and kept pulling ghost.

All I wanted to do was keep the roof from caving in on us. My arm took each shuddering jolt as the truck flipped over and over. I locked my knees and kept my feet tight on both pedals, pushing against the forward part of the engine compartment, hoping to keep the engine in its compartment and not ours.

Jolt. Bang. Flip.

Jolt. Bang. Flip.

At some point the truck stopped flipping ass over end. We straightened out on all four wheels, the truck rocking back and forth until it settled down. The navigation unit screen was out. It had had enough. The radio, too. Even country music had its limits.

There was just me and Jen and a broke truck. In the middle of the largest demolition derby this side of the continent. With cars and demon knights all racing towards us.

Well, the Ushabti couldn't really race. They didn't move that fast. But they were still heading our way.

Jen grinned, and at the same time shook her head. Slightly, as if in a moment of unbelief. "You had one job."

It wasn't hard to see where she was going. I clicked off my seatbelt. "Hey, it was hard to see."

"One job."

"It was a lot of lightning," I protested. "A *lot*."

"You would think you had a lot of practice driving over the past few years." Jen got loose from her belt, too. Tried her door. It had crunched in enough she couldn't open it.

I leaned over, pulled ghost, and punched her door out. It opened with a tearing, crunching sound. "Ladies first."

She gave me a quick peck on the cheek and jumped out. Still smiling. "One job."

I wasn't going to win the argument, so I did something I rarely did. I kept my mouth shut. And then I got out of the truck, looking towards the road we had just tumbled from. There lay a field of scattered husks of vehicles, tombstones of trucks and cars, flipped over or destroyed by lightning on our first pass through them.

The demon knight we had hit was trying to pick himself, or herself, back up. It was going to be hard; the creature looked like its back had been bent backwards over itself. So I wasn't worried so much about that particular Ushabti.

I was worried about the twenty or so more behind that one, marching our way. The couple of groups of vampires behind them, flowing over the landscape. And then the fifty or so cars behind them, tires churning over the dirt in a race to where we had wrecked.

And behind them all, turning in wide circles towards us, like big cargo vessels changing their course over the surface of an ocean, the ten tractor-trailers.

CHAPTER TWENTY-FOUR

The tractor-trailers rolled towards us. Behind them the horizon glowed, the pale blue in the east brightening with the yellow slivered promise of a hot sun. Which wasn't a surprise. Even in December, with Christmas not far away, it was always hot.

To the west, the purple of night was slowly slipping over the horizon. The sky above us was clear of clouds, yet still hazy. The kind of early morning haze you might see around Los Angeles, a foggy kind of mist that left the sky lifeless and gray.

The air smelled hot and dry and jabbed my nose occasionally with sharp pricks of gasoline and burned rubber. My heart thumped steady in my chest, hard, pumping blood at a good rate. I rubbed my arms, feeling the goosebumps there, my body's anticipation of an upcoming fight.

Could we take them?

Probably.

But cars were a hard thing to keep dodging. Especially with all the soldiers coming around. The Ushabti and vampires. It was easy enough to imagine losing focus fighting them and having a car run up my backside.

I could survive a few of those.

I didn't know if Jen could.

"Maybe we should make for the train tracks," I said.

"Eh," Jen said. "They'd run us over halfway there. Unless you fly us. And then we would lead them to the train."

Dammit. The whole point of this was to keep the tracks clear for the Express to run through.

"Fight then?"

A lightning shield bubbled over Jen. Round and sparking. The hisses of tiny bolts stabbed everywhere.

That was my answer.

"Wish we had a hill to fight off of, or a wall or something," I said.

Jen shrugged. "We could make one."

Well, that we could.

No sense in wasting the Five-Fold blade. I grabbed the closest ghost...

He—I—took the edge of the knife and traced the edge of my wrist with it. Felt the edge on my skin, sharp, almost tingly as it rubbed the hair there. The metal pressed inward just a little until a drop of blood appeared. The whole sensation tickled, I laughed, and something swelled in the bottom of my belly. I pushed the knife in deeper, feeling it slice my skin open, watching the skin peel back and reveal white tendrils underneath it, watching the blood run out and trickle to the floor...

Well, that was different.

I pushed the memory down. Pulled the ghost until it popped. Then I found another. My ethereal radar swarmed with spirits, blue and red, burning. I wondered where Hector was out there. There was something I wanted to settle with him.

A rumble of thunder burst over the sky. Flickers of lightning stabbed down to the earth in the distance, trailing further and further away. The ground erupted there, under a line of vehicles headed our way, and two or three of them tumbled out of control.

They were going to run out of cars a lot faster than we were going to run out of lightning.

Though the strain was getting to Jen. I could feel it along the bond. I pushed some ethereal energy that way, feeling the power slip into her. It seemed natural now, like it was something we did all the time.

I ran over to the closest wreck. Lifted it and hauled it back, stacking it on top of our truck with a big crunching sound. Then I repeated the whole process, but running over was too slow. I started leaping over to the closest car and leaping back, like a superhero, picking flipped vehicles over and stacking them like a wall around Jen. Building a fort of cars, like we had done with couch pillows when we were kids.

Sometimes the cars had people still alive in them. A few were vampires of the La Familia Diablo; more were thralls. Or other humans serving Sabnock. I wasn't happy about it; I'd rather take people in a fair fight, but I finished those off with a quick thrust of the ethereal sword, calling the blade and letting it go before grabbing their vehicle.

The car fort got a little grisly. It dripped blood in places. It smelled like burned rubber and melted fiberglass. But it grew. At least big enough to keep the oncoming convoy from running over us. It was a nice bulwark between us and them. I stopped after I had topped it off with the tenth car, the yellow Charger, the paint peeling from where lightning had struck it.

One of the cars seemed intact. A sand rail, one of those dune-buggy looking cars with two seats in a tube-like frame, and a small motor in the back that spun two overly-large tires. There was no one in it, and the motor was still running. I brought that one back intact and set it behind the wall.

It was always good to have an escape plan.

The thunder quieted down. Jen took a large breath next to me. There was a different rumble in the air, a rumble of the oncoming tractor-trailers and the rest of the cars.

And in the distance, the long, thrumming horn of a train sounded.

The Express was coming.

Jen and I exchanged a glance. We would have to hold the convoy here. For as long as possible.

"We both can't go in," Jen said.

I paused. Dammit. She was right. Only one of us could get inside the dead zone. Only one of us had a ticket to the show.

It was something I should have put more thought into. If I was good at the whole planning thing. If I had to say anything, there was probably some half-baked idea in the back of my subconscious, some plan to leave Jen behind, safe, in the vault.

Which Jen wouldn't have been happy about.

"That is correct." Jen's words sounded a little curt. She was reading my thoughts.

Only one of us could go in. And one of us would have to stay out here. My ethereal sword was the only thing that had killed a demon. To me, it made the most sense for me to get inside the dead zone. To be there so I could kill Sabnock.

"It's not about killing him anymore, remember?" Jen said.

She was still reading my thoughts. And she was right. Killing Sabnock would be a plus, but taking out his locust factory was number one on our list. Nullifying the center of the dead zone and removing his ability to create something that could wipe out the human race.

The tractor-trailers had completed their wide swings. All ten were pointed this way. In between their large forms were smaller ones, cars and trucks zig-zagging back and forth. And in the middle of all those were the knights and humans left standing.

Behind them, on the eastern horizon, was a slight sliver of orange. The first crest of the rising sun. Sunrise.

"You or me?" Jen said. Leaving the decision up to me.

I was torn. I almost couldn't make the decision. Leave Jen here to fight the convoy while I went in with our friends. Leave her alone while I protected them and faced Sabnock. Or let her go in on the Express, let her face the demon, and hope like hell she and Nick could exorcise the dead zone in time to let me come in?

I was damned if I did and damned if I didn't.

I was needed in there, and I was needed out here, too.

Jen's face was composed, if still pale. Tired, but determined. I froze for a long moment as memories raced through my mind, memories of the past few days, thoughts and feelings and emotions I tried like hell to hide from her along the bond. Things Jen had said that had stuck with me. All her worries and fears and doubts.

All of this is because of me, because of what I wanted...

How can we figure it out, if we don't know what it is...

A memory slammed into me. I was holding her. Jen, crying in frustration, *I don't know what's wrong with me Gus. I can't fix it and I don't know...*

She blamed herself for this. Some part of her did. It didn't matter that it made no sense. It didn't matter that it wasn't logical. Fear, doubt, blame, those things transcended logic and preyed on the weakest part of you.

There's going to be a cost here.

We're not getting anything free.

I wonder if I can be that strong...

So much doubt in Jen. So much worry and fear. And then, the

tiniest bit of hope back in the truck. The tiniest feel of the real Jen, trying to break free.

It felt good, you know…

I can throw better now…

For the briefest moment she had no fear. She had learned something about herself. But she needed it to grow. To overwhelm the doubt. She had to face her fears and worries and beat them, or she would never be the same Jen again.

"There's something missing, I think." She had said. *"Some part of me I had once, it's gone now. And I don't know how to replace it. I don't know if I can replace it. Part of me worries I'll be this way forever, this person who worries and fears and doubts."*

She knew it.

And now, I knew it too.

Who would I be, to let Jen be that person forever? To not give her a chance? To not let her find herself? To not let her face her fears and grow? Become more?

The decision was easy, after all.

I unsnapped the sheath holding the Five-Fold blade from my leg. Held both out to her. Letting her feel my resolve along the bond. My trust in her, and everything Jen was to me.

Her hand hovered above the blade. Her fingers trembled slightly. Her lips twitched in some emotion I couldn't identify.

So I folded her hand over the hilt. I pulled her close, wrapping my other arm around her, feeling her hair in my fingers. I kissed the center of her forehead, getting a big breath of honeysuckle, feeling strands of her hair tickle my cheek.

The moment wasn't long, it wasn't short, it was just us.

She relaxed in my arms, just a bit.

I kissed her again, this time on the lips. Moved closer to her ear. My words low, just for her. Happy, after all, that I had found the perfect gift.

"Merry Christmas babe," I told her. "Give 'em hell."

When I pulled back tears were running down her cheeks. Her eyes shimmered with wetness, and I knew I hadn't kept my thoughts as hidden as I'd wanted.

Pops sounded behind us. From the east. Tiny shots. Bullets twanged around us as bits of fiberglass and metal were kicked up from the wall of cars.

"Better get running," I said. "You got a train to catch."

CHAPTER TWENTY-FIVE

Louder cracks came from the approaching army. The whines of bullets echoed around us. A few minutes ago there had been just a few shots. Now the enemy was closer, and there was enough shooting that the gunfire sounded like popcorn popping.

Well, it would have sounded like popcorn popping if kernels were made of metal.

The pops weren't really pops. They had an undercurrent of power in them. Of bass. Something punchy that reverberated in the air, along with all the whizzes of bullets streaming around Jen and I. The cracks splitting the air, followed by the thuds of bullets hitting the dirt. The thwacks as they struck the fiberglass of the cars behind us. The twangs as the bullets struck the vehicle frames.

Another bullet made it through the wall of cars. It kicked into my back and felt like a rock thrown at a hundred miles an hour. I rocked on my feet, bracing myself on Jen, steadying myself even as I pulled a little more ghost to keep the skin and muscle and tissue of my back titanium-like.

Jen gave me a last look. It was worried and happy and full of both fear and excitement. Wet trails still lay on her cheeks, though the shimmering in her eyes seemed lighter, like she was ready. Ready for a battle. A battle she would win.

I'd bet on her.

She gave me a kiss, it was neither long nor short, and leaned into me. Her hand lay on my shoulder, the palm warm through my shirt. I let go of a deep breath; the smell of honeysuckle overwhelmed me, and I closed my eyes to enjoy the moment. Gathering a last *feel* of Jen. The warmth of her against me, the press of her breasts against my chest, the stirring of her breath across my neck.

It was a moment worth waiting for. My hand was around her lower back; I kept holding her close, even though I had told her to go. Her cheek pressed to mine, her hand moved from my shoulder to my face, and her thumb rubbed the corner of my jaw, circling once. Twice.

Three times.

The popcorn pops continued around us. Over it came the horn of the train, calling again. Louder. Insistent, as the Express rumbled its way north.

Then Jen, with a whisper. "I'll be back."

I opened my eyes. Caught hers. Stayed there for a moment. "I know."

She looked worried still. Happy, but worried. I flashed a grin at her, one of my real ones. "You know, if you smile more, it'll make your face look better."

Jen's eyes widened. A twinkle quickened through them, turning the irises from the deep oceanic blue of sadness to the happy blue of a clear summer day. She laughed, hugging me tightly to her, letting me feel the happiness radiate from her through the bond, feel each laugh burst from her lungs, let me see her glow in some kind of radiance that was just... her.

The sound carried over the gunfire around us, over the thunks of bullets striking the metal carriages of my impromptu wall, over the whizzes of bullets zipping through the air, the rumbling of an army of vehicles headed our way.

"Go," I said. Holding her close one more time. "I'll keep them busy."

"Don't just keep them busy," she said, smiling that devilish smile she occasionally let loose. "Kick their ass."

I winked. "Deal."

Jen let me go, slowly. She ran to the sand rail and jumped in, buckling herself into the seat. There was a last glance of *her*: happy face, twinkling eyes, devilish smile, and then she must have punched the gas. The sand rail took off, dirt kicking up from the big back tires until they grabbed hold of the ground, clumps of it landing all around me. Then the buggy shot off.

The whole time, the smile had only gotten bigger.

I let out a breath. A small one I had been holding inside. Holding from Jen all the worries and fears I had for her. About her. I had lost her once. I couldn't lose her again. I couldn't lose her or my friends.

But I had to give her the chance. I couldn't fix what was missing in Jen. I had to give her the opportunity to fill it herself. Or she would forever be less than she had been.

When she could be so much more.

I had done the right thing.

I thought.

There was a feeling from Jen. A reaching along the bond. As if she was worried about much the same thing, but maybe about me.

Be careful…

I snorted. *I got this. Go tell Sabnock I said hello.*

She laughed some more. The sand rail left a large trail of dust behind it, streaming up like a cloud as the buggy headed west. I watched a bit longer as Jen angled it a little south; the sand rail bounced up and down over small hills and ravines, leapt over one of the larger ones, always heading towards a long moving line on the horizon, a line of cars being pulled by the Grimm Express.

They missed the mark. We should have called it the Blue Streak. Or the Lightning Locomotive.

The rumbling of vehicles grew around me. The ground vibrated with it. A car raced by me, following Jen. A red four-door Maxima. Then a second one followed, a blue Honda Civic hatchback, the hatchback open and flapping in the back. And then a third, a truck, a white Ford Ranger with someone standing in the back, trying to hold an assault rifle steady on the roof, firing as they could.

All the vehicles were hard on her heels and if they weren't narrowing the distance, they were trying to close it. Another hundred-mile-an-hour rock pinged through the wall of cars and struck my back. This time I had to take a couple steps forward to catch myself.

These guys were getting to be a nuisance.

It was time for them to find out who they were really up against.

I set my jaw, took a deep breath. Felt my lungs swell with it. I jogged my shoulders up and down like a runner getting ready to race. I felt the beats of my heart speed up, goosebumps of energy flowed over my skin, tickled the backs of my arms, My palms tingled with it.

It was time for a fight.

And there were plenty of ghosts around. Ghosts of humans recently flipped over in their cars or struck by lightning. Ghosts of those the plague had descended upon. And spirits of Mexico past, Mayans, Aztecs, whoever. Hundreds, maybe thousands of them, scattered around my ethereal radar.

I sucked them in. One, two, then a dozen or more. Memories pushed past me, one, two, hundreds. Child molesters and rapists, bullies, thieves, my stomach turned at each. People screaming as locusts ate them alive. One particularly sharp memory of a man chewing something rubbery and fat that I didn't think was steak.

I subsumed them all.

Ethereal energy rushed through me. Wings burst from my back. The real ones. My sword came out and for a moment solidified in the air. Became less ethereal. More real.

I leapt into the air.

The four-door Maxima stopped suddenly after I landed on its hood. I crashed through the engine; the car still tried to go forward, and as a result it flipped over me in the air and crashed across the landscape, crunching and flipping over and over, pieces of it ripping off until it tumbled to a stop.

Like playing Tiddlywinks.

I kept playing.

I did the same thing to the next car, the blue Honda Civic, with the same results. Something or someone flew out of the back of the open hatchback. Then it was the Ranger's turn, and I changed the game there, landing on its bed. The guy there had a quick second to look at me until the truck flew backwards through the air, the guy with it.

There might have been time for him to scream.

It was chaos.

I had given Jen a good head start. Other vehicles might have been following, but they wouldn't catch her. She'd make it there easy.

A loud thump came from behind me. I might not have heard it except for the ethereal energy coursing through me. I jumped to the side as a rocket flew past me, leaving a black trail winding behind it before striking the ground a few dozen feet away with an explosion that tore up the earth in a dirt-colored geyser.

More cracks and pops behind me. I turned and bullets struck me in the face, in the chest, in the tender area you may not want bullets to strike. They bounced off in pings, but man it hurt. Especially in the tenders.

Some of the vehicles had pulled to a stop, and the people in them had gotten out. Maybe they had seen the Tiddlywinks game and decided not to play. The vampires and their thralls were close enough that they were taking cover in the little hills and valleys of the fields around us.

Behind them were the Ushabti. It was a large force, almost marching in step, getting closer slowly and inexhaustibly. Oddly enough, I could see tiny shadows of their spirits controlling them, but I couldn't see beyond that. I could see the blue and red twinkling in them, much like I could see the whiteness of the spirit inside humans, and the purple of vampires, but I couldn't see which one was Hector.

I was sure he was there. Waiting for the right time to strike. He wasn't a guy to let something go once he bit into it.

Neither was I. I kept pulling ghost after ghost as I needed them. Subsuming them. One of them seemed to have both human and vampire memories, or at least he wanted to be a vampire. Maybe a thrall. I grabbed a sick memory of him cutting someone's stomach open and sucking down the blood pouring out of the skin.

Maybe he wasn't a thrall being turned. I didn't look closely at the memory, even though I lived it. It was everything I could do not to throw up, the warm taste of salty, coppery blood strong in my mouth.

I raced towards the vampires and thralls. Fast enough that white glittery trails trailed along behind me, white sparkling motes. Fast enough that the bullets missed me by miles, always fired way behind where I actually was. Fast enough that it was easy to watch another rocket fire past me, the smoke trail hanging in the air, like everything else in the world was in slow motion but me.

I got to the first little hill. A tiny rise of three or four feet.

Thralls were there, lying down with handguns and assault rifles. Their eyes slightly surprised as I crested the rise and all of a sudden was among them.

Then they were all dead. The sword made quick work of those that hadn't moved. I grabbed one and threw it towards a few others. The body folded into itself as it struck another man, ripping that man's top half from his bottom.

Then I sucked in their ghosts. I ran to the next rise. Those there perished in much the same way. The third group got wise, or lucky; one person had been holding a hand grenade in their hand. It went off after I killed him; I was caught off-guard, and the pounding explosion rang my ears and sent me flying.

I tumbled across the ground, skin burning from the shrapnel. I pulled ghost as I tumbled, feeling bits of metal and rock and—*was that bone?*—pop out of my skin. I came to on all fours, my knees dug into the ground, fists clenched, skin on my knuckles torn and feeling the hard dirt. Blood covered my face, and I wiped my eyes with the back of my hand. It came away thick with gore and grime.

Gus?

Good was all I could think. Well, all I had time to think.

Something struck me at a hundred miles an hour. Not a rock or a bullet or a piece of popcorn. An actual truck. I didn't catch the make or model. I just tumbled over the ground. Again. Slowing down with each bounce off the earth.

I stopped, flat on my back. Some of my bones ached. Some of them screamed. The side of my ribs where the truck had struck me felt like a lot of the bones there weren't bones anymore. A hot wetness radiated from inside my ribcage there.

And my right leg screamed. I glanced at it quickly and then looked away. The bottom of my leg was at a right angle to my knee, and my toes were pointed in the wrong direction.

The sound of motors rumbled in the distance. The honking

sound of a tractor-trailer blew through the air. One, then another, and then all ten in concert. Maybe they felt like they had me.

I coughed. Blood dribbled out the side of my mouth. I couldn't get enough air.

Maybe they did.

Gus?

I pushed Jen's worry away. Tried to send an okay. Pulled ghost and screamed as the healing tore through me, trying to inflate my lungs, trying to make more blood, trying to figure out how to build a ribcage out of thousands of tiny pieces of bone.

I braced myself and pushed myself up to a seated position. I didn't scream this time, but it was just because I was out of air. A bunch of tiny sharp pins stabbed my chest from the inside out. Blood kept leaking out of my mouth, and all I could do was hope the ethereal energy was making more.

Before I could think about what I was doing, I leaned forward and twisted my foot and leg back around. Pulling more ghost as I did. Feeling little gristly pieces of bone twist and twine through other pieces, like pushing a broken pencil back together.

I threw up again. And didn't quite pass out. I just panted as sharp stabs of pain popped inside me, as bone knitted itself back together. As ligaments snapped back into place. As torn muscles swelled back together.

The worry was strong in the bond.

Okay. I sent.

It was all I had time for. Because they were among me. Vampires and thralls and even a fast-moving Ushabti. They tried to stab my skin with knives and swords and other blades and found they couldn't. They tried to shoot me and found bullets bouncing off my skin and hitting their friends.

I tucked myself into a fetal position. Let the swords bite into my skin. Let the bullets strike me and deflect. There were so many it was all I had time for.

Then something grabbed me.

The Ushabti.

It hauled me up and wrapped me in a bear hug. Like Hector in the dead zone, the creature's strength was enormous. It crushed me against its chest; its arms were like granite, and it was all I could do to pull enough ghost to keep from getting compacted.

The thing kept squeezing. My sight was turning red, though I could see the tractor-trailers. They had all stopped, all their back doors had swung open, and demon knights were stomping down tiny ramps. More Ushabti. Maybe four or five hundred of them, getting out slowly, one after another, like weird dead zone parodies of a clown car.

Black spots swam in front of my eyes. I was glad I had decided to be the one to stay. Glad I had given Jen the chance to go to the dead zone. Because as worried as I was about her, I was suddenly worried about me a whole lot more.

Jen swung the wheel of the sand rail as the buggy slid down an embankment, jerking straight as it hit bottom and took off. She whipped forward; the seatbelt caught her with a tight, painful cinching across her chest, and the sheath holding Gus's blade pinched her hip. She hammered the gas and straightened the wheel; the engine whined in response until the tires caught, then she fell back into the seat as the sand rail launched itself up the next rise, throwing dirt in a spray behind it.

There was time to take a breath. And room to take it. The seatbelt hung loose on her lap; she held the wheel with one hand and quickly ran the thumb of her other hand under the strap, the polyester edging into the webbing between her thumb and forefinger. Jen worked the belt a few times until the mechanism snapped the belt back tightly against her chest.

Just not as tight as before.

The train sounded its horn, long and low, like a ship in heavy fog. A bit into the distance the Express was loco-motioning along, moving left to right in front of her, a heavy thundering machine pounding along the tracks. She aimed for the front of it, angling the buggy across the landscape. The next section of field was fairly level; the tiny hills and small gulches earlier seemed to even themselves out. There was nothing ahead but the dead grass, groups of browning agave plants, and the occasional desert willow, each tree she passed looking like a gallows, dead brittle branches hanging empty in the air.

She took a glance at the rearview.

There were cars behind her. Cars and a truck, red, blue, white. They didn't seem to be gaining, and she couldn't hear anything over the open engine of the sand rail, but she thought she saw flashes of gunfire.

Then something blazing white streaked down from the sky. It crushed the red car; she saw the vehicle tumble across the landscape, a door flew off, and then the white streak jumped back into the air and landed on the blue car.

Gus.

Jen smiled. The sand rail jerked again underneath her, almost pulling the wheel from her grip, and she focused on what was in front of her. Catching out of the corner of her eye the white blazing shape of Gus, leaping up again in the rearview.

Her smile grew wider. She could make out the train now. The white locomotive in front, with the red streak down the side. The words Grimm Express painted in big letters. She could almost feel the rumbling of the machine from the earth.

Though that could just be her imagination. The sand rail did enough bouncing on its own. She held the wheel in both hands now, cutting across the ground, the buggy bouncing as she closed in on the flatcars trailing behind the engine.

Johnny stood on the little machine gun nest on her side. He had binoculars in his hand and was waving her on. Or maybe waving a warning.

Something pinged off her sand rail. A high-pitched whine followed it in the air. Jen didn't look back, just ducked her head a little and kept driving. Thinking and grinning as she did, that ducking in a vehicle made of tubes didn't make a lot of sense.

But she did it anyway.

The machine gun on the front of the train opened up. The one on top of the locomotive. The sound of it firing came like a heavy thumping in the air. Like the heaviest of drum beats, something Jen did feel in her bones. The gun chugged along, the trace of its bullets firing over the top of the sand rail, slicing through the air somewhere behind her.

She matched speed with the Express. The clickety-clacking of the train grew louder. The sand rail bounced along the edge of the tracks, and Jen bit her tongue, the coppery taste of blood flooding her mouth.

This looked easier in the movies.

The sand rail had fallen back from Johnny's car. Jen gunned the engine again; the buggy leapt forward. Johnny had bent over the side of the flatcar, the side of thick metal wall plates welded there in a wall, and he kept leaning as someone grabbed his pants and held him there. He held both hands outward towards Jen. Johnny was turned a little towards her, his face upside down, and he flashed a quick grin and his trademark eyebrow waggle.

It was now or never.

She held the steering wheel with her inside hand. Unclicked the seatbelt with her other and pulled it back over her head. Held the gas as steady as she could as the buggy bounced alongside the flatcar until Johnny was just above where her door would be.

If the buggy had a door.

His hands waved above her. Johnny stretched one as far as it would go. They waved down into her vision.

One wave.

Two.

On three, she gunned the engine quickly and then jumped out of the sand rail.

There was a quick moment where she thought she had made a mistake. A flightless moment where Jen hung in the air, her hands held high above her head, stretching towards Johnny. A moment where everything paused and she could feel the beat of her heart, hear the large clacking of the wheels of the train, smell scents of pepper and sulphur and a glycerin-like sweet aroma in the air around her, whether from the diesel fuel or the machine gun fire, she had no idea.

Then there was a slap of her arm against Johnny's. Jen was falling, her fingers spasmed in the air. She felt Johnny's hand claw down her arm; his fingers slipped past her elbow and slid down her wrist.

Then their hands caught. Her fall stopped with a jerk that she felt hard in her shoulder.

Jen hung in the air. He grabbed her hand in both of his, and she swung wildly, legs kicking, trying to keep away from the wheels underneath the flatcar that were spinning mercilessly. She bounced a couple of times against the hard edge of the flatcar, her free hand windmilling above her. The train wheels kept turning and Jen bent herself backwards in the air as she bounced one more time against the car.

Then Johnny hauled her up. Or, the person holding Johnny

hauled him up, and Johnny pulled Jen along with him. The metal wall tore a little of her skin, but they kept pulling until she was over the welded metal wall, the bulwark, and then she collapsed onto the floor of the flatcar.

The sound of the train motoring along the tracks lessened a bit, shielded by the floor. Jen took a deep breath; the light gray sky of early morning raced backwards over her head, a small whitish cloud hanging right above her. Her heart still raced, her skin stung a bit where the edge of the car had torn it, but she laughed loudly and pumped her fist.

A face appeared above her. Johnny. He was grinning. And thinking along the same lines as Jen. "They make that look easy in Fast and the Furious."

Sarah's face was next. Smiling, too, just a small one. Jen gave her a wink.

"Is Grimm coming?" Johnny asked, looking back towards where Jen had driven from.

Jen shook her head.

There was a pause there. A pause full of thoughts and concerns and maybe even fear. Jen tried not to feel any of it.

He had only been back in their lives a few short months. And he had come to mean so much to all of them. She could understand a little bit of Johnny's grin leaving his eyes, even if the smile remained on his face. She could understand her sister even, as Sarah's head ducked down, briefly.

It all got a little more real then. For all of them. For each of them there had always been a chance they wouldn't make it back, but Gus made them all feel safer. He had an uncanny ability to take the worst of what came, shielding the rest of his friends.

Not to mention, they all counted on him to face Sabnock.

And they had her now, instead.

Fear rose in Jen. Fear and doubt, as much as she fought it. Even her gaze looked back to where she had left Gus, the fight, the convoy, dropping further and further into the distance. Faster and faster.

Maybe none of them could help it. All of them stared. Even if they couldn't see anything, nothing but blazing white streaks over the ground, flashing white brilliance sharp in the eyes before slowly fading away.

It was too far to make out anything else.

Jen's fear swelled until it became a bulging pit at the top of her stomach. Her throat suddenly felt constricted. She couldn't swallow, almost couldn't breathe.

There was Gus, and here they were. He was outside the zone. They were going in. He was holding off the convoy, and they were facing Sabnock.

He would take on as many as he could.

Jen and their friends would have to get rid of the dead zone. Nullify it. Make sure the demons couldn't make more of the plague, stop their plan of ending humanity.

Could they do it? Could *she* do it?

A booming sound came from behind them. It jerked Jen from her thoughts. A tiny explosion of ground burst into the air. With it came a flash of pain from the bond, hot and sharp and wet and... everywhere.

Jen put her hand over the keystone.

Gus?

Okay, came his reply. Though the reply was full of pain and anger and a powerful feeling of rage. It was so Gus, it had Jen smiling before knowing she was doing it. Had her already pushing past her fears.

The pain became less over the bond. She felt him stitch himself together. Felt him push away the memories of spirits he lived. Felt him gather himself up.

Then the feeling of him *muted*, somewhat. Dulled in her mind. In her heart. In the bond. She glanced down to see the keystone glowing a slight blue.

The Express had just entered the dead zone.

Something blasted through the muted feel of the zone. Another flash of pain from Gus. More intense than the last. Something exponentially greater, breaking through the bond and ripping into Jen. She stumbled back and fell to one knee, the train shaking underneath her. Gagging and coughing sounds came from her throat, and without understanding why, she was surprised to *not* see herself coughing up blood.

Her hand gripped the keystone tighter.

Gus?

There was no reply.

Maybe something small in response. Muted. Small.

She forced herself along the bond. Yelled. Screamed.

GUS—

CHAPTER TWENTY-SIX

The Ushabti's arms seemed to only grow stronger. Like the knight had its own store of energy it pulled from, its own ocean of ethereal energy, maybe more spirits swam its way to lend the creature strength. Each arm felt like granite, so hard and thick it was hard to believe the limbs could move at all.

I was getting crushed by a rock.

My legs drummed against the knight; it felt like I was kicking a mountain. The back of my heels burst in sharp pain with each kick. I tried cracking the back of my head against its face; all I got from that was sparkling stars in the back of my eyelids and a warm wetness leaking down the back of my skull.

As much as I pulled from the ghosts around me, I couldn't break free. I had nothing to leverage. All I could do was heal the split in my scalp, heal the bones in my feet, and try again.

I tried summoning my sword. It appeared, but all I could do was wave it around a bit, with both arms trapped in the stone-like grip of the Ushabti.

The other vampires and thralls around me paused and watched.

At least, I assumed the ones in the blacked-out tactical suits were vampires. One of those leaned over to a human standing there and said something. That one, a smaller man with thick dark hair over his tanned skin, raised a heavy, stainless-steel six-shooter in his hand and placed the barrel right on my temple.

He was shorter than me, so he had to raise his arm high. His eyes were animated. Glittering in excitement. His lips curled over cracked, jagged, green teeth.

He pulled the trigger.

I closed my eyes. The bullet cracked into my temple, the metal tip drilled into my skin with an eruption of pain from bone and brain, sudden and sharp and overwhelming my consciousness until it was all I could do to pull ghost. Pull ethereal energy. I yanked it from a spirit's tap until the spirit suddenly disappeared and kept my skin hard, healed the pain, hardened the skin and bone over and over. The bullet compressed itself against my face; I could feel the press of the thin disk against my temple plink off, hissing heat as it flew through the air.

The sharp peppery smell of sulphur came next. A flood of it washed over my face. I must have bitten my tongue or my cheek, because the tang of blood filled my mouth.

And around me, laughs.

More of them lined up to play the game. I pulled ghosts as I could. It seemed too many; the memories overwhelmed me, left me shaky. I retched over and over, which is tough to do in a bear hug. The warm bile leaked from my mouth and dangled from my chin.

Still, I kept pulling. Kept pushing memories aside. Kept throwing up, as everyone lined up to shoot at me. There were so many spirits around; I wondered how many people had died here and hung around, waiting. There seemed too many, even for Mexico.

Where were the good spirits? The good ghosts, like Danny? Had they all left? Had they ever remained on Earth? Or was this, the ocean of spirits I was swimming in, was all this what was left after hundreds of thousands of years of humanity?

There was more laughing. Louder laughing. Talking and bets. Different guns. Assault rifles. An AK-47 that tapped my head a couple of times like a jackhammer. And behind the little group having fun with me, there was the four or five hundred Ushabti coming this way, carrying swords and double-bladed axes.

I tried another reverse headbutt. Got the same star-like pain from the back of my head. Felt the same warm wetness. And healed the split in my scalp again.

This was going to last until I gave up.

Or the army of Ushabti got here.

Or Sabnock himself.

Or the guy in front of me with the RPG. The whole group was laughing and backing away, as someone helped the man hold it up to the side of my head.

They were going to die just to see if they could kill me.

I screamed. Swung my head around. Drummed my legs. Wriggled my sword in tiny, ineffective motions. The blade moved in tiny circular motions, and the guy holding the dark green barrel of the RPG danced a little to the side to avoid it.

Both men lined it up.

I pulled as much energy as I could. Hardened my skull until it felt like titanium. I might have even prayed.

Then looked up.

Where an archangel was descending.

Michael, fire blazing off his sword, fire so bright red, so brilliantly yellow, that spurts of it dripped from the blade and fell to the earth. His wings were huge, spreading outward, slowing his descent just enough that he landed in the middle of the vampires and thralls with just a slight flexing of his knees.

Then he commenced to killing.

I thought I was good at fighting.

This was brutal and elegant to watch. Powerful in the fury of the swings. Graceful in the dance of the blade among the vampires and thralls.

The two men holding the RPG were standing there, laughing, for one brief moment.

Then the top half of the first man, the man holding the front of the barrel, started sliding to the right. A slice of Michael's sword had cleaved him from his upper right chest to his bottom left hip, and he slid apart in two pieces, with no jets of blood, no fountaining arteries. The blade cauterized both wounds as quickly as it had cut, leaving both halves of the body whole as they fell apart.

The second man fell apart much like the first. A smoky, bacon-like burning scent of meat drifted along my face. Though nothing was left in my stomach, I still had to swallow something knot-like down. Which was tough to do; the Ushabti had renewed its effort to make me pop, crushing me in its arms like a boa constrictor.

Michael came around. There was a flash of heat behind me. A melting sound came with it, almost a bubbling. In my mind, the sound was what a large rock or boulder would make as it sunk into a fiery stream of lava. It came with a gurgling from the chest of the Ushabti, and a quick flood of memories from the spirit powering the golem.

A man at a cash register in some small corner store, buying something, as I—as the spirit—walked up behind the man and shot him in the neck. The man fell to the ground, moving a little, just his arms and legs, like a baby wriggling in its cradle. Then the spirit, or me, or both, shot the man a couple of times more, in the head.

I blinked, pushed the memory away. It was strong, powerful. Evil. As I wrestled it, the arms around me relaxed, and I fell to the ground. All the way down. My legs couldn't hold me up, not yet, not now, and I laid face-first for a moment. Taking a few breaths and trying to remember who I was. Taking a moment while Michael was above me, just to put my mind back together.

A lot of my brain felt scrambled.

Bullet after bullet to the temple would do that to a man. The fear of a rocket-propelled grenade had almost made me senseless. But that memory, the pure violence of it, the senselessness of that violence, that had put everything over the top.

A hand pulled me up. Michael. His face was stern but compassionate, yet his eyes struck me. His irises were burning fire. Literally.

"Are you good?" he asked. His voice seemed deeper than normal, reverberating, almost like there was an echo to each word.

I might have needed a few minutes, hours, or days to be good. But I nodded.

He looked at me a long moment. Then the archangel waved his sword towards the approaching army. "These creatures will be tougher to kill," he said, the words resounding in my head. "They were made, long ago, as guardians for the demons. Statues to hold those spirits that have not passed on to their next life."

A part of me came back from the wild fear of death I had a moment ago. A part of the old me found itself again. The evil was always going to be there, the violence, the senselessness. There was only one thing to do, and that was to punish those responsible for it. Send them away. If they wanted hell, they could damn well get a first-class trip to go there.

I summoned my own sword, and it seemed... more transparent than usual, next to Michael's burning blade. Maybe it was just the burning fire, but my sword seemed smaller.

I laughed a bit at a sudden thought. Some of my cockiness returned. Some of what Jen might call my Grimmness. It was time to start punching tickets.

I tapped the point of my blade against Michael's, in a little salute.

What did they say? It wasn't the size of the tool, but how you used it?

"Well," I said. "Seems like we should help them along then."

The sky hung above the train, the muted blue of the morning moving slowly backwards as Jen made her way forward, placing her hand along their welded fort wall so that she could pull herself against the wind rushing past them. The flatcar rattled along, the floor vibrating under her feet.

Her hand still lay on the keystone. She was sure she still felt something there. Some connection, feeling, some tie to Gus. The key still glowed, faint and blue. Maybe slightly warm in her hand. Some images, more thoughts than real, dim in her mind, flickering swords and sweeping axes and flames dripping from the sky.

The images were more things stirring in her subconscious, things she was aware of without being able to really see or feel them, like a movie was playing in the back of her mind. So while Jen worried it all might be her imagination, things her mind was making up to help her believe Gus was still alive, she had to hope that the images were real, and that he was.

In fact, Jen refused to believe differently. She knew, deep inside herself, that he was giving her a chance. And he would give everything he had.

Her hand tightened around the key. She would do the same. She wouldn't fail him. Or fail their friends.

She paused at the front of the flatcar. More firing came from the machine gun mounted above her on the roof of the locomotive. The thumps were brief, heavy bursts in the air. Jen looked, seeing

Gabrielle with a set of binoculars, looking far ahead of the train. She recognized the small form of the vampire, even in her tactical, blacked-out gear.

A moment later, the vampire dropped the binoculars and swung the gun a little northwest, still ahead of the train, pulling the trigger again. The heavy, air-thumping sound of the machine gun reverberated briefly over the rushing of the wind, the rattling of the train, the loud rumbling of the diesel engine.

Jen couldn't see what the vampire was aiming at. Or whether she hit it or not. All of that was hidden by the large diesel locomotive itself, directly in front of her. She stared at the links between the flatcar and the locomotive. The coupling holding the railway car to the train engine seemed to float over the tracks flashing by underneath. The back door to the locomotive opened; Alejandro hung there, holding his hand out, his eyes open and staring at the scene behind her. Jen took a quick breath—she had just leapt from a dune buggy to the train, after all—and took a couple light, quick steps across the coupling to the back of the engine, grabbing the vampire's hand and letting him pull her in.

Then Jen was in the diesel locomotive itself. The rushing of the wind became less muted in the cab, just a dull roar behind them. The floor of the train was more stable here, more firm underneath her feet, no longer rattling to the tracks, but vibrating with the powerful purr of the engine.

There were two chairs in the front of the train; Millie sat in the one to the right, in front of the control stand. The station was off to the right, with a big lever-looking switch mounted sideways on the gray dashboard to her left. The panel in front of the vampire was covered in lights and buttons and gauges. There was something that looked like a speedometer to Jen, a big gauge with its arrow pointed far to the right of the dial. Above everything was the windshield, a large horizontal window from which they could see Mexico City.

228 • CHRIS J. CRANFORD

The city slowly came at them from the distance, the buildings close to the horizon crawling towards the train, the structures speeding up as they neared before rushing by to either side in quick flashes of red and brown walls mixed with gray concrete. They started small, tiny square things with flat roofs blinking by in a moment. Then longer buildings, with long brown walls that might once have been warehouses, with angled black roofs, the long sides colored with graffiti, spray-painted words in big bubble-like shapes that zipped by in bright smears.

Larger buildings lay ahead. Closer to the heart of the city. Taller tenements in the distance, high-rises. Some of the taller structures might have been office buildings, the early morning sun glaring off shadowed glass, their tops oddly shaped and discolored, as if they were dark green buds of man-made tulips, having yet to open.

"We're closing in," Alexandro said. There was a paper map in his hand, crumpled a little in his grip.

Jen nodded. He opened the map and showed her where they were and where the stadium was. It was almost a straight shot there, except for a train station between them. A place where they had loaded cargo, where people might have gotten on and off trains stopping before the locomotives rolled on through the city.

Just a few miles ahead.

The train depot was the spot she was worried about. Was the spot they all were worried about. The spot where Sabnock could have a trap. Where Nick, hopefully, waited.

"How far away from the station is the stadium?" she asked.

"A mile," Alejandro said. "People would take it to games." His eyes looked a little lost, like he was in a memory, and one of his hands moved to Millie's shoulder and hung there.

Even though they all stood next to each other, it was hard to hear him over the rumbling of the train, the occasional thundering of the machine gun, and the wind rushing through the still-open door behind them. "Though I think the plan was to use all these trains for tourists. Take them to all the sites. Cholula, Templo Mayor, Tula. Maybe weekend trips."

The names didn't mean anything to Jen. There wouldn't be any tours anymore. Now, or ever. All there would be was what was left after the plague. After they were done. She was just glad the lines ran close enough to the stadium. That was what they needed.

Her gaze flicked over to the vampire; he looked... not nervous. Maybe impatient. He looked at the walkie-talkie sitting on the dash panel next to Millie. They were closing in on the station. There was a switchyard there, and they would need to slow down and make sure they took the right tracks leading outward. The tracks leading close to the stadium.

"Has Nick radio'd in?" Jen asked.

Alejandro shook his head. "The earth witch did," he said. "Tabitha. Looking for Zoe."

Jen had thought those three had left. Why would they be looking for Zoe?

"Is she with Grimm?" Alejandro asked.

It was Jen's turn to shake her head. Assuming Zoe wasn't on the train, and it would have been hard to miss her, then she could be anywhere. And there was nothing anyone could do about it now. It was something Tabitha and Gertrude would have to figure out.

The city rushed by them, the buildings getting taller around them like the train was entering a canyon, a canyon of tall man-made buildings, of tall metal tulip towers that could hold any number of surprises. Any number of vampires, any number of those knights, anything Sabnock could dream of or make could be held there.

Jen fingered the hilt of the Five-Fold blade. The metal felt charged, almost like the air around her, and she felt that charge like she always did, the storm hidden in the clouds above them, hidden in the blowing winds, hidden from the dim orange rays of the morning sun, burning the gray of morning away.

The train rolled along. Thundering down the tracks. The floor of the diesel engine didn't vibrate like the flatcars did, but still the trembling sensation was there, a muted pounding of the locomotive rumbling down the tracks echoing on the bottom of her feet. The buildings kept swelling around them, large and ominous in their seeming emptiness. A blue spark danced briefly between Jen's fingers and the blade, and the slight tingle of electricity across her fingertips reassured her.

If only the same feeling would come from the keystone.

CHAPTER TWENTY-SEVEN

The dead field around us grew deader. The brown, brittle grass broke under my feet, the dusty earth thickened with a dark green ichor as we went to work on the Ushabti. Michael and I. Him with his flaming sword, me with my ethereal one.

It was slow going. My sword had trouble cutting through the stone or granite or demonic metal the creatures were made of. Like I was pushing a dull butter knife through cold clay, clay streaked dark green with rusty veins of red. I could do it, pulling ethereal energy and putting everything I had into each swing, but it took time.

Time for other Ushabti to grab me. Their arms, thick and heavy, moved slow though. Slow enough that I could always dance away, sometimes—mostly, actually—at the last second. Slow enough I could avoid the heavy swings of the thick swords they carried, and duck the sweeping strikes of the tall, double-bladed axes.

Michael fared a little better. His sword seemed to melt through the creatures, more like a hot, sharp knife through the same cold clay of the demon knights. The flames of his sword sparked and sizzled as it cut through the stone, globs of bright yellow-red flames dripping to the ground with each swing.

I was caught looking at a particular knight, suddenly missing its arm; the rusty green rock-like granite seemed to melt away from the blow of the fiery sword that had hacked off the limb. The wound itself burned a molten red, the glow flaring in the air, and the brilliance of it—just for a moment, a quick flicker of my eyes, nothing more—distracted me at just the wrong time.

A time when one of those sweeping double-bladed axes caught me in the side.

I was full of ethereal energy, so my body was as hard as it could be, as hard as titanium, but still pain burst from my hip as the axe cracked into it. The swing lifted me in the air, like someone punting a football. All my breath escaped me in a rushing *whoosh*.

I fell to the ground in a roll, letting my sword disappear, coming up a good thirty or forty feet away. Covered in dust and brown grass and one large flapping leaf of agave. The end of the spiny stem was thick with sticky goo, and some of it stuck to my palm as I smoothed it off with the flat of my hand.

It was time for a breath. I took a large inhale. My lungs filled and pressed against my ribcage; it ached along the side where the axe had struck. My hip felt a little achy, like the twinge of arthritis. I pulled more ghost; a cold tingling replaced the pain as bones and bruises and joints healed.

Of course, right as I was doing that a crack split the air. Something pinged off my chest. Something hard and metallic and going hundreds of miles an hour. There were still humans and vampires out there, grouped up. Hiding and taking potshots from far enough away that they felt safe.

I worried that there might be more rocket launchers out there. One of those at the wrong time, in the middle of all those Ushabti, that could make a quick end to me. It was hard enough to stay away from the knights themselves, to keep away from two of the creatures wanting to get a chance to play tug of war with a Grimm; well, none of those would be a particularly good ending for me.

It's a tough fight when you have to decide between dodging RPGs and avoiding golems that want to pull you apart between them. I blinked on my ethereal sight a moment, scanning the greenish, rust-tinged stone golems. Each powered by a particularly violent spirit, a ghost looking for a chance at revenge, the insides of their rocky bodies glowing a flickering bluish red. The color of the bad spirits.

I wondered which one was Hector. He was out there, surely. I didn't think I'd know until I killed him. Until it was his memories flooding over mine.

Michael appeared suddenly, landing next to me in a smooth motion. His wings fluttered a bit behind him, then folded up smoothly into his back. His eyes and sword were still on fire. We both surveyed the army of Ushabti around us.

The demon knight with the missing arm was trying to fit it back on. Not the brightest of spirits powering that one. Other knights fanned out now, breaking ranks, trying to put some distance between each of them. A distance far enough that one of the Ushabtis could cover the others, so that the slightest pause in the fight would allow one of the knights to close in on me and Michael.

We had maybe gotten through fifty of them. Maybe. And I was already tired. "Takes a lot of work to kill one."

The archangel nodded. "In the past, they would wear us down with numbers."

Numbers? Hell, we were having a hell of a time just with these few hundred. I wondered how many it took to wear angels down. Would it be an army of thousands? Hundreds of thousands?

"Got a plan?"

The angel smiled something grim. I was surprised to not see fire breathing out of his mouth, too. "Keep swinging and try not to let them hit you."

I let out a breath. Another bullet struck me, this one a heavier caliber, right in the center of my chest. This struck me hard enough that I had to take a couple of steps back. I looked in the distance, among the tiny rises there, the lonely desert willows dotting those rises. Maybe a sniper out there, a real sniper with a .50 cal. "These guys are getting on my nerves."

The constant pull of ethereal energy was getting to me. The constant subsuming of memories, the evil feel of the life of each ghost, the pushing away the nausea from each spirit. Leaving a stain that seemed thicker by the moment.

I pushed that thought away. I would power through it. Live as many memories as I could. Whatever it took until Jen got the dead zone nullified. Until she was back and safe.

That thought had me glance back at the dead zone.

I froze.

Sabnock stood there.

The demon watched me and Michael. He was well inside the dead zone, a good ten feet or so. Far enough back he could feel safe. He was as tall as he had been before, a muscled, ebony creature with gold armor, and that yellow lion pauldron perched on one shoulder. The end of his staff planted firmly on the ground, his hand holding it loosely next to him.

He was smiling. Something thoughtful. But content.

Michael caught my glance, turned to see the demon, as well.

Sabnock held up a hand, and the army of Ushabti paused. The cracking reports of pot shots slowed down, then stopped. The world stilled.

Michael's eyes lost their fire. His sword stopped dripping flames. He stood there, the hilt of his sword white and gold in his grip, before swinging the blade up around his back into the sheath that suddenly appeared to be there.

The two of us walked over to Sabnock. Staying on our side of the dead zone. As equidistant from the line separating the zone from our world as the demon. Like a bunch of gunfighters in an old western, facing each other in a street. The warm air, the air too warm and humid for December, blowing across and through all of us.

"Michael," Sabnock said. "Old friend, the last of the seraphim. Crawled out from your rock, I see."

The angel's jaw flexed. A flicker of flames washed across his irises. "Sabnock. You were never a friend. I remember you. I remember your jealousy. Your flawed creations. You were ever second rate."

Michael seemed to grow, standing there. Sabnock seemed to swell to match. They didn't grow taller or wider, it just *felt* that way. A tension in the air, maybe. A radiance from the angel. A black dimming from Sabnock. I blinked ethereally, catching their real forms, and each seemed thirty, forty, fifty feet high in the ethereal world. An expanding angel, halo blazing, wings stretching high into the air. A monster facing him, horned, clutch claw-like hands, wings black and spiked outwards at the ends to match.

I blinked back. "Sabnock," I said. Being me. "Come to watch us take out your trash?"

The demon grinned, one dark lip curling over white teeth. His gaze turned from me to Michael as if the two of them shared a secret. Maybe a history. It made me wonder what their hidden forms were doing, but I wasn't going to check.

"Humans," Sabnock said. "So cocky, so know-it-all for such a short life span."

I didn't think I was cocky. But I was a survivor. And when you survive enough, you start to grow a confidence in yourself. Why not brag about it?

"Well, I've killed a few demons in my short life," I said. "And I've handled you and your little plague so far. I figure you're just another check on my bucket list."

The demon chuckled. "You think so?"

I figured he was here to watch what was going on, maybe catch Michael and I napping. Maybe he thought he'd see his Ushabti get lucky. So the demon's next words surprised me a little. "There's a plan for you, Grimm. Something you may not expect."

The surprise wasn't that he had a plan for me. It was the confidence of his statement. It rattled me a bit. Still, if the demon was here bandying words, then he wasn't in Aztec Stadium. And the longer we kept him here talking, the better off my friends would be. The better chance they had at getting to the center of the dead zone and taking it out.

It was time to get on someone's nerves.

And I was pretty good at that.

"You've talked with Azazel, I'm sure," I said. "He'll tell you I'm a little more trouble than you think I am." I paused, as if a thought had surprised me. "In fact, you might ask him why he's okay with me coming down here to take care of you. I mean, I'm pretty sure he had to know where I was going. He the type of guy to sacrifice a friend to save his own skin?" And another pause. "I kind of think he is."

Michael chuckled a bit at that, a mockery of Sabnock's earlier laugh.

"Azazel." Sabnock blew out his giant breath. "What do you really know about him? About me? Azazel has plans for his plans, he schemes and plots, but this—" Sabnock waved his staff over the dead zone. "This is me. The dead zones *were* me. It was my plan. My scheme. This is constructing something more permanent than you know. I *plan,* human. And I build."

"You build this?" I waved my hand around in an imitation of the demon. Over the dead grass, the brown fields, the locust-eaten trees and plants, the blown-up vehicles and the dead Ushabti, humans, and vampires littering the landscape. "It's a bang-up job, Sabby. You must have been hell finger-painting with the other kids."

The demon's jaw set. His words become dark, guttural. "To build something, you must destroy it first. There has to be clay in order to mold." Another big breath. For an architect, the demon sure got angry. "You will see, human."

A pause. A small smile. "Well, *you* will not see. But humankind will. Your friends, as well."

Well, as long as he was here talking, my friends would be okay. And I wasn't worried about me. As definite as the demon sounded, there were enough ghosts and spirits around to keep me going, so his army here didn't concern me. As long as I stayed conscious and pulling energy I'd be okay.

I was more worried about my friends. I couldn't feel Jen, not really. Just a dull, foggy wall along our bond. A fuzzy feel of her, maybe, on the other side of the key. On the other side of the dead zone.

"Maybe you should come out here and say that," I said. "To me, it seems like you've traded one prison for another. What with the key, and now the dead zone." I took a large breath, blew it out, like I was breathing in the freshest of air and not a gun-smoked battle-field. "Come get some."

"One day," Sabnock said, then repeated himself. "One day. When I'm finished what I'm building here. Right, seraphim?"

Michael shrugged. "I've seen what you're building. It's a poor imitation." His words carried quietly, spoken in a matter-of-fact manner. "But of course, I've lived in the city of the true master builder."

Something about that comment seemed to get to the demon. I tried to tie it together with the jealous comment earlier. It made me wonder what the demon had been, before he had fallen. Before he had turned from a haloed angel with wings into a black-winged monster. Whatever it had been, it had happened thousands upon thousands of years in the past.

I would likely never know.

Sabnock's face twisted a little, his eyes narrowed, his dark lips curling a bit, revealing white, even teeth. The wind picked up a little, stirring my hair, fluttering the feathers in Michael's wings. The gunfighter feel of the scene grew stronger.

"We going to stand here all day?" I asked. "Is there something you want to say? Or do?"

The demon seemed to gather himself. The intense feeling of him growing larger faded away. His head cocked as if he was asking himself the same question. I wondered if he would answer.

"There's a beauty in destruction," he finally said. "It captivates me. That what existed before will be no longer, and will become something else. Sometimes I catch myself, I feel the desire to watch the world burn, the excitement of it all, and I wonder what it is that really draws me."

I was surprised. The answer was something felt from the demon's inner heart. Maybe something that had drawn him, so long ago, to balance on his own precipice, before his fall.

"You know from where that voice came," Michael said. "You listened to it. And look where it's gotten you."

Sabnock's eyes seemed turned back in time. His gaze caught me. I saw him reflecting. I might have caught a hint of sadness there. Of a decision in another place of time.

Then the demon shook himself. Not literally. Figuratively. His eyes focused on me, and they were angry, blazing with a black fire that drew me in.

"You ask, human?" Sabnock said. "I came to tell you I know about your friends. About the storm witch. The shadow walker. The death siren and the vampire's pet. I came to tell you I know about them all, where they are, what they plan. I know all about your plan, and this…" The demon waved his arm over his army, "This is just something to keep you occupied. I came to tell you, to rip your heart out, so that you will know they die alone. In *my* land. In *my* kingdom."

His eyes were like twin black holes. They pulled me in even as I fought it. The rage in them, so intense, flooded me. My heart all of a sudden burst with a feeling of hopelessness. With the anger in each of Sabnock's words. His promise. "Know that. Know that they head into a design of my creation. At a time of my choosing."

Fear burst through me. Fear of the unknown. Fear of being unable to help. Fear of some angle Sabnock had thought of that I hadn't. Whatever my friends were about to run into, whatever Jen was going to run into, they would have to handle it on their own.

Still, him stealing the Mad Max plan from me gave me a little hope. So I kept poking him. Smiling my Grimm smile. "I haven't been too impressed so far, Sabby."

Sabnock's return grin was full of malice. Envy. Hate. "I guess we'll see. Or I'll see. I'll come back to let you know just how they died. I'll come ready to see how cocky you are then. Ready to see if I'm still a checkmark on your bucket list."

And then the demon disappeared.

The air rushed by the Express; Jen heard it in the rushing roar behind her, the wind whipping through the open door in the back of the locomotive. There was the roar and the pounding rhythm of the wheels powering over the tracks, the side rods pumping so fast the sound of the tracks underneath became a wooden rumbling of a vibration felt on the floor of the locomotive. The train moving so fast they seemed to float above the tracks.

The feeling of the canyon increased. The buildings closed around them. Taller now. Old apartments, some brick, some stucco, with white-paned windows. Office buildings and other taller structures just ahead reminded Jen of tulips with their bulbous, stained-green tops. And while the buildings weren't the size of a mountain, as the train moved underneath, it still felt like everything towered over them.

Jen looked at the tulip bud-shaped bulges. Wondering how many locusts could be left. How many more Sabnock could have made in just a few days.

There had been a lot of people at one time in Mexico City.

And that city looked abandoned now.

The feeling of a trap grew. The depot was just ahead. A mile or two. Jen's eyes followed the tracks north, to where they joined other tracks, all heading in the same direction. Other trains and cars sat on the tracks, one blue locomotive faced the Express. And, finally, as she watched, a tall, two-story building appeared off to the right in the distance.

The station.

Where Nick was waiting.

Then, maybe because they were all expecting it, the radio buzzed them.

"Abort." Nick's voice. "Abort."

His words spurred action. Alejandro cursed and bent forward, scanning in front of them. Millie's hands reached to the side, to the brake switch there, but her eyes—full of worry and fear and something else—locked on Jen.

Jen had already grabbed the radio. Her fingers pressed down on the speak button, feeling the click. Nick had sounded frantic, so she made her words short. "Nick. Abort?"

"Trap," he said, the word coming out in a gasp. Jen listened to him take a deep breath and repeat himself. A little more composed. "It's a trap." His voice surprised Jen, because Nick was usually quiet. Deadly. In control. "They're waiting for us. I don't know how many—"

A buzzing came over his walkie-talkie. Then silence, as if Nick clicked off. Alejandro rushed back past Jen and out the door, shouting something to Gabrielle, but the heavy machine gun had already started firing. It was too far to make out anything, but Jen saw forms on the tracks by the depot. Small in the distance, a little over a mile away, but Jen could gather the size of them. The knights. They were maneuvering something across the tracks. What looked to be the taller passenger cars of a train.

Millie's hand stayed on the break. Jen shook her head. For now.

"We don't have much time," the vampire said.

Jen nodded. "Nick?" Jen said. "Tell me something. Anything."

There was a long moment. Then Nick came back. His voice low and fast. "It's too light out now. I'm trapped north of the station." His breathing slowed. "I was there waiting, making sure the switches lined up when vampires stormed it. Some of those golem-things, too. They're all over the place."

They must have come at dawn. Where the shadows were less. Enough that Nick had made it out, but not enough to stick around. Jen heard Nick swallow, hard. "I was lucky, but they were even waiting—" He stopped himself. "You've got to stop the train."

Millie shook her head, not even glancing to see how fast they were going. "We're not going to stop in time."

Jen thought quickly. Measuring the distance and speed. They might have a minute or two, tops. She tried some quick mental math and realized she didn't have the slightest inkling of how long it would take a train to stop.

Her thoughts came amid the pounding of the machine gun

above. Occasionally one of the bullets was a tracer, a bright flash of metal darting towards the station ahead. Towards the small forms there.

A minute, maybe. Hopefully.

"You're safe though?"

A pause. "Yeah," he said. "For now. But the station is packed."

Jen's free hand, her fingertips there, still lay on the hilt of the Five-Fold blade. Or the cars. What the size of any of them really were.

She was going to have to try anyway.

This was going to be either the longest minute in history. Or the shortest.

"Save who you can," she told Nick.

He swore, even as she clicked off and turned back to the open rear door at the back of the locomotive. Alejandro hung to the side there, looking above the train. Probably at Gabrielle. The heavy gun had stopped briefly, and it looked like he was climbing up to help with something. Maybe a reload.

They might not have that kind of time.

Jen tapped his shoulder, shouted in his ear. "We're ditching the train."

Alejandro glanced at her, quickly. Jen felt the precious seconds slip away. The vampire seemed to get it though, and bounded up to the roof.

At least Jen hoped he had gotten it.

Behind him, behind the locomotive, were the flatcars. They bounced heavily on the tracks. Sarah knelt just across from Jen, across the coupling, right behind the wall of the hastily made fort on the car, the barrel of an assault rifle poking up next to her. Sarah's hair whipped behind her in the wind, and their eyes met briefly.

Johnny was back in one of the machine gun nests. One of the smaller guns they had mounted on the sides of the cars, smaller than the gun Gabrielle stood behind on the roof. Jen thought Gus had called the big one in front of the vampire an M2, a Browning something-cal. There were a couple more Brownings on the first flatcar, right behind the engine, one to either side. Then four more of the smaller machine guns, built on nests on either side of the last flatcar. All of the nests manned.

"Trust me," Jen shouted at both of them.

Sarah nodded. Her sister, so serious now. And always sad, even now. Johnny just waved cheerfully and hunkered down behind his gun. It was such a Johnny thing it had her smiling. It was good to have him back, himself again.

"Give 'em hell," Jen shouted, repeating what Gus had wished for her, the words she had been told so recently. She grabbed the hilt of the Five-Fold blade, leaving the knife in its sheathe, and called a bit of lightning. A spark of blue electricity blew apart the coupling linking the cars to the locomotive. Immediately the flatcars started to slow down.

But the engine stayed at speed. Ten, twenty seconds had gone by. The depot was coming on quicker. Passenger cars lay across the tracks, as well as some of the knights. More were coming, though, flooding the area in front of them.

Millie had already buckled herself into her chair. Jen jumped into the other one, one hand pulling the belt around her and doing the same. Her other hand still tight on the blade's hilt. Still calling the storm.

Calling the lightning.

Not from the sky, though. Around Jen. She built her lighting shield like she had other times before. But she wasn't building it around herself. She was building something larger than she had ever built before. Larger than her body.

She was building it around the entire locomotive.

Jen pulled from the Five-Fold blade, feeling energy pour into her, a cool tingling sensation that felt like a thousand cups of coffee. Her heart raced with the surge of power. The blood seemed to rush out through her body, thumping through arteries and veins under the hard beats of her heart. So hard and fast her limbs, her fingers and toes, they all seemed to swell with the flow.

Her one hand still held onto the hilt of the blade. Her knuckles were white. Still, Jen pulled more and more energy, called more and more storm, feeling the electricity tingle across her fingers, over the backs of her hands, the skin of her forearms. Feeling the electricity flow over the outside of her body, much like the blood raced inside.

Time seemed to slow. The crowd of golems stood in front of the Express. Not a hundred feet away. Not fifty. Closing in fast. Some held swords, some axes, some large crossbow-looking things. All of them seemed still, in Jen's storm-calling perception.

Behind the golems were the passenger cars, the cars stacked one behind the other. The first car's metal side was ripped and torn and littered with bullet holes from the heavy machine gun on top of the train.

The windshield of the Express cracked once. Twice. The third crack left a thick bolt stuck in the middle of the glass, spiderwebbing cracks spreading to either side of the vibrating shaft.

The train sped on. Jen kept pulling from the blade. Kept calling the lightning. Kept calling the storm. Out of the corner of her eyes she saw Millie staring at her, eyes wide, wide open. The golems were RIGHT THERE in front of the train.

Blue sparks gathered around the Express. Sparkling bolts, brightly blue and thick, popped into place in front of the train. The bolts fluttered in the air there for a quick moment.

Then two.

The Express tunneled through the knights, shuddering as the bodies flew up and over the train. As the cowcatcher plowed through them. The train mowed through the creatures, trembling and shuddering as the wheels ripped through the bodies, shaking as the machine lurched through the crowd, as if the Express itself was afraid of what might happen when it struck the passenger cars behind them.

The lightning shield held. It bowed under the weight. Spat as pieces of golem struck it. Sizzled as bodies hung to the side of the train.

Jen kept pulling. Sucked in the energy from the blade. Wondering at the amount of it all, at what she was doing. A sound broke the air. A scream. It took Jen a moment to realize the sound was coming from her.

The lightning shield locked in. Held. A comet of blue raced along the tracks, a teardrop-shaped shield of lightning, throwing sparks and hisses as the train thundered through the crowd of golems.

Right as the train crashed into the passenger cars.

CHAPTER TWENTY-EIGHT

I slammed into the dead zone wall.

Like before, when Jen and I had tried it, the zone resisted me. Forcefully. It felt like I had run headlong into a mountain. Headfirst into one of those Ushabtis. Or a speeding car.

I fell to the ground. My head split with pain. I shook it and tried it again. Screaming this time. With the same results.

In the distance, in my ethereal sight, I saw flashes of energy to the north. Bursts of blue, maybe. I pushed along the bond and felt nothing but the faintest of fear from the other side. Maybe a screaming.

I echoed the scream. And slammed back into the wall. Pounded it with my fists, over and over.

Then a hand on my shoulder pulled me back. I turned quickly, ready to summon the sword, but it was only Michael. His face worried. His hand on my arm.

"What's wrong?" he asked.

I yanked my arm away from the angel. "He's going after them."

He looked closer at me, as if trying to look inside me. "I know.

We know. But why..." Michael mimed the motion I was making, the beating against the wall of the dead zone. His hand, though, actually went past the border.

I realized he didn't know. One of the many things I hadn't had a chance to talk to him about. To understand more about myself. "I can't go in."

His eyes narrowed. "I've seen you go in."

I shook my head. I wasn't thinking clearly. Not with how Sabnock had left. Not with the feeling of fear in the bond. The flickering energies to the north. "I can, but not if Jen is in there."

Michael looked puzzled. I showed him the key on my chest, where it glowed, ever so faintly. "I don't know why." I tried to explain. "But if one of us is in there, the other one is locked outside." I wanted to cry, and I wanted to scream more, both at the same time. "I don't understand."

The angel's head rocked back a bit. As if a sudden realization had hit him.

"What?" I yelled. Demanded. My eyes welled with wetness. "What?"

His hand was still in the dead zone. Michael pulled it out, looking at me as if seeing something new.

"What?" I shouted. Jen, my friends, they could be dead by now. Dead. Torn apart. Suffering under Sabnock. "Tell me, what?"

His mouth moved. Slow, as if Michael was forming what he wanted to say. Then the words came. "It means you share a soul, Grimm."

Share a soul? What did that mean?

He took a deep breath. Let it out. He tried a reassuring smile. "You are worried. I worried you," he said. "It's a good thing, Grimm. It's just something... It's just something I haven't seen in a long, long time."

"Seen what?" I asked. Still scared. Heart pulsing rapidly. Not able to settle myself down. Not trusting the angel's words.

"A great love," he said, his words low, as if he still wondered.

Those words gave me pause.

"A love so great," he said, his voice almost wistful, "that the two of you share a soul. You share a love greater than most know. Than most will ever know."

His hand open, his fingers splayed over the wall of the dead zone as if revealing it to me. "These places. These dead zones, they mark the boundaries of a part of hell. And in Hell, only one soul can enter, only one soul can exist, at its own time and place, for its own reasons."

I took a breath. Tried to calm myself. It was the hardest thing I'd ever done, I thought. Jen and I shared a love? I knew that. We *both* knew that, Jen and I. We shared it constantly, not just in the bond, but in life.

But a great love? What did that mean? She was my rock. I thought I was hers. We were together in all the ways that people should be together. We would do anything for each other. Everything.

I should never have left Grafton, but if I hadn't, maybe I wouldn't have realized how much I couldn't live without her.

And, I believed she felt the same about me.

Still. Sabnock was there now. In the dead zone. Leading my friends into a trap. In a place I could not get to, could not make, no matter how hard I tried.

I stared north. My hands were clenched. I could not help them.

"It's not explaining anything," I said, finally. "It's not helping."

"I can't help," he said. "I can just try to explain." Michael's eyes remained wet, yet turned wistful. "With such a love, all things are possible."

His eyes went past me. To the flickering of the ethereal energies

I had seen far in the distance. To the north, where the stadium lay. The Crown of Bones.

"A love such as yours…" Michael said, his voice taking a wondering echo to it, "can change the world."

Jen shook her head for what felt like the thousandth time. She couldn't figure out exactly where she was; Jen only knew she had an arm around Nick and that he was half-carrying her, half-dragging her down a street. Only knew they were running from something. As fast as Nick could drag her.

The rest of it, the rest of what happened, it all came in flashes…

Like the last moments of the Express. The whiplash-like jerking of the locomotive as it barreled through all the golem-knights, through the stacked passenger cars, through the crowds of vampires and humans, the banging of Jen's head against the seat, against the wall, the sizzling and popping of the lightning shield, the feeling of weightlessness as the train had left the tracks, soaring through the air, lightning bolts flickering away from the train until it finally came back to Earth like a low-lying meteor, furrowing through the ground until the locomotive abruptly came to a stop, on its side.

There was a pain in her head. In Jen's skull. She tried to shake her head and stopped as a nauseous, sick sensation erupted from her stomach. She tried to keep everything down and ended up gagging on bile.

Nick stopped. Sarah came into view, and Jen felt a moment of frustration. *I'm fine*, she wanted to scream. But she wasn't. Her head hurt bad. Like someone had hammered her skull with a spike.

Something warm ran down the side of her face. Jen tried to wipe it with her hand and missed. She looked at her fingers, confused, thinking they had struck something hard, straight, and smooth, like a pole. That couldn't be right.

Sarah said something to Nick, then her sister thumbed Jen's eyelids, one at a time, peering deeply at each...

There had been Nick cutting Jen out of the chair she hung from. Cursing the whole time, telling Jen it was going to be okay. That she was going to be okay. Just to hold on.

There had been Millie, who was not going to be okay. The vampire lay underneath them, crushed underneath the control panel, as it had bent backwards into the front of the train. The sweet scent of diesel fumes thick in the air. Millie's scar was bright red against a too-pale face; she waved a closed fist at the two of them, a fist holding something square and black, waving at them to go, go, go...

Jen seemed to blink, and they were running again. In a different place. Her head almost on fire with pain, with cracks of single-shot gunfire coming from behind them, the cracks echoing along the tall buildings the group ran between.

Johnny was helping Nick carry Jen now, his dark face marred with blood and dirt, a long tube slung around his back and a rifle in his other hand. He seemed stronger than usual to Jen.

He glanced over, saw Jen recognize him. She tried to tell him she was okay, that her head hurt but that she was *okay*, but nothing came out of her mouth, and then Johnny's gaze slid by her.

"I think she's coming around," he said.

The sharp burning pain continued. A stabbing in her skull. It seemed to pin the fogginess to her thoughts, to hold it there so Jen couldn't think or speak. It was like coming out of the deepest sleep, when you didn't know where you were, and all you saw was darkness. Darkness and pain. Flashes of pain and flashes of memories...

Alejandro, lying on his back, somewhere along the ground behind the train. Buried in part of the furrow along the earth. Just the top of him, the lower half of the vampire had been sheered away by some force of the crash.

His eyes still twitching back and forth, lifeless but twitching, as if he was still trying to see what killed him, as Nick carried Jen by.

A flash of the flatcars which had come to a stop around the station. Just a quick image of them, overrun by the golems, by the vampires, even as the people-shredding machine guns tore into them.

One gun blurred to a stop as its operator became entangled in a fight. Then the next. One after another as the army of Sabnock collapsed onto the cars.

Another blink. Johnny carrying Jen now, carrying her like she was a baby, her head bobbing to the rhythm of his stride. His head was turned, Johnny shouting as he ran. Shouting at someone or something behind them.

Jen tried to hold down the nausea her bobbing head brought up. Tried to keep from throwing up. Her face was wet still, the front of her shirt sticky. Had she already thrown up? She couldn't remember.

She focused on the air above them. Tried to find a point in the sky to keep the sickness down. But all that was there was a dark cloud, a gathering shadow, that seemed to be overlapping the group from the south.

Locusts, thick and dark and sounding like the buzzing of a million bees, the buzzing growing louder and louder as the insects buzzed lower and lower...

A flash of an explosion. Right as Nick was carrying Jen away from the depot. Away from the cars. Sarah was screaming at Nick, Sarah and Gabrielle standing at the corner of a tall building down the street from the depot, when an unseen hand blew into them from the Express, tossing Nick and Jen and Sarah and Gabrielle amidst a cloud of sulphury blackness...

And then the screams. The screams and Jen felt someone pull her up again. The shouts and screams behind them, from the station. The screaming from Jen herself, from the spike of hot pain in her skull...

The stadium loomed large in front of them. The Crown of Bones. The skeleton fingers of concrete ringing the outer walls, the columns holding the structure in their bony grip.

It seemed impossibly tall. The group of them small, below the crown. Still, they ran into it. Johnny still carrying Jen. Still holding her like a baby. Gabrielle running at his side.

The pain in her head was less now. Jen wondered if that was a good thing.

Gunshots rang around them, no longer echoing in the empty air. Just pinging off metal bars, thwacking off the concrete. It was hard to hear with the buzzing of the locusts, lower and lower, the guns and the insects herding them onwards.

Nick and Sarah held a pair of glass doors open. The three of them ran through it. Well, Johnny and Gabrielle, Johnny carrying Jen. He paused briefly, trying to shoulder past the door and keep Jen tucked into his chest. A pane of glass shattered to their left, and Sarah cried out.

The group ran on. Past the concession counters with empty popcorn boxes, empty pretzel stands, empty hot dog carouses. Fled as gunfire followed them. Fled as single locusts traced after the group, winding through the air as if marking their location.

Then they were in a tunnel. A dark, flat thing made of stone and concrete, with a tiny arch curving above them. The tunnel had a slight decline, as if it ran down all the way to the stadium field.

The gunfire stopped then. Briefly.

The four of them stopped as well. Johnny lowered Jen, sitting her back against the wall, her legs straight out. She tried to pull them in, to cross her legs, but they barely twitched. Johnny held her shoulder, as if to keep Jen from tipping over.

I'm fine, she wanted to say. But couldn't.

"He's got to be waiting," Johnny said.

"Yeah," Nick said, his hand on a knife. "Yeah."

"It's not the fight we wanted," Johnny said.

"When is it ever?" Nick asked. His knife had a glow to the hilt, something small and blue, etched with circles. Something about that glow clicked with Jen, and her fingers twitched next to her leg.

The glow wasn't just noticed by Jen. Johnny saw it too. He looked at Nick for a moment, then back to Jen. Then he bent down over Jen, looking into her eyes for a long moment, as if silently apologizing. Something unsnapped along her leg, and Johnny brought up a second knife, snugly wrapped in a sheath.

Her knife.

The Five-Fold blade, Jen thought. Or wanted to say. The pain in her head spasmed, as if pushing away from the blade. From what could heal her.

They didn't know.

Her fingers twitched again. She desperately wanted them, needed them, to put the knife in her hand. But they weren't aware; they didn't know she could be healed, that whatever was wrong with her, the splitting pain could be *healed*. All they had to do was lay the blade in her fingers and Jen thought she could fix whatever was wrong with her. She knew she could heal herself; she *knew* she could with the knife; she just had to remember…

"We can't leave her," Sarah said. Suddenly, out loud, as if a decision had quietly been made among the friends. Her sister's hand was pressed against her own arm, lines of blood dripping down along her forearm.

Just put the blade in my hand, Jen screamed. Or tried to scream; whatever voice she had seemed to circle around her brain, circle around the pain in her skull, but no sound came out. She barely even moved.

There was something more about the blade. Something more about the knife and the energy it held. But the thought disappeared under the throbbing pain in her head. All Jen could do was record everything in front of her, watch her friends, her sister, desperately wanting them to just *give her a chance...*

Nick went to Sarah, his hand going to Sarah's arm. She pushed him away, still looking at Jen. There was a long pause. All of Jen's friends stood around, looking at each other. They all looked beat. Covered in dust, black mud, maybe blood. And tired, tired eyes.

Tired, and sad.

Nick was the first to break the silence. "We just have to find a way to cut the power off to the zone. That's it. We do that and Grimm gets here."

Johnny gave one of his grins. "That's it, huh?"

Gabrielle snorted, one of her hands rubbing Johnny's shoulder. Leaning on him a moment. Almost at the same moment, Nick and Sarah were next to each other too, Nick's arm around her sister's shoulder, pulling her close.

"We can't leave her," Sarah said.

Who? Jen wanted to ask. Tried to ask.

Nick's voice was soft. "She'll be as safe here as anywhere."

A sob broke from Sarah, loud, echoing down the tunnel.

Nick's voice seemed even softer. "The sooner we do this, the sooner Grimm gets here."

Another sob. A scream from Sarah.

The word. Grimm. The knife. Energy, to heal. Pieces putting themselves together in Jen's mind. Linking the two. But it wasn't Grimm; that wasn't the right name.

That wasn't his right name.

"Okay," Sarah finally said. "Okay."

A gunshot cracked behind them. The bullet pinged and whizzed down the concrete, zipping by the group. As if the army that had herded them to the stadium had given the friends enough time.

Sarah gained something. Stood a little taller. As if a weight had fallen off.

"You guys deal with Sabnock," her sister said. "I'll take care of these guys."

Nick pulled Sarah close, pressing his forehead to hers. "Give 'em hell, babe."

Those words, Jen knew those words. They tumbled through her brain, screaming at her to remember…

Her sister kissed Nick. "You too."

Then they let go of each other. Her sister took a few steps backwards, and as she did, Sarah started to transform. Started to become someone else. Some*thing* else.

Sarah disappeared as thin, whiplike things flew out from where her sister had been standing. A grayish-black fog burst from her body, a fog from which the tentacles whipped around the tunnel, the cords slapping the stone, and through all that there was a keening sound, a chord, a song…

And then her sister disappeared back up the tunnel, the gray-black fog blending into the darkness of the shadows there, the slapping of the tentacles, the keening song following her. Growing only stronger as Sarah headed up the ramp.

And then she was out of Jen's sight. There was just Nick, and Johnny, and Gabrielle. Nick stared after Sarah. There was a slight curve to his lips, and a fiery glint to his eyes. Then Johnny slapped his shoulder, and her three friends turned, heading down the tunnel. Downwards, towards the field.

The light there seemed to swell. Grow brighter. Until it swallowed them.

Leaving Jen.

She lay there, unable to move. Unable to speak. Nothing in her mind but a memory of a burning spike of pain in the side of her skull. That memory, and thoughts of the knife. Of the power that could have healed her.

Of another thought, too. Of Grimm, though she knew him as someone else. Of that someone else and something important between them. Of Nick and his *give 'em hell, babe*. Of the last sight she had seen of them, of her sister being swallowed by a darkness, and the shadows of her three friends, as their forms were swallowed by the light.

It all swirled around in her brain, among the pain there. Recording it all, as Jen could only watch her friends walk to their deaths. Nick's last words to Sarah ringing around her mind as if there was something there, something she should remember, but just could not.

CHAPTER TWENTY-NINE

I stood there, facing the north.

Lightning had played over the earth there. The remnants of it stayed as afterimages I saw on the backs of my eyelids. There had been a bright blue glow, some kind of flickering sapphire bolt that had travelled over the earth. A low rumbling had accompanied it, in the distance, echoing all the way back to me.

Then, after a moment, silence.

And then, a burst of pain. Enough that I had to kneel under it. My head burned with it.

And then slowly, the pain bled away. Enough that I could stand.

My heart raced as emotions tore through me. Hope and Fear. Fear because Jen was in trouble. She was hurt. In pain. I felt it in me, a hard stabbing in my skull.

Hope because I could feel her through the bond. That the muteness laying between us wasn't caused by distance, wasn't caused by the sharp edge of the dead zone, that the muteness was something I could work past.

Even if the pain scared me to death.

I tried to push energy to her, got nothing in response.

I shoved it through the bond, pulling it from the ghosts around me, slamming the energy into the bond like someone tamping the earth. Giving Jen everything I had, and getting nothing back.

I screamed. It seemed to go forever. The sound echoed across the empty sky, around the battlefield, past the Ushabti behind us, and on and on and on. The rest of the world was lost to me. Bullets struck me in the back, in the skull; I felt none of that and healed it all without a thought. They came with a heavy, peppery smell of charcoal, which I noticed only when I stopped screaming to take another breath. They came with the challenging screams of the hundreds of Ushabti closing in.

And they came with the feel of Michael's hand, once more on my shoulder.

"Come," the angel said. "Let us finish this group. And then see what may be done."

He wasn't wrong.

He wasn't right.

It was just something that needed to be done when I could do nothing else. Nothing for Jen, and her pain. Nothing for Jen, not when she needed it *most*.

So I went to killing.

My heart was out of it, though. I was constantly aware of the bond. The flickering flashes racing through it, glimpses I didn't understand. The Express on its side. The rail cars covered in vampires. An explosion. And running, always running, with a glimpse of the morning sky above. A sky slowly eaten by a dark cloud.

None of it made sense. But I stayed connected to the bond. I stayed aware. I kept pushing ethereal energy that way, praying, hoping, praying.

And while I did all that, I killed. The sword seemed sharper now. The Ushabti melted before it. I wasn't sure because I wasn't focused on it, but it seemed as if a white fire burned along the transparent edge of the blade.

Saying the whole time, Jen, oh Jen, take the energy.

Take the energy. Please.

Come on babe.

The killing of the golems, the vampires, the thralls who were left, it was more a mechanical motion to me now, than anything else. Something I did because it needed to be done. Like chopping wood. There was a lifting and falling of the sword, then a moving on to the next golem. The next vampire. The next thrall.

Always glancing north. Never paying attention to what was before me. Hoping to see something, anything.

Hoping to *feel* something, anything...

Give 'em hell, babe...

The words kept rolling around Jen's mind. Mixing with her other thoughts there. Her chance to heal herself. Her thoughts of Grimm-not-Grimm and what they shared. The three words avoided the stabbing, painful area. But they surfaced constantly; they stayed conscious, swimming at the forefront of her brain as if they were trying to tell Jen something.

She didn't know what it could be. All she knew was a cold, dark feeling. The cold of the stone under her legs. The same cold stone, the stone of the tunnel, pressed against her back. All of that coldness leeched the last of the energy from Jen.

No bullets kicked down the tunnel anymore. The loudest sound was the keening, a dirge-like echoing along the tunnel, growing and fading in volume from up the ramp. The siren call muffled soft, fading screams underneath its song.

Then blackness. Not blackness, but the closing of Jen's eyes. She shook her head. Tried to shake herself awake. The nausea that usually came with the shaking was gone. As if her stomach was empty. As if *she* was empty, gone.

Give 'em hell, babe...

Give 'em hell—what?

Gone. All her friends. Her sister. The tunnel was empty of nothing now but blackness. There was nothing but Jen and the glimmering brightness far below her, the growing morning light that must have been the field.

What was it about those four words? What Nick had said to Sarah? Why were they so familiar to Jen? Why had they brought such an urgent message to her brain? Why did they circle so hard in her skull?

She had died once. She thought she was dying again. When she had wanted to not fear death, when she had wanted to become herself again. And if not herself, something greater. So why, when she was dying, did those words keep circling her brain?

Give 'em hell... Give 'em hell... Give 'em hell...

Merry Christmas, babe. Give 'em hell.

Everything came together.

And with that everything, a feel of *him*. Of Grimm-not-Grimm. GUS!

The memory swelled in her brain, pushed past the spike of pain. An image, a thought, a vision of him and her, of the two of them by the wall of cars outside of the dead zone, the horn of a train blowing, long and low in the distance.

Gus pressing the knife into her hand. The Five-Fold knife into her hands. What she had needed, what Gus had given her, so that she could come in and tear Sabnock's world down around the demon.

Merry Christmas babe...

And then, *give 'em hell.*

The feel of him, of everything he loved about her, of everything he wanted to, along their bond.

The Bond!

The thoughts crystallized, and Jen became aware of him. Of Gus, so far away. Of the bond that would always tie them together. Of all the fear and worry Gus held for her, the screaming pain he radiated, so full of ethereal energy he burned brightly on the other side of their bond. Burned with ethereal energy. Fiery in his power.

The bond. The keystone. What Gus had once jokingly called the keydrop. What had always been the knife, what had given Gus the idea in the first place to build the knives in the first place.

Jen reached out along the bond, her thoughts, her figurative hand, shaking.

What was a normally solid, firm connection between them felt thin now. Vague. She wandered along the bond, crawled along a blank space, staggered in the void between them. A heaviness weighed on her as if she walked a dark mist, each footstep taking immense strength, and yet she felt nothing as her foot touched upon the ground.

Time stretched. Her head ached. Darkness swirled around her.

Then she felt Gus. Felt the power he held. Felt him holding it all for her. Pressing the ethereal energy towards her, forcing it down the bond between them.

And she took it.

Took it all.

Healing herself as she did.

Icy chills burst over and around and through her body. The pain centered in her skull, the iciness becoming a numbing, then a sharp pain with something tugging there. Something in her skull, tugging outwards from it. She poured more energy into her body, taking it from Gus, and there was an explosive eruption of healing as bone and tissue and brain came together in a loud smacking, crunching sound.

Jen gasped. Something clattered to the ground. Part of the bolt that had been stuck in the windshield of the Express. As if, during the crash, the bolt and become free of the glass and finished its journey, thunking into the side of Jen's head.

She fingered the shaft; the bolt was thicker than her index finger. Her eyes opened at the realization. Then narrowed, as Jen remembered where she was. What was happening.

Anger burned through her then. Anger. Vengeance. Thoughts of her friends, of her sister, out there fighting. Thoughts of them almost being without her. Thoughts of her failing them, failing Gus.

She would not let that happen.

Jen found herself snarling.

A faint cry from Gus. A question. Hidden behind the power she was drawing from him. Drawing through their bond, from the keystone.

I'm good, she thought back.

She was better than good. The healing kept up throughout her; the coolness washed over her body and became a peppermint-like icy sensation floating across her skin. Like a chill winter breath had gusted across her.

Following that sensation came the tingle of electricity. Powered by a hundred ghosts. Powered from the bond between Jen and Grimm. A thick tendril of it, invisible through the air but a bright, brilliant white in her mind.

Radiating. Pulsing. Swelling. Powered by Gus, but also powered by her fury.

Lightning burst from Jen. It flickered through the tunnel, lighting it all up in flashes of electric blue. Sparks of bolts lifted her up off the ground and tiny fork-like bolts burst out from her every step as Jen strode down the tunnel into the bright lights of the Crown of Bones.

Onto the field. Against the demon and his army there. Into the madness of the fight.

Sabnock had herded them all here. Had wanted them in the stadium, for whatever reason he had. He would get more than he bargained for.

I am the storm.

Game on.

CHAPTER THIRTY

The press of stone-like bodies pushed down on me. There was a weird, sweet, sickly scent to them. As if the clay they had been made from was rotting inside, as if the kiln that had hardened their bodies had baked that smell in.

The golems seemed to weigh as much as a car. Once a couple of them were on top of me it took every ounce of energy I could pull to push them off. Push them away and then swing the sword. Another time, I had to summon the sword so that it punched through the creature so I could roll out from under the golem. But I always killed, killed each one, sucking their ghost away, disappointed each time when I found the spirit wasn't Hector.

That ghost was still out there. Somewhere. Waiting.

I had lost Michael. Something had exploded near us, I thought another rocket. Whatever it had been had blasted the angel's face with rock and pieces of metal. The last vision I had of him had been his eyes burning in fire, the fire bursting from his face, and him leaping into the air to descend wherever it was that the rocket had been fired from.

Michael hadn't been lying, when he had said the Ushabti had worn them down with numbers. It still made me wonder how many there could have been back then when the few hundred left here were taking everything we had and kept coming. Kept pressing onward. Kept swinging their swords and axes, kept dragging me into their crowd.

Even ethereal energy had its limits.

Well, the energy itself had no limit. Not that I had found. The limit was in me. In how much I could force myself to keep pulling.

And I was nearing an end.

My muscles ached with effort. The ethereal sword, so light in my hands, seemed to weigh more than the golems. Still, I swung. Still, the ethereal sword's edged burned in a white flickering flame. Still, I kept one eye on the Ushabti in front of me, one eye always, always, on the bond.

On the pain I felt there. The splitting pain from her echoing in my own skull.

Jen, oh Jen, be okay.

A bullet struck my forehead and bounced off. It hit hard enough that I stumbled back. Losing focus on the Ushabti. Shaking my head to clear it.

And the golems grabbed me again. One. Two, three piled on top. A stone sword thrust at my stomach; I felt the tip of it press inward, push on the organs underneath, and I screamed as I pulled more and more energy. Swallowed more and more memories. Hardened the skin and organs against the press of the sword.

And then, from the bond, an awakening.

JEN.

She came across the bond, shaking with the effort. I could feel it, her light brush of mind and soul against mine. She flooded me, and the sickly smell of rot and decay went away. Became the sweet smell of honeysuckle. The hard sweat on my skin became refreshed with the feeling of a cool rain.

I almost let go then; I was so happy. Thrilled to feel her. Even as the ethereal energy I held was sucked from me. Sucked along the bond. Torn from me like a black hole takes in everything around it.

I gave it to her. Everything I had. Until the stone sword of the Ushabti almost punched through my skin. I still gave her more, and more, feeling her body heal itself, feeling the icy chill radiate through her, feeling the pain in her brain disappear in a particular chilly blast of healing, and then, I felt her anger, her anger at the demon.

Then, all I felt was lightning. Bursting from my Jen. Bursting from her in a way that it came back through the bond. The lightning flickered through me, crackled from the sword, blew apart the golems that held me in a way that left heavy, rock-like chunks falling back down in the air around me, pieces of boulders thumping into the ground.

I smiled to myself.

Then gathered myself.

There was some killing to do.

The stands of the stadium ringed the field. The seats alternated color, so that the bottom bowl seemed gray, circled above by a thin ring of yellow, and then more gray, gray all the way to the top of the stands.

There a partial roof circled overhead, just far enough over the field so that most of the seats all sat in shadows. The only section not in darkness was the western side of the field, where the morning sun had risen enough that yellow rays lit up the gray seats there.

The rays were only broken up by the metal plates Sabnock had raised up above. Tall square plates, each the size of a wall of a house, circling the hole in the roof above the field. Circling it and angled so that the metal faced the field. The face of each plate seemed oddly shiny.

The field itself was brown, the thin wispy brown of dead and dying grass, as well as the lighter patted brown of dirt, from millions and millions of trampling feet. From all the humans Sabnock had forced into the center of his dead zone. From all the people that had become locusts in the center of the pentagram.

From where Sabnock stood, even now. The tall, dark demon standing in the center of the field, gold glinting from the lion on his shoulder, the golden plate on his chest, the links of gold hanging between pieces of his armor. There was a deep, black crater to his left, as if a grenade or a rocket had missed the demon, exploding off to his side. Otherwise, the demon was surrounded by the golems, with their weird rock-like bodies streaked with dark greens and crimsons, with their skulls, like helmets, the plume of some feather or something sticking out from the back of their head.

Much like the bolt that had struck Jen.

Her hands clenched. She strode from the tunnel, onto the field. Seeing all that. Smelling the smoke of guns. Hearing the cracks of gunfire, single-shots and bursts. Hearing the shouts and screams that came from a pitched battle.

A quick glance showed Jen her friends. Johnny, to the left. Behind a low-lying concrete wall, the lowest wall that always sat in front of the first row of seats. The long tube of the RPG lay thrown off to the side; he was ducked behind the concrete, sneaking up only for a quick burst of his assault rifle.

Gabrielle was much further down from Johnny. In a crowd of vampires and thralls, and a couple of the golems. The vampire had a blade in one hand and a shorter, compact gun in the other, and was slicing and shooting in the middle of a crowd.

Nick blurred in, here and there, in the shadows.

He would pop up quickly to the side of Gabrielle, cutting someone with a knife. He appeared once behind Johnny, pulling him down as gunfire split apart the chairs behind him. Nick held his Five-Fold blade in his hand, flickering around the stands, cutting anyone around the ring that stood close to a shadow.

Jen saw his problem. Sabnock stood in the middle of the field. Directly under the center of the hole in the roof. Directly in the center of the Crown of Bones, in the morning sun, where no shadows lay.

At least, no shadows Nick could appear out of.

At best, her friends were held to a standstill. The demon stood in the center of his place of power, in full light. Bullets that struck him didn't seem to hurt Sabnock. They seemed to just disappear. Almost wink away.

And the demon himself seemed to stand there. Jen could almost see his smile. She definitely thought the lion pauldron, the golden thing on his shoulder, had an expression that was almost laughing.

Well, she could fix that.

If the demon wasn't in the shadows, he was under the sky.

And Jen ruled the sky.

She called lightning. Pulling power from the bond, pulling it from Gus, who seemed to be pulling even more to give to her. She could feel the memories he lived at the edges of her consciousness, feel him push those memories away and pull even more.

The power surged through Jen.

Sabnock saw her, then.

Just as lightning drummed down through the hole in Crown of Bones. As the bolts tattooed the earth, thundering around the golems and the demon. Thundered in flashes so big and bright everything on the field disappeared under a glow of brilliant sapphire.

STORM OF SOULS • 269

Then silence. A deafening silence. The rumbling, the thunder, echoing away until her ears could hear the little things again. The ticks and tacks of bits of golem as they rained around the field. The screams of those on the field that were still alive.

The shouts of her friends.

Nick appeared to her, then. Stepping from the shadows to give Jen a quick hug. He spared no words and disappeared as quickly as he came.

Then he surged from the pit in the center of the field. The hole made by a grenade or maybe Johnny's RPG. The hole made even larger by Jen's barrage of lightning.

A hole with a deep, dark shadow inside it.

Nick leapt from the pit, leapt from that shadow, the Five-Fold blade bright in one hand. He was fast and quick and merciless, taking one step and bounding into the air, falling on Sabnock, the demon struggling to get up.

Nick plunged the blade deep into Sabnock's side. Right underneath one of his arms.

The demon screamed. No, not screamed. Roared, a thundering roar of a thousand voices splitting the air. A roar that shook the stadium, shook the Crown of Bones.

There was another flash. This time of red, bright red. Like the flashing of red alert strobes. Nick went flying, still holding onto the blade. Sabnock was there, getting on one knee, a staff suddenly in his hand. A black staff with a gold blade at the top of it, something sharp and pointed, with something that looked oddly like a gold sun underneath it.

Things started to happen all at once. Johnny ran onto the field, Jen's Five-Fold blade in his hand. Moving faster than a human could. Firing his assault rifle in one hand, cutting down the occasional golem-knight, or vampire, trying to stand. Ducking and bobbing and weaving past the creatures as he ran. Gabrielle close beside him, cutting and shooting to help clear the way.

Johnny got close enough to the demon to cut him. Slice him along one arm. There was the brief flash of energy, the scream again by Sabnock, the stadium-shaking roar of a thousand voices, and then the staff whipped out. There was a crack, and Johnny flew through the air, tumbling over and over the field, until he lay there, motionless.

A scream from Gabrielle. A paused moment where she stood in front of the demon, Sabnock standing now. Then a blur of motion as the vampire danced with her blade, shooting her compact pistol so fast it seemed like it was an automatic.

The staff whirred, met the blade. The bullets disappeared as if they became mist drifting past the demon. Then Gabrielle slipped, and there was a second crack.

And another motionless body.

Jen strode out onto the field. Blue sparks flicking out from each step. Bits of dried, dead grass flamed out in bright winks under her feet, leaving blackened prints behind her.

Sabnock was standing now. Standing in the center of the penta-gram. A brilliant red glow around the demon, a glow coming from bright, crimson lines around him. Thick crimson lines in a star-like pattern, repeated larger and larger as the pattern expanded throughout the field.

The pentagram.

The demon stood in the very center of the pattern. The very center of the smallest star. The very center of five lines, tracing the shape of the center, smallest pentagram. The red flowed from all the lines into the demon's body, flowed up his limbs, healing the wound in his side, the cut along the arm. It flowed into his hands, forming big red blazing fists.

The pentagram was powering up, and the demon was taking part of that power into himself. There was a relationship between the two, between the Zatar, Gus had said Sabnock had called the pentagram, and the demon. Sabnock stood there, the redness running from the lines into his body, powering himself up.

Two could play at that game.

Jen walked closer, stopped about ten paces away, and drew from her bond. Drew from the ethereal energy there. From Gus. The pulsing white radiance with the tiniest of blue centers. A blue core of power under the white brilliance.

She let the lightning play along her body. Spark as it worked itself up her legs, around her stomach, her core, fork into flickering sapphire tendrils as the bolts worked around her shoulders, her arms, her hands.

Her fists of lightning.

Sabnock grinned.

"So, storm witch," the demon said, in a deep, echoing voice. "We finally meet."

Jen stood there a moment. Her lightning hissing and spitting as the bolts flickered. They were bright blue and brilliant, but also small when up against the glow of crimson that lit up the stadium. Like the smallest flashlight pen, lying in one of those red-light rooms.

There was some motion behind the demon. Nick, struggling to get up. He lay face down, his arms moved weakly. One leg drew itself up.

She wanted to distract the demon. But she wanted even more to be herself. Be the old Jen. The one that had lived through Grafton, fighting Raphael. The one that had taken on Kimaris with Gus. The Jen that had walked with Gus into the cemetery in New Orleans, lightning balled around her fists.

"You wanted me here," she finally said. "You'll regret it."

The corner of Sabnock's lip curled up, slightly. "Hubris. Just like your bastard angel."

"It seems to me the other way," she said. "You've been out of this world for a few thousand years, and you come back and get all angry about *my angel* threatening you."

She *was* angry. Furious. Tiny sparks of lightning spat from her hand and fell to the ground, hissing the entire way. Burning the grass there. "Tell me, why would a little old threat like that bother a big, mighty demon like yourself?"

Sabnock's mouth opened, but she cut the demon off. Because she knew the answer. Knew it intimately, and maybe, just maybe, had finally come to terms with it now.

"Because you fear the truth."

Nick was on one knee. Shaking his head as if to clear it. One hand pressed to his temple. The other around the Five-Fold blade.

The demon's mouth remained open. It took him a moment to close it. When he did, his eyes narrowed in the same motion.

"You think I have nothing to say."

Nick's head turned. Looked at the stadium wall. Found Jen and Sabnock. His hand went to his knife.

"None of us likes someone who talks too much, at the end," Jen said. Pulling more energy from the bond. Getting ready, bringing up a second fist, lightning dripping from that hand as well.

"Maybe one thing, before we fight," Sabnock said. He swelled before her, slowly growing taller. As if the energy of the stadium had filled the demon to bursting and was pushing his body outward. "Call it the stakes of the game, if you will."

Jen was ready. She was full of power and fury. She was full of anger and energy and wanted more than anything to take this fight now. To wipe this demon from the Earth, and with him his plague of locusts, his armies, and most of all, to wipe away her fear forever.

The timing was perfect. Nick had started running. A few more steps and he could dive into the shadow. Come out of the hole at the same time as Jen started throwing lightning.

It would be easy with the demon still talking. Still *explaining*. Jen would wipe his mocking smile from his face.

"Here, in the very center of my power, I build things. I *change* things." Sabnock's fists swelled with more and more crimson, the red lines thicker along his fingers, as if veins of dark red blood slithered over his hands.

There was a slight pause in Jen's anger. Her fear. Her thoughts followed the demon's words.

"Let me ask you, storm witch. You've died once already. Do you think your angel can bring you back again, if you die again and become a thousand locusts?"

Her pause became uncertainty.

One of Sabnock's hands made a fluttering motion, the red glow streaking lazily behind his fingers. "Buzzing so prettily around the air?"

Her uncertainty became fear.

Nick dove for the shadow that lay between the wall and the field.

Sabnock snapped the fingers waving in the air, the red streaks sharpening up behind the motion, as if the streak had snapped its ghostly fingers, too.

At the same time all the metal plates, the ones ringing the top of the stadium, angled so that they faced down into the field, all those plates lit up. Lit up brilliantly with that red glow, like the lava-like burning of the center of the sun. Like the fiery center of a million suns.

And in that moment, shadows ceased to exist in the Crown of Bones.

Nick hit the wall and fell to the ground. The knife tumbled from his hand.

Jen's fear froze her.

Sabnock laughed then, a mocking laughter with its deep echoing of a thousand other voices laughing underneath his. The laughter filled the stadium and seemed to burst outward into the air.

Her fists almost fizzled out. The demon had planned for them to come here. Had planned everything, even for Nick. Had planned to bring them here and make them all locusts. Like he had millions of other people.

What would happen to her then? Would she be dead? Could Sabnock stop her soul at the gateway between life and death and take her to some land of undead? Could he remake her as a thousand locusts? A million?

She was scared then. Really scared. As she hadn't been, ever before.

Until a thought surfaced. One that had circled round and round in her brain. Something that had stayed close enough in her mind that it broke through her fear, as if that thought had known she would need it. The thought that had awakened her back in the tunnel.

Give 'em hell, babe.

It was just a thought. It didn't banish her fear. But it was enough for her to be aware of it. It was enough to have her push her fear away, enough for her to focus, even as it buzzed around her like the locusts had. Like the bullet had, zipping through the air, aimed at her heart.

Those were just thoughts, though. Her fear was just a thought. And as soon as she wanted it to be, it would be gone. It could be gone. She would give Sabnock hell. All the hell he could handle. It would be him or her, in the end, and she *would not* let her fear decide it before it even began.

Her fists sparked up again. They blazed. Lightning poured from her hands, waterfalls of sizzling electric blue bolts crashing to the ground and spilling across the field.

And then Jen became the storm.

Lightning burst through the hole in the stadium. Large bolts, thicker than cars, striking towards the earth. Striking towards Sabnock.

Where it stopped. Halfway in the stadium. Meeting an equally large bolt, a thick red crimson, that had burst *up* from the ground. Like a geyser of red lightning.

The two bolts met. Blue and red. Where they mashed they became a deep, radiating purple. Forks of blue lightning split off to the side, dancing through the air. Flickering blood-red arcs met those forks, a hundred thousand red and blue sparks met and spit and hissed and burned.

"So," Sabnock said. The demon seeming even taller now. Bigger. Pushed outward and upward by the thick, red glow. "It begins."

CHAPTER THIRTY-ONE

I fell to a knee. The burst of fear along the bond had shocked, surprised me. There was a feeling of a fight, of need, of a battle for life and death.

And the fear, pausing Jen. The uncertainty. The sound of a bullet and the buzzing of locusts. Some of it confused me, but most of it angered me.

With that anger, I pulled ghost.

I would make sure it was life for Jen. And death to Sabnock and his fucking plans.

I popped one ghost, then the next. I banished them to wherever it was they went and pushed their energy through the bond, to Jen, bursting one ghost after another, swallowing the spirits and their memories and their energies, pushing down their screwed-up lives, and pushing energy along the bond.

I had my pick of ghosts. The field was littered with them. The land was littered with them. Mexico was an old, old place. I pulled, even as the Ushabti pressed against me. I pulled even more, sending it to Jen.

And, to top it off, as I pushed the energy to her I screamed *give 'em hell babe*.

It was then I felt Jen's fear turn to anger.

It was then I felt her pull on the bond, take all the ethereal energy, and then felt the storm coming down on Sabnock.

Around me the Ushabti closed in. The swords, the axes, the hands hacked at me, grabbed at me. I hardened my skin and prepared for the worst. Stone axes descended like anvils on my head, my skull ringing with the blow. Stone swords struck my chest, the reverberations shaking through me.

Still I kept on. Staying on one knee. Ignoring what I could. Pulling ghost after ghost and feeding Jen.

It was more important to me to power her than protect myself.

I thought the Ushabti started to laugh. Though the sounds the golems made were funny. Their mouths didn't seem to move much; they were hollow, grim holes through which cavernous sounds echoed as they swung.

So I ignored them. Pulling. Banishing. Pushing power through the bond. I ignored the strikes of their swords, the pounding of the axes.

All that mattered was Jen.

And that's when I knew we had it all. That's when armor burst through my skin. Sliding over my arms, my back. The blue-black plates swelled over me until I was covered in them.

Swords broke when they connected. Axes shattered. It was me who laughed then. Laughed and pulled and banished.

A grin broke from me. And a scream. No words, just a challenge. A roar. A *defiance*.

All the while sitting in my armor of faith, protected from everything, a generator of ethereal energy, transmitting all the power I could to the one person who needed it.

The stadium, a field that had hosted soccer teams and football teams, with stands that had once held hundreds of thousands of people, had quickly become an arena for just two.

Jen and the demon.

No one else moved. No one else could move. Nick lay where he had hit the wall, seemingly out of it. Johnny and Gabrielle hadn't moved at all. Both of the Five-Fold blades lay near each of them, near Johnny and Nick, but Jen felt like she was on her own.

There were other bodies around. Dead vampires, dead or dying humans. People who had fought for Sabnock. And then there were the stone-like golem-knights, most of them blown to pieces, with arms and legs lying over the field, moving on their own as if trying to find the body they had been separated from.

And then there was Sabnock.

Red lightning blasted upward from the ground, thick red bolts crashing around Jen in geyser-like eruptions. Each crimson bolt was met with lightning she called from the skies above, thick bright blue streaks thundering from the heavens to pummel the earth, meeting the crimson lightning in brilliantly purple blasts of light.

The demon swelled with his power. He was two stories tall now, thick red lines coursing around and through his dark body as if a sickness raced through his skin, his veins. The lines broke out of his body and dove back in, and through their fight the lines just got more and more distended, pulsing with bright globs of power.

Sabnock laughed.

Jen screamed.

And pulled more lightning down on the demon.

The bolts struck and clapped down his golden lion's pauldron. The lightning bounced off his golden armor, reflected like a mirror, and zig-zagged along the field. Ozone thickened along the ground like fog, the scent mixed with charred meat and something like rotting eggs.

She felt Gus pushing energy towards her. She sucked it all in, almost inhaling it, feeling the power course through her body. Feeling electricity tingle along her skin, the charge of it raising her hair along the backs of her forearms, even her scalp.

Still, it wasn't enough.

The demon reflected every bolt that struck him. His crimson lightning met Jen's sapphire bolts along the field. He laughed at every rumble of thunder.

And he waited.

Waited for Jen to tire.

Because even where the mind was committed, where the mind was strong, where Jen was focused, her body could only do this for so long.

She had called a lot of lightning this day. It had begun back in Cuernavaca. It had continued with Gus, where they had met the oncoming convoy. It had gone on in the train, where she had almost died.

And now, this.

There came a moment when Jen stopped calling lightning. The demon did the same. She stood there watching him smile, watching Sabnock, all the while taking deep breaths. Her muscles trembled with the power she had called. Her knees felt weak, like they could give out at any moment.

And the demon knew it.

"Like I mentioned before," Sabnock said, white teeth glistening behind grinning dark lips, lips now running with threads of crimson. One hand moving to encircle the field under the Crown of Bones. "Humans."

Everything about the demon was big. Too big. Both feet planted on the center of the Zatar, in the middle of the center of the pentagram that stretched outward across the field. The red lines powering the pattern pulsed and ran up his legs and into his body.

"You fail to understand your limits," Sabnock said. "It is what kills each of you, every time. The reaching for something you can never have. Flying too close to the sun. You become angry when the sun swats you. When we put you in your place. Thousands of years, and you never, ever learn."

Jen locked her knees. Fought to stay standing. It seemed like she couldn't get enough air.

"Look at you, storm witch," Sabnock continued. His voice getting deeper. Echoing harder. As if all his voices were angry. "Weak, the flesh. *Weak*." The demon motioned around. "Here, here are your friends. Look at them. *Look*."

Nick's hands were on his head. One leg moved, weakly. Drumming the ground once, twice. As if he was trying to pull himself up by force of will.

Johnny, finally, had started to move. One arm had levered himself up. The other looked broken. His gaze was blurred; he caught Gabrielle lying there and froze.

The demon sneered. "And your sister? The death siren? She lies outside the stadium, storm witch. Lies where she fell because she, too, was weak."

Jen closed her eyes. Let her emotions wash over her. Let the fear and the worry and the pain flow over her, running over her skin like water, and wash away.

Then she opened her eyes. Put on her best Gus-like grin. If it was going to be it, she was going out with a bang.

Jen?... came the distant thought.

It's okay Gus, she said. And it was okay. She had come to terms with it. With death. With whatever it took to save the human race.

Some things were worth that sacrifice.

And with that thought, she began reaching high into the air, higher than she ever had. Calling a storm unlike any she had called before, calling a storm from the heavens themselves. Pulling more and more energy from Gus and still needing more.

Give me everything you have.

Gus strained from his side of the bond. Jen felt—weakly felt— things striking his body as he pulled on the ghosts around him. She felt him roar his defiance and anger, even as she felt his stomach turn at the memories flooding through him.

And that strengthened her.

For someone to love her like Gus did, to go through what he was going through for her, to always have sacrificed that for her... that was a strength all its own.

Jen?

More, Gus, she said. Reaching higher. Gathering the storm. *More.*

Sabnock's head tilted a bit. As if he knew something was happening, but couldn't understand quite what it was. The time seemed to slow, like it always did at the end. Like the last few moments of the bullet before it struck.

The demon gathered his crimson power. Grew another story taller. Swelling and swelling, gorging himself on the energy. The red lines ran so thick around him they were no longer separate; a bloody sheet of power flowed over Sabnock.

Jen pulled the same amount from the bond.

Nick's leg thumped another time.

Johnny lay his good hand on Gabrielle's shoulder.

And Jen reached higher, pulled more, so much ethereal energy from the bond that it seemed to empty, briefly, into her.

More.

She heard, more than felt, Gus scream as he stopped pulling

ghosts one or two at a time. As he pulled ghosts by the dozens, then the hundreds. His scream became a sharp exclamation of defiance, a gathering of strength, a roar of rage, followed by pain.

Power exploded into her. The bond itself erupted with ethereal energy. It felt like a firehose was pouring power into her. Ten fire-hoses. A thousand.

Sabnock screamed as crimson bolts erupted from the stadium, large red geysers bursting in the air, one after the next, racing towards Jen.

At the same time, Jen screamed and pulled the storm she had been calling down.

And as everything met, as sapphire and crimson collided, a bright orchid flash exploded over the stadium, blinding everyone. It blew Jen back; she tumbled to the ground, and she couldn't tell if her eyes were open or closed. Either way, all she could see was darkness, darkness the color of dark plums.

Then the color brightened, became a brilliant afterglow of blue. A pure blue with no hint of red.

And then the blue faded, faded into the sky above them. A sky of pale blue, dotted here and there with tiny, puffy white clouds.

And dotted with other things as well. Tiny white crystals falling from the heavens. Dozens of them. Then hundreds. Then millions.

Snow. Huge flakes of it dropping out of the sky.

In Mexico.

Jen looked from where she lay on the ground. Sabnock lay in the middle of his field, his back to the ground, his dark body darker with char. The demon was smaller now, the size of Jen, and his form did not move. Nick and Johnny were exactly where they had been, both of their faces now upturned.

Already the snow was covering the field, but the crimson lines of the pentagram were gone. The *lines* were gone, the things built by Azazel. The Zatar had been broken, the pattern shattered. Nothing left.

The dead zone was gone.

Jen closed her eyes, exhausted, empty. Letting the cool flakes light upon her skin, enjoying the cool sensation of snow, reaching out to Gus to tell him the good news.

CHAPTER THIRTY-TWO

I felt when Jen won.

Not the fight with Sabnock. The battle within herself. The overcoming of her fear and doubts and worry. The understanding of the sacrifice she would have to make to save her friends. The *being okay with it*. And not just being okay with it, but being committed to giving everything she had, even her life, to save those she loved. To save the world.

There was power in that. Power in understanding what you could do and what you couldn't stand for. Power in understanding your worth in the grand scheme of things. Power in the lessening of fear, of the knowledge that you would gladly give your life for something greater than yourself.

Merry Christmas, babe.

I hadn't known any of that would happen. But I couldn't be happier that it did. That Jen was my Jen again, was someone capable of facing down giants. Of being the rock of all rocks. Of calling a storm unlike any other.

Even now I could see it, see *her*, reaching high into the skies above Mexico City. Flickering thin tendrils of ethereal energy, maybe invisible to everyone else, invisible to the world, reached up into the air like thousands of fingers, reached higher and higher, a giant's hand forming to claw the very heavens and drag it all back down.

She was going to wipe Sabnock from the face of the Earth.

She was planning to sacrifice herself in the attempt.

It was my job to keep that from happening.

Spirits surrounded me. Ghostly forms, shimmering white and blue, some tinged with red, stood in a crowd, stood in waves circling me. They spread out as the distance grew, spread out over the earth, but I could see them on my radar. *Feel* them around me.

Just like I felt the axe breaking over my armor. The occasional sword shattering. The grabbing of my arms by the Ushabti, holding me there on the ground, one knee firmly planted in the dirt.

I pulled ghost like I had never pulled before. Two at a time. Three. Four. Memories flooded into me: some girl stabbing a cat, some guy stabbing a girl, some guy in an old truck running over someone on a dark street and then driving on.

And those were the good ones.

I pulled more. Four at a time. Ten. Until the ethereal energy almost burned in me. Pushing it along the bond, letting it power Jen's storm of storms. When the bond started to resist I just pushed harder, pushed with the force of energy I was pulling.

Twenty ghosts at a time.

A hundred.

I pulled them all. Memories flooded through me—rapes and murders and thieves, puppy-kickers and child molesters, a group of guys in a barn, doing who knows what there. I roared my rage and gathered more strength, banished everything in waves, banishing all the spirits, the child molesters, the puppy-kickers, the stabbers and the murderers and the guy still driving his ghostly truck down the road.

I screamed aloud and sucked everything, all the spirits, and in the same motion, banished them all.

Holding more energy than I thought possible. The ethereal plane around me was empty. Each ghost, gone. Every spirit, banished. There was me, there was Jen, there was the bond between us pulling at me, powering up the storm Jen was calling.

More...

I started pushing more towards Jen.

That was when Hector struck.

A sword burst from my chest. A thick sword glowing a crimson red. Glowing with the same power I had seen a long time ago, powering the lines of the pentagram in New Orleans. Glowing with the same color I had seen in Hector's dark spirit. Madness. Rage. Hate.

The pain was immense.

My scream turned into a cry of pain. Then nothing, as all the breath left my body. It seemed like I could see myself; I was outside of the Grimm kneeling on the dirt, a thick, crimson stone sword jutting out of my chest, the hilt flat against my back, Hector standing behind me with one foot planted firmly on my leg.

I could see the storm Jen was creating, the giant stormy hand, the splayed fingers, reaching higher and higher into the stratosphere. I could see the bond between us, almost breaking under the strain of ethereal energy I was sending to Jen. I could see the land around me, empty of ghosts or spirits.

I was dying.

Hector was killing me.

But not just in this life.

His spirit tore into mine. I felt his ghost around me as I drifted outside my body. His ghostly hands burned as he gripped my head and tried to tear it from my ethereal corpse. I could hear him, laughing madly, trying to drag me down to wherever it was he lived.

It would take everything I had to keep me alive.

And that would cost Jen her life.

Which really wasn't a choice, was it?

With no breath, I screamed. I raged.

I swung my ghostly arms and pounded into Hector. I saw, with my ghostly eyes, Michael in the distance. Descending in the air towards me.

Hector's laugh grew stronger. His spirit dragged me further and further away from my body. Down, always down. I could feel two things: my spirit in flames, and my body growing cold. Even now I was halfway out, my ghostly being dragged from out of my chest, my face, transparent in the air, screaming with no sound.

I was good at one thing. I was good at swinging until the end. Stubborn, to a fault. So, even in the face of death, I gathered and pushed everything I had into the bond. Sent all the energy from every ghost I had banished, sent every pure thought I had along with it, anything and everything that was a part of me I pushed along towards Jen.

The stormy many-fingered hand wrapped around the heavens. A huge burst of ethereal energy flooded up the hand, along the fingers, sparking out into the stratosphere. Clouds formed among the fingers, appearing as if they had always been there, thick bolts of lightning striking back down to the earth from among them.

And after the lightning had struck. After the thunder had rumbled. After everything had been blown away by a brilliant blue flash, there was a sound of silence. A sound of peace. And, in that peace, tiny flakes drifted down from the heavens. Cold flakes of snow, sparkly even in the distance, glittering like a million diamonds falling from the sky.

Not a storm of storms.

A storm of souls.

I sat forever, watching the flakes swirl and lower and dissipate as they fell. Watching souls fade. Watching snow fall. Images flickered through me. Nick, popping in and out of shadows. Johnny, with his trademark grin. Sarah, playing the guitar.

And Jen. A million images of her. The night on the water tower, looking down on the tiny lights of Grafton, her hip pressed against mine. Finding her in the factory there, years later, saving her from Azazel. The two of us, back-to-back, in New Orleans.

And the one of us at Christmas. A large snowfall outside, the snow covering a house like a blanket. Inside was a warm couch, a crackling fire, and the two of us huddled together with some hot chocolate. With marshmallows. The Christmas tree with many-colored lights and a slightly tilted star. And Sinatra playing from a scratchy record; a warm, comforting feeling of family, of peace.

The song played on in my mind, but the sound faded, as if I was moving further and further away from the player. The bulbs of the Christmas tree blinked slower, and slower, and even slower still. They turned on and off in long, patient breaths, in dying glimmers, the greens and the blues and the reds winking out, one by one.

The snow fell on. The fire dimmed in the fireplace. One by one the bulbs burned out, leaving just the star at the top of the tree, streaming its bright white rays, valiantly struggling against the oncoming night.

It grew a little chilly. The inside of the house got darker. The blanket, the couch missing; I shivered. The sweet mug of hot chocolate was just a memory on my tongue. Sinatra grew more and more faint in my ears, as something dragged me further and further away…

I tried to catch myself. One last gasp of the living. Drag myself back to the song. Back to the house under the blanket, with the crackling fire and the couch and the hot chocolate and Jen, but there was nothing to grab. Nothing to pull back to. Everything around me was black, and the image kept fading until it was finally gone.

Have yourself a merry little Christmas babe.

I'll miss you.

Make sure to give 'em hell.

CHAPTER THIRTY-THREE

J en screamed.

Her scream went on forever until she choked at the end of it. Took another breath and screamed until her voice grew hoarse. She lay there with tiny flakes of snow dropping out of the sky, the chilly flakes melting as they touched upon her skin, reaching for Gus over and over. Reaching for him and finding nothing. NOTHING.

The bond was gone. Severed, maybe. Where Gus had been there was an emptiness. A hole. A darkness from which came the image of a Christmas tree, star slightly tilted, the colored bulbs winking slowly, winking as if to the slow beating of a heart, each bulb growing dark on its own, never to brighten again, one by one until all that was left was the star...

And then it too, faded.

Something had happened. And now Gus was gone.

And she knew why. She had felt the pain of it happening. The incredible storm of energy crashing down the bond after his burst of pain. She had known what he had done, and she had known why, and she wanted to curse him for it, but couldn't.

However long she had screamed, she finally stopped. A hardness swelled inside her, something built of iron and steel, of fire and fury, and maybe a touch of darkness. Slowly she came to, struggling up, getting to her feet, and finally standing.

In the middle of the Crown of Bones. A broken crown now. The roof shattered. A part of the stadium blown outward. The center of the field, where the pentagram and been focused, looked as if the ground had erupted. A tiny white dusting covered it all, tiny flakes of snow falling over everything, falling around her, falling on the bleachers and the broken wall and the field.

Covering her in a chilly dampness.

There was the demon, Sabnock, lying on the ground. The tall figure blackened and torn and not moving. There were the Five-Fold blades buried in the turf. Sticking out like broken fingers. One close by Johnny, the other near the wall where Nick had been thrown. They radiated to Jen; she could feel them from here, they were so full of energy.

Her keystone, too, the tiny stone almost hummed along her skin. Ethereal energy coursed within her, Jen was full of it, and she pulled the smallest bit of it. The melted drops of snow burst from her in a cloud of electricity. It sparked and hissed until she controlled it, controlled the storm, pulled it all back until it lay within her.

She marched over to the demon.

Sabnock lay there. His dark skin charred and split all over. From each one a dark greenish fluid leaked, along with the smell of sickness, the sweet, sickly smell of rot and decay.

His lips cracked, smiled. Over teeth still too white. His voice came out in hoarse, echoey gasps. A laugh chuckling among the gasps. "I got one of you, didn't I?"

Jen's hands were clenched tight enough that pain came from her palms. Her nails had cut into her skin. Her eyes ran with tears. They streamed down her face to drop onto the demon's face.

Sabnock laughed, a choking thing. "I did, didn't I? The one that mattered." His eyelids fluttered, and the demon's head relaxed. "I told you, storm witch, you humans fly too close to the sun."

Jen said nothing. Just knelt next to Sabnock. Placed a hand flat against his chest. Found her place and called the storm within her.

The demon burst into a million fragments of ash, each piece of ash fluttering through the air, sparking in tiny glints of electric blue, tendrils of lightning dancing from one flake of ash to the next, burning each flake before leaping outward in thousands of forks of lightning, bursting outwards in the air. Rumbling, rushing outward, on and on and on.

For what seemed like forever. Jen remained there, on her knee. Her open, flat hand empty in the air. She had no sense of time, how much had passed, how much would pass.

There was just Gus.

And him no longer being *there*. Not in her bond. Not in her mind. Not in the place she had always sensed him, even after he had run away.

For a long time she had waited for him to come back to Grafton. She had known, from when they were kids, that he was different. That he was special in a way that many people couldn't be. That from his face, which would always look better if he smiled more, would be the face of a man who could change the world.

And now he was gone.

And now she would look up into the night sky, see the full moon there, the stars, and know that whatever she thought, she would know he wasn't there, thinking that same thought as well.

A hand touched her shoulder. Carefully. Slowly. As if Jen was a wounded animal.

She blinked. Once, twice, as many times as it took for her eyes to clear.

Nick stood there. He had found Sarah, and was holding her with one arm tucked around her waist. Her sister looked exhausted and so pale she was white, and could barely stand on her own.

But her sister was there. She had turned into her own storm, a storm of death, holding off Sabnock's army outside of the stadium, and Sarah had survived.

"He's gone?" Nick asked, simply. Understanding over his face.

Jen couldn't answer. Her arm fell to her side, and she huddled there on her knees, huddled into herself. Trying to breathe, trying to find a *reason* to breathe, until a big breath escaped her in a giant sob, a sob that racked her body and had her collapse back on the field.

She didn't feel Sarah falling next to her, holding onto Jen. Or Nick kneeling there beside her. Or Johnny and Gabrielle coming over, standing around them all. Each of them looking at each other, wondering what to do, while Jen cried on and on and on. Until she was empty. Until she knew for sure that he was gone.

CHAPTER THIRTY-FOUR

A while later Jen found out what had happened. What had really happened. The angel had flown in; Michael landed in the stadium, his white wings torn and blackened, his chest covered in gore. His eyes sad. His words quiet. His eyes closed.

"I was only a moment late."

The chill air in the stadium grew colder. A blast of it blew tiny dustings of snow around them, white flakes swirling madly for a moment before setting back into the field of white. The Crown of Bones had taken on its namesake, a bare skeleton of white concrete on a whiter field.

Jen had yet to really feel the cold, not inside her. Inside her was empty. There was the damp touch of the cold flakes on her skin.

Nothing seemed to penetrate any deeper.

"Did you kill him?" she asked.

A pause. A shake of the head. A slow subsiding of the warmth of the angel.

The angel knew who she meant. Hector, the spirit that had been so wrong, so evil.

His eyes flashed quickly with flames.

"I killed everyone."

And that was that.

Jen had wanted to see. So the five of them had gone back out there. Nick and Sarah. Johnny, his arm wrapped in a splint. Gabrielle, a thick knot swollen on the side of her head. They walked out of the stadium body, past hundreds, maybe thousands of dead, pale bodies there. They walked down the city, past the train station that was no longer there, the bits and pieces of the *Grimm Express*. Past where Alejandro and Millie had died.

It was a long walk, but they all walked it. Walked it until they got to *his* body, surrounded by hundreds of dead Ushabti, a sword still stuck through his back. He was kneeling, and facing north, facing the Crown of Bones, and his head bent forward, chin tucked against his chest, like Gus was just taking a break. His body almost still felt warm, but there was nothing within. No Gus. No feeling of *him*.

Jen had thought she was out of tears. But she hadn't been, by a long shot.

They cleaned Gus up and buried him there. By one of the lone desert willows. It was hard work, not the digging, but the doing of it.

The cleaning hadn't taken long. They didn't have much to clean him with. He looked empty, so empty. Limp. His head lolled some, until Jen couldn't bear holding him while she cleaned. And the wound in his chest was so wide...

The key was gone from his chest. Maybe torn in the battle. Jen searched for it for a while, lost in thought. Her eyes stayed there, even as she searched along the bond. It felt sheared. Gone. Flat.

Then they buried him. They stood there for a long time, Nick at the bottom of the grave with his hand on a shovel. A tool they had found along the way. His eyes, behind his glasses, laser-focused on something in his own past.

"I remember me and Grimm and Johnny burying Father Ben," he said aloud. Not really talking to Jen, but just talking. "I would have said then, Grimm would have been digging my grave first."

Jen didn't say anything. She let the shovel fall from her hand and leaned against the cold earth, damp and chill against her back. Snow still fell above them, a lighter snow with thin, delicate flakes. A Christmas tree kept popping into her thoughts, the last image she had had of Gus, the last thing he had given her, the winking lights and the dying star.

Finally, her words rough. "I know."

They wrapped him in what they had. The locusts had eaten most of everything, so just a blanket. A gray thing, scratchy, dark with stains. They wrapped that blanket tightly around Gus and buried him deep.

By then the group had collected again. Standing around the mound. The snow almost gone now, just an occasional glimmering of a flake in the darkening sky above Jen.

Nick said a quick prayer. His words quiet, almost thin in the chill air. There was no echo in them, no timbre; they were taken by the wind and gone as quickly as he spoke them.

Jen shivered. Everyone stood around. Nick, sad. Sarah leaning against him, her face turned towards the grave. Johnny's arm in a sling; his other arm around Gabrielle, her face swollen. Michael standing alone, almost swollen with something that might have been fury.

There was quiet. No crickets chirping. No birds calling. Nothing left in this land, nothing but this small group. *Them.*

A light piece of chilliness touched Jen's nose. The snowflake melted there, quick, became a damp spot to join those on her cheeks. She took a breath, a shuddering breath, and thought, underneath the breath, she could hear the old record player playing. Frank Sinatra singing his song. And though she heard the words, they meant nothing, not anymore.

It was Sarah that asked the question, then. The one on everyone's minds. "What do we do next?"

Jen wiped her face with the back of her hand. Quieted the Frank Sinatra in her mind. Took a long glance at the grave beneath her feet and the man underneath all that dirt. The man who had come for her when she had died. When she had been a ghost, he had made it his mission to bring her back, no matter what.

Then, though, she had been there. A ghost, but there. She couldn't *feel* Gus now. Not like she had, looking up at the night, knowing what he was thinking. Not like she had through their bond. Not like she had felt him, huddled under the blanket on her mom's couch, his body warm against hers and the two of them sipping from the same mug of hot chocolate...

Her hand lightly touched upon the shape of the key, still hanging underneath her shirt.

Gus...

Gus...please...Please just answer. Just give me something.

The answer was the quiet of a grave. The quiet of the land around them. The quiet of her own voice, in her answer. "We finish what we started."

Her hand clenched the shape of the key through her shirt. Even rounded, the amulet dug into her palm. There were more demons to answer for this. For Gus. More demons, more dead zones, and *the* demon, Azazel himself.

Jen remained there a long time. The breeze picked up, rattling the branches of the desert willow. The flakes of snow, the few that remained, fluttered in the air and occasionally lit upon her skin, melting in little drops. Each of her friends stood there, her sister stood there, they all waited for a while, with silent comfort.

Still, she stood. Her jaw set. Her hand clutching the lifeless key. Staring to the Northeast, over the lands, over the waters, to another continent. To other dead zones. To the demons there.

One demon in particular.

One by one her friends left. The angel. Her sister last, giving Jen a quick hug. Overhead the darkness came, on the same breeze of wind rattling the willow, a blustery darkness full of anger and hate and rage, full of demons and fear and the unknown.

She stood there for a long time. Not hearing the first shouts from her friends. Not seeing a figure climbing the dunes to the south. Not seeing a small figure there, waving something high in the air. Something round, something that glowed.

AFTERLOGUE

Afterlogue

STOP.

I had heard the word before. It had a ring to it, a bell-sounding toll that seemed to charge through wherever it was I was. A black place, a place of darkness, a place where it was just me and Hector locked in an eternal struggle, his elbow locked around my throat, my hands over my head, trying to tear myself from his grip.

The madman—the mad*spirit*—laughed. Said something in Spanish, something quick and guttural and full of a promise of pain. His words were hot in my ear, and his breath smelled like shit.

He just kept laughing. Kept breathing that foulness over me. Kept laughing, over and over, his arm locked around my throat.

I kicked. My legs hung in the air. *We* hung in the air. In whatever dream world this seemed to be.

STOP.

The words rang again. Washed through this world of dreams, this spirit world, and as the word washed over me, it also seemed to crystallize. Everything didn't quite freeze, but became more clear. The darkness had an outline to it. Hector's arms became more real, ropy, wiry arms of a smaller man.

The very air vibrated with the word's power. The word soaked into my skin, holding me in the spirit world. Or holding this world to me. The darkness shook, like the fuzzy edges of hair on your arms, next to a bass speaker. It shook, and then a point of light appeared far above me. Far above us.

There was me. And there was Hector. His elbow locked around my throat. Still dragging me down, down, down. Slower now, after the word had been spoken. But downwards, nonetheless, down into his pit of darkness, his face a rictus of hate and anger and fury.

STOP.

The word washed over Hector a third time, washed over his dark, furious spirit, and it was this time that the word washed him away. Fading into the darkness, leaving dark trails of ethereal spirit. As if he had blown away on a ghostly wind.

Then there was just me. Me and the vibrating power around me. Me and the darkness around me, dark except for that tiny globe of light hanging high above in the dark night. Almost swinging, like the tiniest lightbulb hanging from the thinnest cord.

The light grew, swelled above me. It was as if someone held it, brought it down, closer and closer to me. The light swelled and became a rounded surface of light, like a beacon in this dark world my spirit swam in. As it grew closer I saw the curve of the light was wrong. It wasn't round, like a bulb. It was more concave than convex. The light curved outward around me, as if I was in a globe and looking out.

Or, as if someone held a globe and was looking in.

A face appeared. Zoe, I thought, though the brightness of the light and the distortion of the glass made it hard to tell. There was a pair of glasses with tiny wisps of hair around the arms of the glasses. One eye was closed, and the other pressed close; the eye was gigantic to me, peering into the globe even as I looked out from it. Zoe's lips moved, as if she was speaking to someone next to her, a person I couldn't see.

Then the globe grew smaller. The light became less. As if someone was pulling it back away. Zoe's lips moved frantically, as if she was telling me something important, as if she thought I could actually hear her.

The darkness returned, darker now because once there had been light. A thick darkness, like the blackest soup. Maybe it was the relative motion of everything, but I seemed to be drifting down.

Well, my spirit seemed to be drifting.

The light became the size of a quarter. A dime. A pinprick.

Then it was gone.

I kept descending into the dark soupy blackness. It growing darker the whole time, like I was descending into the very depths of a black ocean. I could almost feel a pressure on me, on my ethereal form, pushing in on my ghostly skin, like the press of balloon against me, all around me.

Then, a long blow of the whistle of a locomotive. A forlorn cry in the darkness. A sound that lit upon my spine and shook my soul. I knew where I had heard that sound before. I had thought it could have been the Grimm Express; I now knew I had been wrong.

The cry of the whistle seemed to pull me down. I waited a long time. Floating in the unseen currents. Drifting downwards until suddenly I saw light again. Light below me, a swelling light of a reddish hue. As if a dying sun had been buried in the ground below, yet still burned with a light, simmering with anger.

Buildings appeared in the red landscape. Tall buildings, growing upwards, towards me. One, then another, then blocks of them, tall constructions of brick and metal, with water towers on the tops of some of them, windows and fire escapes along the sides. Buildings that rose high in the center below me, spreading outward around me.

A city.

And then, following that thought.

A city of the damned.

Shit. I guess I knew it was where I had always been headed, but still, it hit me hard. Somewhere along the way of my life, I believed I had done better. Maybe deserved more.

In the end, maybe the good we do never outweighs the evil.

Figures.

Mountains ringed the city, tall peaks. So tall they could never be climbed. It was like the city had been set at the bottom of a very steep cup, though one mountain dominated all the others. Like the cup of mountains had a handle poking from its side, a bulging handle that swelled over the side lip, a handle more like a cancerous growth than something to hold on to.

Tracks circled the city. Train tracks. I found the train, chugging around below me, ashy puffs of a dark cloud leaving its stack as it circled along the tracks.

Its whistle cried again, and again I recognized it. Again it sent a shiver of pain and sadness down my spine.

I drifted lower, down among the buildings. The office buildings, the banks, the apartment complexes. High-rises of metal and glass, tall buildings of red brick, some faced in a white concrete that was streaked in veins of concrete, under the angry sun. The metal frames of the water towers, the fire escapes, the ladders, all of the metal lightly stained with rust.

Forms appeared below. Ghostly forms drifting in and out of the buildings. Walking the streets. Occasionally, in the apartment complexes, shouting out of an open window. As if living lives they had left behind upon their deaths.

No one particularly paid attention to me. Maybe this was how people appeared in this world. Maybe they were used to the damned people of the world above just dropping in. Maybe other forms were following me down, getting dragged deeper into this ocean of hell. I kept drifting, my spirit dropping down between two buildings, right into a little dead-end alley.

And then my feet touched the street. It felt like a real road. Like blacktop. Only colored with blood. I tested out a breath and found that I could breathe in and out, and that the air smelled like burned ash. Like someone was smoking a cigarette around me.

I took another breath of ash. Wondered if this was Hell or some other place. Wondered about Zoe and her globe, high above all of this.

Then I heard a voice. A voice I thought I'd never hear again. But one I recognized.

"Well, fuck me, it's Grimm," Lilly called out from behind me. "Game finally over, huh?"

I know how this one ended. I know it, and I felt it, and I wanted nothing more than to get back in there and write the next story. So that this one didn't end and we all didn't have to wait until the next.

So here it is. Ready for you. It was supposed to be something short and different and a little exciting, and it became so much more.

City of Second Chances

Thank you readers for being a part of this world, this group of friends, with Grimm and Jen, and enjoying this ride with me.

chrisjcranford.com

ABOUT THE AUTHOR

When Chris isn't trying to figure out how to write a bio, he spends time contemplating the fate of the universe. Probably while walking into a door jamb. He's accepted the two go hand-in-hand.

He currently resides in Florida, though he has some Magellan in him, and loves to wander.

It is his dream to write stories that – through their telling – influence others to live a little better. Stand a little taller. Smile a little wider. Hold someone a little longer. Fiction should be the dream real life aspires to be.

Dogs are his buddies. Football is his hobby. Books are his passion.

Find out more about Chris here:

www.chrisjcranford.com

 facebook.com/chrisjcranford

X x.com/chrisjcranford

 instagram.com/chrisjcranford

www.ingramcontent.com/pod-product-compliance
Lightning Source LLC
Chambersburg PA
CBHW031335020726
47499CB00005B/1278